# A Justifiable Madness

### A B Morgan

To Lesley

I hope you enjoy
the story

Ali Morgan. x

www.bloodhoundbooks.com


Print ISBN 978-1-912175-59-8

For Andy, who always believes in me.

# Chapter 1

## No Turning Back Now

Mark deftly removed the last remaining item of clothing between dignity and nudity: the sarong around his waist. He departed through the train doors almost directly from the toilet where he had left his oldest t-shirt and abandoned his train ticket.

It had been a warm night for the first week in September, and there was not even the slightest hint of chill in the early morning air. In fact it was quite muggy, heralding a hot oppressive day ahead for those off to work in the city. Facing Mark, as he alighted from the train, was a sea of commuters. Most were jostling their way past other travellers, pushing through train doors, desperate to find an available seat. Those in his direct path gave Mark a very wide berth indeed. Bare and exposed for all to see, with arms outstretched, he looked up to the heavens. Strolling slowly and deliberately further onto the platform, he muttered a language of vague Arabic origin.

Having caused more than a bit of a stir, he stopped abruptly and honed in on a bespectacled man in the crowd. Lowering his head, Mark stared him directly in the eye. Then, in a theatrical manner, he placed his hands gently upon the man's shoulders and let loose a stream of incantations, as if striving to produce a public miracle healing.

The shocked commuter remained motionless, his eyes beseeching his fellow travellers to intervene; none did, and no rescue was forthcoming from any quarter. People in the crowds were finding it difficult to avoid coming into contact with Mark because of the heaving mass of humankind squashed onto the platform, endeavouring to access their morning trains.

Mark then raised his game in both volume and behaviour. He began to chant, and to spin like a Dervish with his arms again outstretched. Every now and then he would punctuate his rotations by halting without warning, to lovingly touch and bless whosoever he could target. He gazed down upon those he was praying for, mesmerising them with his hypnotic eyes and melodic prayers.

Mark looked magnificent. His long dark wavy hair was flowing across his shoulders, and his lean muscular body was tanned and glistening with nervous sweat. He was so tall that, nudity notwithstanding; he was already easily distinguishable from the surrounding throng.

# Chapter 2

As people surged onto the trains, the platform became less populated. Mark therefore had more room to showcase his naked Messiah performance, which was having the desired effect on the morning travellers. Most were either shocked or irritated and Mark had become aware of one or two commuters who had laughed nervously as he passed them by. Their reaction was at the most unusual sight of a nude man who looked remarkably like Jesus, wandering purposefully along a busy train station platform. Mark was as naked as the day he was born, apart from a pair of well-worn leather sandals.

It was merely a matter of luck that there were two British Transport police officers on the opposite platform, lying in wait for a serial fare dodger.

'What's all that fuss about?' remarked one to the other. In response to the commotion, they made their way to Mark's vicinity, and as they glimpsed through the crowds, they saw a man who appeared to be lying prostrate on the platform. They anticipated having to deal with a medical emergency, but as they approached the scene, they soon realised that the man was conscious, lying on his back, legs akimbo, with his genitals on public display. Mark had his hands together as if praying, and was spouting a lengthy but unintelligible string of suitably made-up words, as he gazed again at the heavens above.

'Heavens above!' remarked the first policeman with a huge grin on his face. The second, his sergeant, rapidly took control of the situation, and from the gathering circus of passengers and station staff, he chose a number of people to help shield the scene from those of a more delicate disposition.

'Right; you, you, and you three. Stand together, facing outwards and form a shield please.' There were young children and ladies present, most of whom had already turned their backs to the offending sight. Inevitably, there were also voyeurs who made certain that they had an uninterrupted view. One high-heeled bleached-blonde woman drew attention to herself as she shrieked loudly about how delighted she was at the quality of the assets on show.

The sergeant, a lanky man, took a high visibility vest from one ponderous member of the station staff, and swirling the waistcoat like a toreador, swiftly covered Mark's prized possessions. The other policeman, a rather chubby constable, tried unsuccessfully to talk to Mark who was determinedly praying and chanting.

'Come along, sir. Let's keep covered up, shall we, there's a good chap. Now, what's your name? Can you tell us where you're from? Do you speak English? No, possibly not then ...'

The local police were contacted, but they had 'no available officers to deal with the incident at this time.' Therefore in an unusual step, the two British Transport police, who were not local to the area, were left to deal with a naked ranting Messiah on platform two. They decided to escort the praying flasher to the local hospital's A&E department, and let the mental health services deal with him there. 'He's off his rocker,' noted the endlessly cheerful chubby constable. 'Doesn't he look like Robert Powell in Jesus of Nazareth? Really uncanny that,' he remarked.

Mark was praying and chanting in the direction of both policemen as they debated between themselves the best way they should get him up from the platform and onto his feet, without further indecent exposure occurring as a result.

Mark wished they would get on with it. He was becoming uncomfortable in the places where grit from the dirty platform irritated and abraded his back. Optimistically he had assumed that he wouldn't have to wait too long before they whisked him smartly to the hospital, but these two were dithering and debating to such a degree that it seemed an age before any action occurred.

Lying there, listening to the Keystone Cops attempting to access an acceptable, practical idea between them, Mark had time to review his own work. Overall he was pleased with how well his performance had been received. He could only hope that it was enough to secure the desired outcome, and that he had not overacted. It was difficult to gauge.

'Fetch us something to cover this man up a bit better, would you?' asked Sergeant Thin. He was duly given a slightly worn but relatively clean blanket from a couple of members of the station platform staff, who were openly laughing at the mayhem.

Handcuffs were employed as a precautionary measure inside the police vehicle, keeping Mark's hands tied to prevent him from removing the blanket wrapped around his waist.

It was only once they had arrived at Hollberry Hospital did the two policemen realise that this was not entirely effective. Each time Mark stood up, the blanket fell down of its own accord, and Mark made no attempt to hold it in place. He was concentrating hard, trying not to smirk or to laugh.

'Right, I'll lead. You follow, and hold the corners of the blanket in place,' instructed Sergeant Thin. Constable Chubby appeared to find the whole scene highly amusing. He chortled loudly as the three men stumbled their way through the main doors to A&E at Hollberry Hospital. As a pair, the two policemen resembled the Chuckle Brothers from children's television fame.

The triage nurse greeted them with a smirk, and by the way she looked at him, Mark knew that she had been struck by his resemblance to Jesus. She didn't move for several seconds, momentarily hypnotised as Mark fixed her with his saintly stare. He looked at her lovingly. She smiled back at him with nervous sympathy as she put the phone to her ear. 'Switchboard? Could you bleep the on-call psychiatrist for A&E please? Prompt response required. Thanks.'

Mark was continuing to produce an award-worthy religious performance for the benefit of a handful of people in the A&E waiting room. He did the same for Dr Siddiqui, the psychiatrist, when he finally made an appearance. Mark had deliberately discontinued his dramatic verbal ranting, and had lowered the overall tone. He didn't want to overdo the effect, so kept the volume low.

'Once the doctor takes him away for assessment, we can get straight back to what we were supposed to be doing.'

'Yes, Sarge. Lovely day for it.' Unfortunately for the two policemen, Dr Siddiqui had other ideas, and appearing somewhat nervous, he instructed the police to remain.

'I strongly suggest that you should be using the police powers of the Mental Health Act, in case the patient decides to run.'

'What did 'e say?' whispered the constable, leaning towards the sergeant's left ear. Despite working in the UK for years, Dr Siddiqui retained a strong Indian accent, and when nervous, spoke at the speed of a firing machine gun.

'Thanks for the suggestion, Doctor, but the man came with us willingly. He won't be going anywhere with those cuffs on.' The sergeant was reassuringly emphatic.

Dr Siddiqui conceded by nodding, or in his case by shaking his head in a peculiar figure of eight motion. This was even more bewildering for the inexperienced constable, who looked for assurances from his superior. 'That means "yes", Constable.'

Dr Siddiqui nodded his way to a cubicle in which to carry out a psychiatric assessment, and with pen in hand, took details of the chain of events at the station as reported by the two policemen. It was the sergeant who answered most of the questions. Constable Chubby remained quiet with a puzzled expression fixed upon his rounded face. It seemed he was unable to understand the vast majority of Dr Siddiqui's enquiries.

Mark listened intently as they described his morning's work and debated his future. Truth time. Had his performance been good enough?

'You're telling me that this man here ... he's touching the members of the public and people who were from the crowds on the train station platform? Is that right? Now then, when he, ummm, exposed his body parts, did he frighten members of the public on purpose with his behaviour?' the doctor asked.

Mark thought that Dr Siddiqui seemed embarrassed by his own questions and unnerved by the answers. The psychiatrist then turned his professional attention to Mark, who had become mute, pretending to pray silently.

Mark decided, as a finale, to suddenly stand up in order to bless Dr Siddiqui. Startled, the doctor sat back in his chair so violently that the whole chair flexed unnaturally. He was visibly alarmed at being confronted, full in the face, by Mark's genitals as again the blanket slipped inexorably to the floor.

The result of this pantomime was that Dr Siddiqui, with eyes wide, hurriedly left the cubicle.

He returned minutes later with reinforcements in the form of a beige, square-shaped, flustered lady who he introduced as an approved social worker. Dr Siddiqui, who had remained shaken by his pelvic encounter with Mark, abandoned the social worker to make her own attempt to ask Mark some questions. The beige lady, a Mrs Anna Brown, made a valiant effort to get an intelligible verbal response, but failed. Mark said nothing. He smiled beatifically.

Mark eventually decided to allow himself a few more made-up Arabic type incantations, and tried to bless her too.

'Do we know anything about this man?' she asked in exasperation as she stepped back out of range.

'Sorry, not a thing. He had no ID with him, and when we detained him he was only wearing those sandals. That's it. Not a stitch on. We're not even sure he speaks English. So far he has just jabbered away in some foreign language.' The sergeant sounded weary of repeating himself.

\* \* \*

Mark, the constable, and the sergeant were then deserted for a good hour or so, and Mark was left wondering what on earth was happening.

The sergeant looked at his watch. 'Christ, what can they be buggering about at?'

'Dunno, Sarge. Never been to one of these mental assessments before.'

'Right, that's it! I'll wait here with the naked Messiah, and you go and see if you can track down that bloody doctor before I charge him with wasting police time.' On such an uncomfortably muggy day, the thin sergeant took offence at being kept waiting for so long. 'I've better bloody things to do,' he muttered.

\* \* \*

Even Mark had to admit that the waiting had become tedious. He too was finding the lack of information wearing. The day was becoming warmer and more oppressive while the three of them remained abandoned in an airless room with nothing to drink. With no communication from hospital staff about what was to happen next, tension rose for Mark as the time dragged on. He began to have doubts: *Have I done it? Christ, what if they've sussed me out already? Impersonating a nutter … is that an offence?*

\* \* \*

When the chubby constable returned, he reported proudly that he had found Dr Siddiqui and Mrs Brown the social worker, completing paperwork.

They arrived moments later, forms in hand.

'Right, sorry to keep you waiting. In the circumstances, we have completed the necessary paperwork to detain the unknown gentleman from the train station, under an emergency Section of the Mental Health Act. Dr Siddiqui will call the acute psychiatric admission wards in the next building and liaise with the nursing staff. If you could kindly deliver this man to the ward, and un-cuff him there. Thanks.'

This request from square, beige Mrs Brown left no choice open to the sergeant and his constable. It would have been counterproductive and wasted even more time to argue the point, so they didn't bother.

Mark was rather surprised at the ease of his admission. Relief flooded through him. That useless doctor hadn't made any real effort to communicate with him. All he had done was to take the vast majority of the details from the police, which was helpful to Mark in many respects. He felt he had given his best performance at the railway station, and had rather enjoyed the pandemonium he had caused. He was now in uncharted territory, even so, he stuck firmly to his original plan. He went into total mute mode. *I've made it this far*, thought Mark. *So far, so good.*

# Chapter 3

## A New Arrival

'Monica, you're going to love this,' Emma said as she winked at me impishly.

'Go on then … pen at the ready. Let's have the gory stuff first,' I said.

'Okay, I'll try, but Dr Siddiqui's accent is so thick, I may have the finer details wrong.' She sighed. 'It appears that British Transport police had to arrest a man at Hollberry Station, because he was behaving bizarrely on one of the platforms.'

'Nothing unusual about that.'

'That's what I thought, but as I understand it, he had no clothes with him and no ID, and is declining to speak. He entertained the morning commuters on their journeys to work though … apparently. The police who picked him up reported that the man in question, had been praying and preaching, and all with no clothes on. Nice morning for a bit of wanton nudity, if I do say so myself. So, in short, as we are the nearest acute psychiatric unit to the station, we have the pleasure of his company.'

My interest was piqued at the word nudity. 'Are you sure? No name, no clothes, and not talking. What's that about? Has he lost his memory do you think?'

'Not a clue. I was only told that the police are bringing him over on a trolley, but I don't understand why. There was no information from Dr Mutter-a-lot indicating that the naked man couldn't walk. He must have prayed himself to a standstill, I assume.'

* * *

On that Monday in September 1994, the day 'Jesus' arrived with us, we had one available admission bed.

The ward telephone had rung loudly, making Emma and I jump, breaking our concentration. There were only the two of us in the oppressively hot ward office at the time, trying desperately to finish updating patient records and prepare handover information for the next shift. As it had been such a warm, sweaty, sticky-gusset day, we were tired and a little tetchy.

Emma had growled when she'd picked up the phone, but managed to disguise the resignation in her voice as she announced brightly, 'Pargiter Ward, Staff Nurse Emma Foster speaking.' She and I had exchanged tense glances, and collectively held our breath, praying that we could finish the shift without a new admission.

Emma had jotted down the details given over the phone from Dr Siddiqui, the on-call psychiatrist stationed in A&E, and as she did so, I couldn't help noticing that she had become a tad irritable.

Emma had looked at me despairingly and mouthed a few choice expletives, indicating her exasperation. She then made a gesture with her left hand, forming an okay sign, placing her hand towards her forehead a number of times. Helpfully she mouthed the word 'dick-head' leaving me in no doubt as to her opinion of Dr Siddiqui. I admonished her with a threatening stare and firm shake of my head. I motioned to the surrounding large windows, which were required for an effective level of patient observation, but which resulted in a goldfish bowl of an office, within which we were permanently on show. In the summer months, the goldfish bowl became a see-through sweatbox. Most unpleasant, as working environments go.

'Okay, Doctor, we'll expect them in the next thirty minutes or so. Can you please ensure the police know to ask for Staff Nurse Monica Morris when they get here? Oh and thanks for the heads-up on the clothing issue, we'll see what we can find.' It was my turn to complete the onerous admission paperwork and organisation. Emma knew this and was wearing a smug expression as she put down the phone.

\* \* \*

Several minutes later, with the rest of the staff informed of the pending arrival, a bed space in a dormitory prepared, and a brief moment found to make use of the staff toilets for a wee, the police made an appearance via the lift with a man handcuffed to a patient trolley. 'Are you Nurse Morris by any chance?' asked a tall, thin policeman.

'Yes, gentlemen, that's me. You've found the right place. I'm Monica Morris. Welcome to Pargiter Ward. Would you mind wheeling the gentleman this way?' I instructed the two officers to wheel the gurney onto the ward and into a wide reception space away from the main corridor.

'We're calling him Jesus,' the shorter, more rounded of the two policemen proudly announced. He was a cheerful, chubby man with dimples embedded indelibly in his cheeks from permanently grinning. 'He looks like Robert Powell. You know, Jesus of Nazareth.'

'He's more than likely some foreigner who had a smoke too many in Amsterdam, silly bastard,' the tall, thin sergeant volunteered. Adding unhelpfully, 'Looks a bit Spanish.'

'Then we can't call him Jesus, it would be "Haysoos",' was the swift riposte from the cheerful constable.

I decided to put an end to police banter before they became more carried away, and asked why it was that 'Jesus' was handcuffed to a gurney. I was actually concerned that no one had thought to inform us that this Jesus was a bit on the violent side.

'It was the easiest option,' offered the chubby constable by way of explanation. 'When he walked cuffed between us, his blanket kept falling off and he's a generously endowed young man. You know. Well known in Australia ... big down under!' He then laughed uproariously at his own joke.

'Thoughtfully put,' added Emma, who had joined the welcome party. It was at that moment that Emma and I looked down at the young man on the trolley, covered in a grey blanket. He had dark wavy shoulder length hair, olive skin, and the most beautiful face. I believe it was his serene expression, well-muscled shoulders, swarthy good looks, and glacier blue eyes that prompted the most unprofessional of responses from my colleague.

'Jesus!' exploded Emma, spitting out the remnants of a ginger nut biscuit she had hastily grabbed before leaving the ward office.

I produced a weak 'bloody hell' under my breath, but the constable didn't miss a trick.

'I told you, ladies. Jesus of Nazareth as I live and breathe.'

'Yes, thank you,' I replied curtly. 'Can you help us to understand why you handcuffed this man to a trolley?'

'Oh yes. Simple really. It's because he had already exposed himself to the general public, so we thought it safest to cuff him to the trolley and that way he couldn't pull the blanket off, if he suddenly had the urge to do so.'

'Oh, so no particular risk of violence we should know about?' I asked, just to be quite sure.

'No, not that we are aware of,' confirmed the tall, thin sergeant.

I turned to our new patient. 'Oh crikey, I'm so sorry, sir. This is not how we welcome patients on to our ward, but they do usually arrive on two feet and not on a trolley. Let's see what we can sort out for you in the way of clothes, and then we'll settle you in. Okay?' I felt ashamed at how badly Emma and I had both reacted. Even though I didn't know whether or not this man understood anything I had just said to him, I had to apologise. 'Would you like a cold drink?' I asked. They all looked as if heat exhaustion was not too far off.

\* \* \*

Once the trolley had ceased to squeak and sway, Mark knew he had arrived at his final destination. He had no idea exactly where he was. All he had seen of his journey through the hospital were fluorescent strip lights on ceilings, but he knew he had made it. He congratulated himself. The acute psychiatric ward; part one of the mission accomplished. Throughout all the banter, Mark had lain silently on the trolley. He was still having trouble not reacting to the witty repartee as the ludicrousness of the situation had suddenly struck him as being most amusing, especially when a nurse had showered him with biscuit crumbs. What a welcome!

Focusing incredibly hard not to respond to comments being made about him, he managed to remain resolutely mute. This part of the plan was important to get right, he realised. The minutes ticked by, and due to the tension of the situation, Mark was becoming hot and sweaty under the blanket. He was thankful when at last the two nurses and the policemen joined forces to help find him clothing, uncuff him and allow him to dress. Even more relief arrived when he could accept a plastic beaker of refreshingly cool water.

\* \* \*

Having partly regained his dignity once the handcuffs were removed, Mark was able to sit up on the trolley. He took a good look around at the neglected décor of the ward, where he set eyes upon the nurses who had welcomed him so vocally to Hotel Bonkers. He was unsure as to what was in store for him next, and he was going to be wholly reliant on picking up clues from the staff.

\* \* \*

'Thanks, gentlemen. We appreciate your help.' I said to the two policemen. 'I'll leave you in Emma's capable hands. If you're lucky, she'll let you have one of her biscuits.'

'Yes, not a problem,' Emma replied from the chair she was standing on with her head in the lost property cupboard. 'Oh dear, it's a shame we haven't much in the way of clothes that actually fit. I'll keep rummaging for a shirt,' she suggested. I was more concerned that we couldn't even find a pair of underpants for Jesus. What did that say about the state of the NHS?

Jesus remained strangely calm and silent throughout the admission proceedings. When the blanket was removed, it was clear that he wore only sandals, and not a stitch of clothing. Scruffy, well-worn leather sandals were the only thing he had in his possession, but he had neat feet and they didn't smell, I noticed. He didn't appear to be a member of the great unwashed; his hair was clean and shiny, he was a healthy weight, and had neatly manicured hands. All of which would indicate that he was not likely to have been street homeless. Apart from those incidental observations, we had nothing to go on to help us to identify the man now in our care.

'Right, let's get these necessary forms filled out. Name: not known. Address: not known. Age: not known. This isn't going to take long, Em. I'll have to put down the same as they did in A&E.'

'Yep. Can't see any other option.' She nodded approvingly.

'Okay then. Name: Mr Trainman, it is.' And that was what we decided to call him for the duration, or at least until he offered to inform us of his true identity.

Clerking him in as a new admission to Pargiter Ward was challenging. We had no facts to record, other than the presence of an extraordinarily handsome young man who looked like the actor Robert Powell and, or, Jesus. Emma and I decided that calling him Jesus would potentially offend any sensitive souls, so we kept that name for our personal use only.

Jesus Trainman was shown around our dingy and dull, but otherwise clean ward where we tried to keep the atmosphere settled and secure. On the whole we succeeded in achieving this, however, young Greg was not too settled at that particular time, possibly because Margaret on 'one-to-one' duty had developed a sore throat from reading out-loud non-stop for over an hour.

Greg was becoming restless and was talking to himself about the devil and demons and suchlike, and was pacing up and down in his room with his troubling thoughts on show for all to witness. Jesus looked saddened at this sight as he passed by.

It had been much worse the week before. Greg had been so disturbed that he had managed to barricade himself into his single-bedded side room where he had smeared his own faeces over the walls. Everywhere. We had to call in reinforcements to deal with the chaos and the smell. It was grim! Things improved once we had sorted out different medication, and through creative invention, discovered that the spoken word was soothing for this young man. After that we read to him out loud, everyday.

It was Margaret's turn to read to Greg. A seasoned healthcare assistant, she was sitting in a chair positioned inside the doorway of Greg's side room, and was conspicuously distracted by our new patient as he walked past her on his way to the dormitory beyond. I walked beside him, paperwork in hand.

Jesus Trainman was wearing a pair of beige belted trousers that were far too short for such a tall man, and consequently they flapped around his calves. Emma was still searching lost property for a suitable shirt, and so our Jesus was bare-chested, and that chest was incredibly well toned, I happened to notice.

'Margaret,' I hissed out of the side of my mouth as we passed by. 'I can see what you are thinking by the expression on your face. Shame on you at your age.'

Margaret blushed with the embarrassment of being caught out, but despite this could not take her eyes off Jesus Trainman, and neither could I. As part of my job, I was required to ensure that our new patient was comfortably settled on to the ward, and carefully observed. I convinced myself that I was not staring in a lecherously appreciative manner. I was.

With the help of 'Gina the cleaner' our diminutive but unflappable Sicilian ward cleaner, I rustled up tea and biscuits for Margaret the healthcare assistant to ease her sore throat, and for Jesus, who accepted these with a slow gentle nod. There was no hint of suspicion, no guardedness, and he seemed to look right into my soul with those crystal-clear blue eyes, framed by impossibly thick long dark eyelashes.

He simply did not speak.

\* \* \*

Mark continued to take in his shabby, paint peeled surroundings. The walls were a pale NHS green, as was the lino on the floor. *How uninspiring. Was green supposed to be a relaxing colour or something?* It had also been a depressing sight to see the troubled young man in his room pacing back and forth like a caged animal. Mark was even more appalled when he realised that he was being led along a corridor towards a dormitory. *God! I hadn't predicted that*, he thought. Sharing with other blokes was not what he had in mind. He had stayed in some rough hotels in his time, but never had he been required to sleep in a dormitory full of mad men!

He caught sight of himself in the reflection of a Perspex-fronted noticeboard and was mildly amused by how bad he looked in a pair of ankle-flapper trousers. *Hardly a winner in the fashion stakes.* Apart from this dreadful sight, the other sense being assaulted, was his sense of smell. Everywhere was tainted by the stench of cigarette smoke; stale dog-ends. Revolting. He then tuned in to the sounds of the ward. There was a persistent humming, which turned out to be emanating from an extraction fan within the stinking hole of a patients' smoking room. The hum of the fan was overlaid by an endless babble coming from at least two televisions. Mark assumed these were being watched by patients in a lounge area elsewhere in the ward. He would have an exploratory walk around the whole ward when he had the chance, he decided. Not too far. With no underpants on he was all too aware of the potential for chafing! Mark laughed at himself for that one. There were plenty of times in his life when he'd had to go commando. *I think that may be the least of my troubles*, he predicted.

Being mute had its disadvantages, and these were becoming increasingly apparent. He couldn't ask advice, for directions, for information about the ward or about the staff. In fact he had disabled himself quite considerably. He could only listen and watch in frustration.

Through a set of oversized windows, he could see directly into the main ward office, which was centrally located, giving an all-round view of the corridors and the ward entrance. How convenient. Despite a deliberate search, Mark could not see any CCTV cameras, so he had to assume that they did not exist. Good. He watched through the glass as the two nurses chatted and busied themselves.

# Chapter 4

## Who is Jesus?

E mma and I desperately needed to communicate with each other to discuss our new guest. At the earliest opportunity, we rushed off to the ward office, leaving 'Gina the cleaner' chuntering away to Jesus in her unusual mix of English and Sicilian. He seemed to appreciate this as he watched her working, mopping, dusting, and chatting.

'Bloody hell,' Emma said, a gleeful look on her face. 'Bloody, bloody, bloody hell!'

'I know what you mean. He's gorgeous.'

'Bloody hell.'

Emma and I continued in this way for a while, interrupted only by brief silences and the odd giggle. Pathetic. We put our heads down, not wanting to be seen behaving like a couple of teenagers.

'Is he foreign do you think?'

'Could be. But foreign or not he doesn't look barmy,' I ventured, while making up a case note file for Mr Trainman (*real name unknown*).

'He doesn't have that usual haunted look, I must say. He certainly isn't manic, and what's more he doesn't come across as obviously being depressed, just tired. So, we can only conclude therefore, that it must have been a rapid recovery between Hollberry railway station, A&E, and here? Did they give him any sedation in A&E? And where is that damn doctor. He needs to finish clerking in and to decide what needs doing next.'

'There's nothing on the paperwork from A&E to say he was given any medication when he was there,' Emma replied to one of my streams of questions. 'Those eyes are so amazing,' she added distractedly. 'But you're right, he doesn't seem Billy-bonkers. Still, time will tell.'

Emma then remembered to inform me that the police had promised to try to trace the mystery man's train journey via CCTV at the stations on that line, in an effort to work out where he had come from.

'They said they would be checking missing persons and various other avenues of enquiry, and they agreed to keep us updated as to any progress they made. Most helpful of them, I thought. We could do with finding a relative, I suppose.'

'Yes, he must have parents somewhere.'

'Mary and Joseph Trainman?' Emma suggested.

'Not funny!' I grinned nevertheless. Our efforts to obtain useful information about Jesus were proving less than fruitful, and the usual assessment and history-taking approaches yielded scant results. The written information from Dr Siddiqui was not much better. It did however, go into a bit more detail about Jesus being seen to be preaching and praying, naked on the station platform, before being detained by the transport police, who by-passed jail and came directly to hospital A&E.

'He must have been speaking at that point,' I suggested, 'because how do you preach without speaking?'

I raised the same observation with Dr Siddiqui when he came to the ward to complete his part of the required admission documentation. Dr Siddiqui was a rather short, balding Asian man with eyes that were puffy and tired looking, and he had unusually pointy ears. Ordinarily this would have made him vulnerable to the obligatory nickname, based purely on physical looks, however in his case, he was often referred to as 'Dr Sticky', because that was how he pronounced his own name. I always felt that he was rather nervous on the whole, and not at ease with either patients or staff.

Arriving on the ward, Dr Siddiqui and Mrs Anna Brown decided unilaterally not to bother trying to speak to our Jesus again, as this had been entirely unsuccessful in A&E not an hour before. Strangely, Dr Siddiqui outlined a working diagnosis of: 'psychosis, possibly drug induced'. This was a bit peculiar because, apart from the passing comment from the policeman earlier about Amsterdam, there was no other mention of drugs being suspected. Not even as a possible cause for a young man to go flashing a platform full of commuters, although it was entirely possible. Jesus did not smell of cannabis either, I realised.

'Monica, I have written a prescription for the Mr Trainman for PRN Lorazepam and Haloperidol, in case he becomes disturbed later on. You can give it if necessary. He needs to be seen first on the list in the morning at ward round, by Dr Sharman.' I didn't need reminding of this fact, as I was not looking forward to the event.

Dr Charming Sharman, the consultant psychiatrist for the unit, was so called, by the staff, because he was not. He was far from charming. His ward rounds were tense affairs for patients, for their relatives, and for staff, and it was no place for the weak, ill-prepared, or incompetent. No one seemed to challenge him about his dreadful behaviour, and only the sycophantic or well-endowed attractive female had the ability to shift any decision, once he had made up his mind. I was neither of these.

He had only joined our ward team six months previously to replace lovely old Dr B, who had retired after decades of sterling service to the NHS. Dr B had an impossibly long Sri Lankan name, which resulted in nobody ever bothering to pronounce it. Fortunately the man himself was perfectly happy being called Dr B. When Dr Sharman had arrived as his replacement at the unit, it was rather like experiencing an earthquake with numerous aftershocks. It was devastating.

The staff nurses of Pargiter Ward, as a group, raised concerns with our managers about Dr Sharman's harsh treatment decisions, and bullying approach. Our delegation to the senior management was dismissed as evidence of troublemaking.

'Whether you like the man's attitude or not is irrelevant,' said Gordon Bygraves, the unit manager. 'You will have to make the necessary adjustments to accommodate our new consultant. He has an exceptional reputation and is highly thought of in the world of psychiatry. Surely you are all aware that he has written numerous research articles and he's been published in national and international psychiatric journals. Impressive don't you think?'

The nursing team was not impressed.

'You cannot accuse him of bullying, so I suggest that if you're not happy working here then you start looking elsewhere for a job. We've had no other complaints.' I knew that last remark was quite untrue. There had been a number of complaints by relatives. These must have been swept under the carpet, which would explain the lumps in the flooring of Gordon Bygraves' office.

Given the challenges that our consultant presented us with, the best plan of action for the rest of the staff was to be well informed and thoroughly prepared. So I made it my business to organise the standard baseline physical health checks for Mr Trainman, in anticipation. The usual: blood pressure, pulse, temperature, urine sample, height, and weight.

Often this was impossible to achieve for new admissions, as our patients were, in the main, significantly disturbed when they first arrived, or simply unable to cooperate fully. Not in the case of our very own Jesus. He appeared to understand English perfectly well and was not at all distracted or distraught. In fact, he followed me around, watching, and almost scrutinising everything I did. A couple of times I made him smile, but he never uttered a word. Not once.

# Chapter 5

## Mark has Doubts

Mark instantly took a liking to Nurse Monica Morris who had taken the trouble of introducing herself properly as his named nurse, and had shown him around the ward. He had managed to hide his disapproval at being shown a single bed in a dormitory. He would have to make the best of it, and he couldn't complain to Monica, he wasn't speaking. Mark thought her to be unconventionally attractive. Tall and slim, Monica carried herself with an air of efficiency, without appearing too bossy. He liked that. She smiled easily and was engaging and welcoming. Mark noticed how the other staff responded positively to her, especially the almost incomprehensible Italian cleaning lady, and the other staff nurse, Emma Foster. She who had showered him with biscuit crumbs on his arrival.

He did find it strange at first that none of the staff wore a uniform of any description, and that most were casually dressed in trousers or skirts and short-sleeved shirts or blouses. The only things that distinguished them from the patients were their name badges, he realised. He supposed that this casual dress code was designed to put patients at ease and avoid the look of authority or the expectation that the classic white coat would be the order of the day for all psychiatric staff. No one had come to take him away … He had manufactured his own admission to a psychiatric ward. Very successfully.

Mark wasn't nearly so confident about how he would be received by his fellow patients. He was aware that anxiety was creeping in and that he was becoming more nervous as time passed by. When he had planned his dramatic performance he hadn't thought about the consequences fully. Concentrating more on his efforts to convince professionals that he was mad, he had not really considered how the other patients would relate to him. His arrival had attracted attention from the resident patients, some of whom spoke to him briefly just to say hello. Others made a beeline for him, and chatted away, seemingly unaware that he was not joining in the conversation. *It's a damn good job I'm mute,* mused Mark. *At least I don't have to worry about saying the wrong thing.*

There was one particular lady who spoke at him for a considerable amount of time, barely pausing for breath. She was animated and emotionally overexcited, but Mark allowed her to carry on ranting while he nodded politely. He couldn't think what else to do, as he didn't want to upset her. *What was she rambling on about?* Plainly the subject matter was significant from her perspective. The brightly dressed lady in question was wittering on about how 'only the mad have an understanding of the mad' in a takes-one-to-know-one way, and she had obliged him with a theatrical wink as she said it. Mark wondered if he had been revealed as an imposter already. He could argue the case, as he was certainly mad for putting himself through this whole charade.

*Hell! There's a relief,* thought Mark, as the lady in the bright clothing finally buggered off. He had coped well until that point. His levels of anxiety had even eased. What had started as amusing, was now striking Mark as being a test of his resolve. Reality struck home: *I've only been here for a matter of hours. God knows how I'm going to last long enough.*

Although never entirely peaceful, overall the ward was a lot less chaotic and intimidating than Mark had expected. He had assumed, in anticipation of his stay, that there would be people wailing and talking to themselves throughout the day, and he was almost ashamed that he'd had that thought.

Mark soon concluded that the vast majority of the patients were elsewhere in the hospital. He would meet them all at around teatime, as Monica had pointed out when she explained as much as she could to him, keeping the language simple. Mark appreciated that she had no idea if she was addressing a person who understood, or spoke English, and he admired her patience. He was slightly dreading having to meet his fellow dormitory mates, and for this reason he tried to keep within sight of the main office and the staff. He was not sure how the other patients would continue to react to him not replying to questions, and not joining in conversations. For Mark, isolation and fear of intimidation were shadows that lurked nearby.

He was not nearly so worried about being seen by the consultant the next day. He had planned for that scenario, and had pre-empted the likelihood of being prescribed tablets. That was going to be the tricky bit. Knowing this, he had practised at home with headache tablets, and had managed to develop a technique whereby he used his tongue to poke the tablet into his cheek, appearing to swallow it with water. The only weakness to his carefully rehearsed madness was whether his efforts would not only be believable enough, but be so for long enough to achieve the required results. *I can but try*, Mark assured himself as he settled back on his bed to read a scruffy old Reader's Digest magazine. He wondered what was going on in the outside world.

# Chapter 6

## No Clearer

By the time the next shift had arrived, Emma and I were none the wiser about the identity of our new arrival. We were no clearer either as to what mental health problem he was actually experiencing, if any. We had watched him orientate himself to the ward, find the toilets, and we noticed that he passed by the smelly smoking room, where most of the patients spent too much of their free time.

'Blimey, that's unusual,' remarked Emma, 'a patient that doesn't smoke. I wonder how long it will be before he starts chain-smoking like the rest of them.'

I didn't expect Jesus to smoke. He hadn't smelt of cigarettes or anything else on his arrival. 'Emma, you know how other people notice when someone has B.O.? Do you think we've become desensitised? Jesus smelt clean. Did I only notice that because everyone else who gets admitted smells as if they haven't washed for weeks?'

'Yeah, good point. Do you think I can rely on you to tell me if I smell?' Emma had her own way of looking at the world. She and I watched as Jesus spent time flicking through the pages of an old Reader's Digest magazine. He looked at the patient information leaflets strategically placed around the corridors and on noticeboards. When he spotted a leaflet about the Mental Health Act, he seemed to find what he was looking for.

So, on that basis, I assumed he could understand and read English.

Eventually, Jesus Trainman settled down to listen to Janet, the healthcare assistant who had taken over from Margaret. I could hear her relating to Greg, an interesting travelogue from a National Geographic magazine that the late shift had arrived with minutes previously. Once or twice, other patients would try to speak with Mr Trainman. In return, he looked at them and smiled politely, but he never once engaged in conversation. Interestingly, he made good eye contact with the other patients when he met them, and remained unruffled.

Throughout the rest of the afternoon, Emma and I tried many times to encourage Jesus to write something down, but he only shook his head, indicating his decline of this offer. Emma made one last attempt before we had to go home for the day. 'Look, just keep them with you. You never know. You may decide that doodling will help you pass the time.' At last, he was persuaded to keep hold of the paper and the pen, which we both took as a hopeful sign.

After a long busy shift, we were glad that the end of our working day had finally arrived. When Emma had finished the handover to the next set of staff, we both trooped slowly towards the lockers to grab our personal belongings before we gratefully headed home. We didn't refer to Mr Trainman as Jesus when we discussed him with any of the other staff. We kept his nickname to ourselves.

On the way to catch our respective buses, we chatted as was usual but this time more animatedly than was normal after a tiring day. The topic soon turned to the next day's ward round and how well Jesus would be received as a new patient by Dr Charming Sharman.

'Oh great,' remarked Emma, 'old Charming is going to give us, well you, a rare grilling tomorrow. We know nothing about this man and we have no evidence for any obvious mental health problems.'

'Actually, there is a fair bit that we do know, so I'm going to impress The Charming One by sticking firmly to the facts.

Our new patient may well not have a mental health problem, but he doesn't seem to have a physical health problem either. The baseline physical checks are done, with nothing abnormal to report. Blood tests are ordered for tomorrow morning, and the CT scan has been requested, and what's more, we have an update from the police to say they haven't any further information … yet. I don't think being mute, on its own, is an indicator for any drastic mental illness, do you?'

'Nah … So …' Emma said as the truth of the matter seemed to hit home, 'It's actually Dr Sticky that is going to get his arse chewed, because he admitted a man who shouldn't be here. Poor Sticky.' She then indulged in wild imaginings. 'What if he is the real Jesus?'

'Right …'

'Or what if he's here to escape from the police and he has actually committed a terrible crime, and losing his clothes, etc. and pretending to be mad helps him evade capture by Interpol?'

'I doubt that very much,' I replied. 'However, you have a point. Why would anyone who wasn't unwell or who wasn't intent on avoiding the criminal justice system, want to be admitted into a psychiatric unit? Maybe he has lost his memory and can't say anything because he can't remember who he is. Either way he is lovely to look at and it is free to look, isn't it?'

Emma reviewed these latest offerings. 'I think he would look a lot more bewildered if he had lost his memory though, and he doesn't even look distressed, in fact, mildly anxious at best which is peculiar in itself … so maybe he is Jesus.'

'Bloody hell, Emma. He's in trouble. If he decides to talk tomorrow and tells Charming that he's Jesus, he'll never get out of the ward. The Charming One will slap him on a Section 2 as fast as you can say bonkers.'

We had reached my bus stop where Emma and I usually said cheerio.

'Have you marked up your calendar for next weekend?' Emma enquired. 'I know you don't want to, but it's high time you were back on the market again, and there's no better place for finding a real man than at the rugby club. Jake's mate Max still fancies you.'

Emma was teasing me, but I knew that any attempt at resistance was futile. 'Yes I'll come along to shut you up, as long as you promise that we'll still go to the cinema as well.' She nodded. We would see each other at the lunchtime handover the following day. Emma was due on the late shift, and I was to be on an early one managing the ward round, for my sins.

# Chapter 7

### First-night Nerves

Following a staff shift change later in the afternoon, four o'clock heralded the return of more patients to the ward from their groups and activities. As a result, the overall volume of noise increased on the ward, as did the people traffic along the corridors, in the dayrooms and dormitories. Mark picked up from the snippets of conversations around him, that the general topic amongst the patients was about medication, and getting off the ward. Several of the patients had permission to leave Pargiter Ward to go into the hospital grounds, or even to the local shops.

Much to Mark's surprise, the ward doors were not locked, but instead the staff monitored the comings and goings of patients and visitors. He watched, fascinated as the vast majority of the patients had to be formally signed in and out, because they were detained under the legal provisions of a Section. This seemed to keep the two staff nurses on duty permanently occupied. He watched them intently through the generous windows of the ward office.

On each occasion, a patient would approach the big glass office, knock, and wait to be given permission to leave the ward. Mark quickly picked up on the fact that each patient had a set of papers in a file, which detailed the exact permission that they had been granted. He could overhear most of the conversations.

'Yes, Rodney, you still have six hours' unescorted leave left today, so we're happy for you to go to your sister's for tea. Have a lovely time and don't forget to smuggle a slice of cake back in. Oh, hang on. What meds are you on? No, it's okay, as long as you're back for nighttime meds by ten o'clock.'

Mark had observed how carefully the nurse had checked the papers and what he assumed to be a prescription chart, before giving the nod to allow Rodney out of the main ward doors.

The beige square social worker, Anna Brown, who Mark had met briefly in A&E, had inferred that he too was under some sort of Section of the Mental Health Act. However, she had been disappointingly lax in providing him with any written information, which would have clarified his position. He didn't even know whether he had any permission to leave the ward.

After searching along the corridors and on various walls, he found the leaflet that he was looking for, but it was pinned to a noticeboard, which was glazed: no it was Perspex … He could only see the leaflet's front cover. This frustrated Mark's efforts to clarify what Section he was on, and what that might mean. *Am I on a proper Section or not?* Mark asked himself. He could only wait to be told. He had done a lot of waiting that day.

Feeling brave, Mark decided to test the possibility that he could at least go outside for fresh air as a welcome release from the smelly smoky atmosphere of the ward. He approached the office with determination, and once he had caught the attention of a male nurse, he pointed towards the ward doors.

'Sorry, young man, according to the paperwork I have here, there's no going out for you I'm afraid. You'll have to wait until the consultant in the ward round has seen you tomorrow. He's the only one who can grant you any leave.' Mark nodded and shrugged. That answered his question. He was on a Section.

With the ward events such as medication and meal times creating a regular routine, Mark found to his surprise that the rest of the day went by fairly rapidly. Despite being an intense day, he eventually went to bed after eleven, where he endured a restless fitful sleep, interrupted by his usual nightmares. He woke up sweating profusely in the early hours more than once. He was certain that he had shouted himself awake.

Earlier that evening, he had seen a girl with deep self-inflicted wounds, which had thrown him a bit, but he couldn't put his finger on why. After all, he was used to seeing wounds, but not ones self-inflicted by such a young person. This had been playing on his mind, and must have led to his predictable set of terrifying flashbacks. The flashbacks, which played like internal live-action films, were of incidents that he had been exposed to in the last few years. These indelible memories resurfaced most often when he was sleeping. On occasion, he had waking replay of these events, during which he could smell the metallic sulphur of gunfire, the blood, and the dust. When this happened, he experienced full-blown terror as if it were in the present.

Mark sat up in the single bed, and put his head in his hands to ground himself and become re-familiarised with his surroundings. *Crap. Did I wake everyone else up?* He wondered. He didn't appear to have done so. The five other men in Mark's dormitory had disappeared to bed after having their nighttime medication and had been asleep within the hour. A cacophony of snoring had commenced shortly afterwards. Despite Mark's nocturnal disturbances, it continued unabated.

* * *

Lying awake, churning over endless irrelevancies in his head for the rest of the night, he listened to the snoring and mumblings in the dormitory. Most of the patients hadn't been too scary or as threatening as he had feared and many had stayed in their rooms, actively avoiding the company of others.

Mark was thankful that he had achieved the first part of his task. He had been admitted to the ward, as planned, and could look forward to his first ever psychiatric ward round. It would be the first step towards getting himself out again. A week at the most would be all the time he would need. The challenge was on.

# Chapter 8

## Holding Court

'Morning, Monica. Morning, Charlotte.'

'Morning, Bob. Good nightshift?' I asked, keen to hear how Jesus had settled in. Bob, as the nurse in charge, was always a solid and dependable man. In the handover meeting, the nightshift team supplied the early morning staff with the latest update on all the Pargiter Ward patients, large and small. I was sharing the staff nurse duties with Charlotte that morning.

'Generally it was a quiet night. No significant disturbances. In fact I'm led to believe that the whole ward was relatively settled in the afternoon and evening too.'

'That's unusual. I can't think of the last time we had a settled ward at night.'

'I think credit should go to the healthcare assistants for talking themselves hoarse reading to Greg. It's definitely working. That and the medication probably,' confirmed Bob, who, along with Charlotte and myself, was waiting for latecomers. In the meantime, the general chatter amongst the nurses who had arrived for duty so far indicated that the staff teams were intrigued by our new mystery guest.

The night staff had noticed that Mr Trainman's sleep was exceptionally poor. 'Even by the usual standards of a person's first night on a psychiatric ward, he had a rough time,' Bob said. There was a consensus of opinion that night terrors were being demonstrated.

'No wonder the poor man looks so tired,' I said.

The nightshift staff had also been keen to report that Mr Trainman had willingly assisted one of the younger patients with a jigsaw puzzle that she was trying to finish, and they noticed how taken aback he had seemed when he spied the self-harming scars crisscrossing her forearms. One or two of those wounds had been relatively fresh, and deep.

The young girl in question, had not yet come to terms with the death of Nirvana lead singer Kurt Cobain a few months previously, and her pattern of self-harming had become increasingly dangerous. Before this, she had never imagined finding herself in a psychiatric hospital. I don't suppose she ever dreamed of completing a jigsaw puzzle with help from Jesus either.

'I don't reckon that our Mr Trainman has ever been in a place like this before. But I also think he's a bit of a cool customer. He's too relaxed and there's a confidence about the way he walks and moves, the way he watches everything. It could be paranoia … I'm not convinced. Weird. And he looks just like Jesus,' Bob said. Those present agreed with this observation: It was impossible not to. It seemed that the whole team were puzzling over Jesus as much as Emma and I had done the day before.

\* \* \*

In a desperate effort to be well prepared for the morning, I checked the ward round list while breakfast was being handled by the rest of the staff, and swiftly organised the pile of patient files that had to be available in the large soulless office where the ward rounds took place.

'Do we know who's coming in for ward round today?' I asked Charlotte who had her head in the ward diary. 'Apart from the doctors, I mean.'

'Barbara from the community team. That looks like it … no psychologist again. He doesn't want them on the ward, does he?' A rhetorical question from Charlotte, who was referring to Dr Sharman's open dislike and disapproval of our psychology colleagues. He viewed them as an unnecessary hindrance. As a professional group, they had been pretty much excluded since his arrival at Hollberry Hospital.

'Good, I like Barbara. At least I'll have one ally. Any of the CPNs coming along?' The community psychiatric nurses were also our allies. They were assertive and dynamic. I aspired to be a CPN one day.

New admissions were always seen first, which bought me only a matter of minutes to try to squeeze a titbit of useful information from Jesus Trainman before his appearance in front of Dr Sharman. Luckily, Jesus was up, fully dressed, and in different trousers that fitted decidedly better than the ones we had found the previous day. I met with him in a small office to let him know what the plan was for that morning. Not letting his alarming good looks interfere with my professional role, I outlined slowly and carefully what ward rounds consisted of.

'We would like to know what to call you, and I'm sorry if we are causing offence, but at the moment you are being referred to as Mr Trainman.' I hesitated and then added, 'Perhaps you could write your name down for me on this paper …?'

But Jesus only smiled politely and shook his head.

I resorted to closed questioning. 'Are you Spanish?' He did look Spanish, I thought, harking back to what one of the policemen had said the day before.

Jesus shook his head. This was tremendous progress, because previously this approach had failed miserably.

'English?'

Nod.

'Do you know where you are?'

Nod.

'Did you understand what I explained to you just now, about the ward round?'

Nod.

'Excellent. Tell me, do you believe you have a mental health problem?'

Shrug.

'Do you hear voices when there is no one there?'

Shrug.

This was getting me somewhere, but not fast enough. Just as I had started to crack the uncrackable, I had to leave my golden opportunity for assessment, because Dr Charming Sharman had arrived with his entourage, and he was demanding cups of tea or coffee for all. He was unerringly specific about his refreshment requirements, which were provided on a tray with a plate of biscuits: plain mugs, a jug of milk, bowl of sugar, pot of tea, and a cafetière of decent quality ground coffee. Dr Sharman took black coffee, one sugar, and on each occasion, without fail, in his fine bone china cup and saucer. God forbid this should be forgotten. He expected drinks to be poured by the staff nurse in charge of each ward round.

A tall slim man, immaculately dressed, everyday Dr Sharman wore a pristine, pinstriped tailored suit. His finely manicured hands confirmed that the heaviest things he ever lifted were his cup and saucer, and his pen. Dr Sharman had the sallow complexion of a man who rarely ventured into the daylight, and piggy eyes that were too close together for my liking. Over his wrinkled brow, hung a mop of dark unruly hair. The grey at his temples gave a distinguished look.

'Right then, shall we get on?' he announced in a wonderfully exaggerated public school accent. He then took a sip of strong coffee from his china cup, before the proceedings commenced. 'New admission, Nurse Morris?'

'Yes, Dr Sharman. Admitted yesterday afternoon to the ward. Dr Siddiqui saw this man in A&E, and he's on Section 4, which commenced at 13.30 hrs yesterday. The approved social worker, Anna Brown, from the assessment can't be here I'm afraid.'

'Never mind, we don't need her. Siddiqui, please present your case,' pronounced The Charming One.

Dr Siddiqui opened a thin set of hospital notes, and shaking visibly, attempted to give a summary of the facts about Mr Trainman (*real name unknown*). He stumbled over his words and reached the point where he had to explain why he had made use of Section 4.

'What the hell were you thinking, man!' exclaimed Charming. 'No one uses Section 4. It is for emergencies only. The police had him in a place of safety in A&E, so you had no need to make such a ridiculous decision.'

Dr Siddiqui bravely explained the dilemma he'd had the day before. Apparently the police officers were not local, and also were not familiar with whether they could keep the patient in a place of safety under Section 136 of the Mental Health Act in an A&E department. According to the trembling Dr Siddiqui, they had sought advice but to no avail, and therefore as there was purely by chance an approved social worker in the department at the time, she and Dr Siddiqui had used Section 4 to detain the patient as an emergency. They felt the patient was 'at serious risk of hurting himself or others.'

'Right. Understood,' said Charming unexpectedly.

Certainly it was unexpectedly as far as I was concerned, because I didn't understand what it was that Jesus had done. What was it that had indicated to the doctors that he was such a big risk to himself or others? Had I missed vital information? It was the same old comedy routine. Apart from the odd moment of belittling from the consultant, doctors usually stuck together like glue, and backed each other up regardless of the facts. I should have learnt not to be so surprised when this happened, because it did, on a frequent basis. Something to do with old school ties, I believe. A brotherhood, a herd of doctors, a dose of doctors or could it be a consensus of doctors? Whatever the collective noun was, they were a law unto themselves at times.

When Dr Siddiqui announced that the patient had stripped off on a station platform, and performed religious rituals and prayers during the morning commute, Charming was even more impressed, despite the details of Dr Siddiqui's account not being exactly the same as the ones we had been led to believe the day before. He gave the distinct impression that Jesus had been aggressively intimidating and threatening violence towards members of the pubic.

'So, he was handcuffed when he arrived on the ward. Risky chap then. Well done, Dr Siddiqui. Good risk assessment, and I'm pleased to see that you used your common sense in this case. There we have it gentlemen, we have a man who declines to inform us of his name, with no known relatives, we are not sure from whence he hails, but we do know that he's presenting with a severe mental health problem.'

Do we? I thought. That was a hell of a leap in assumptions on Dr Sharman's part, in my view. So it was that I was compelled to interject, to ensure the facts, as few as there were, were accurately reported. 'Umm, I'm sorry to interrupt Dr Sharman, but would you like the nursing report, as we have a few details to add that may be helpful?' I received the usual irritated look, the one that said, '*If you really must, Nurse.*'

Given the go-ahead by a condescending nod, I provided a succinct account of the admission, including the real reason for the use of handcuffs and trolley by the police. Confirming that our patient understood English, I added that there had been 'no observations which indicated a disturbed mental state.' That was my first big mistake, and it acted as the flame to blue touch paper, a catalyst to a series of unpredictable events.

'Yes, I'm sure that's what you do think,' came the reply, with a sarcastic emphasis on the word 'do'. 'Shall we meet Mr Trainman? Please bring him in, Nurse Morris.'

Charming was on the offensive.

As Jesus entered the room, I could see that he was understandably nervous. Anyone would be in that situation. But despite that fact, as he strolled towards a chair to my right, he still looked like someone who had recently returned from a beach holiday, including the weary look of the jet-lagged traveller.

Charming pompously introduced himself and his team. He excluded the senior social worker Barbara from the community services, and he excluded me. We happily introduced ourselves for the record.

'I'm Nurse Monica Morris,' I said. 'We have met, but just to clarify for those present, I'm your named nurse while you are with us.'

Jesus nodded but with no smile apparent this time.

\* \* \*

Mark had enjoyed his one-way chat with Monica before the ward round, when she had cleverly used direct questions to try to extract a tiny fact or two. He had played with her by giving nods of confirmation. In return, he was amused to discover that his paperwork identified him as Mr Trainman. He had secretly suspected that the staff teams were referring to him as Jesus, as the two policemen had done the day before. He would too if he were them.

Mark had entered the ward round feeling relatively confident, but as he walked in front of the men in suits, nervous butterflies bubbled up in his stomach briefly. Maybe, he thought, it was because he was aware that he had woken in the night shouting, and was considering the chances of this having been reported by the night staff. *Was that a bad thing?* He wasn't sure.

His nose was pleasantly tantalised by the fabulous aroma of good ground coffee wafting in his direction as he walked into that large room full of people. Mark deeply regretted not being able to access a cup of equal quality right then. He could do with a stimulant effect to help his concentration after his night of poor sleep.

It was not hard to identify the man in charge. The pompous parody of a buffoon, who had introduced himself as 'Consultant Psychiatrist Dr Giles Sharman,' began. He asked Mark a series of leading and rhetorical questions, most of which he then answered. *At least he's worked out that I won't be replying*, thought Mark.

'So you don't recall your own name then? No. And you divested yourself of all clothing in front of a large crowd at the station. Yes? I understand that at this time you were somewhat elated, and believed you had special religious powers to heal others by praying for them, that's right isn't it?'

Mark tried to remain impassive.

* * *

Barbara and I glanced at each other. She raised her eyebrows confirming that she had not heard this in Dr Siddiqui's presentation, and was wondering where this new information had come from. I was watching the scene carefully; Jesus did not respond other than to shrug intermittently.

Charming then spoke to his group of fresh-faced, eager, trainee doctors in a booming tone. 'The patient is guarded and suspicious. He appears to be responding to unseen stimuli, and I strongly suspect that he may have an underlying psychosis. In which case, we need to continue to assess, and treatment with antipsychotics will undoubtedly help to address these symptoms. Then he will speak to us when he's not so paranoid.'

I could contain myself no longer.

'Sorry. Dr Sharman … I'm confused by this assessment. This man has been calm and settled, and apart from not speaking, we haven't seen anything indicating psychosis. I wonder, well … Dr Siddiqui thought it may be a drug-induced episode?' I proposed.

My intention was that Dr Sharman might consider this as the reason behind the apparent rapid recovery made by Mr Trainman since his arrival on the ward the previous day. Unfortunately my helpful suggestion only served to aggravate the situation.

'Well, Nurse Morris, that's why I'm a consultant and you're not.'

Withering look.

'I'm qualified to diagnose, Nurse Morris, and you're not. I'm also in a position to make a decision about care and treatment which you will ensure is applied.' He then took a deep breath, and staring at Jesus, with his audience of junior doctors waiting for the exciting conclusion, he announced the following, 'Section 3! I will complete the second recommendation to add to that of the Section 4 assessment yesterday. We will commence on ...' He paused for effect. 'Haloperidol and Lorazepam.'

I reacted instinctively and without hesitation.

'Haloperidol?' I questioned. 'Could we perhaps use medication that is less sedating to start with?' I put forward this idea while accepting that the chances of success would be slim. I was trying to avert a potential nasty experience for Mr Jesus Trainman, assuming he was a first-timer in psychiatric care.

Charming was furious at my challenge and seethed for everyone to see. 'No, we will not.'

A cold sensation which originated in the pit of my stomach, spread up my spine, and I felt a little sick. I was mortified. What had I done? Had I made this happen? Had I made Charming take his revenge on Jesus for my insubordination?

There I was, a nurse doing her job, and trying to advocate for her patient, but by doing this, I might have changed his future prospects. Bloody effing Nora! Haloperidol and Section 3. There were countries that could refuse an entry visa if you had a Section 3 on your medical record. Oh God. What about his future employment? Shit. What if Jesus was a teacher or a law student?

\* \* \*

As Mark had left the large meeting room having been seen in an acute psychiatric ward round for the first time in his life, he had felt more than a little confused and disconcerted at the series of events that had played out in front of him. He had been immensely proud of his acting skills and performance, which had led with such ease to his admission the day before. It had been relatively straightforward and had played out exactly as planned.

Then he had met Dr Sharman. Mark had immediately taken a strong dislike to the man as soon as the consultant had pretentiously introduced himself and his silent fawning team of doctors. *What is that man's problem?* Mark wondered as he walked out of the ward round and down the main ward corridor.

He had no doubt that he was placed under a Section 3 of the Mental Health Act, and that the consultant believed he had psychosis, although there was no diagnosis mentioned. He was puzzled, however, as to how that had happened solely on the say-so of one man. *What did I do to deserve that?* He had pitched his admission perfectly. Not too exaggerated, no risk to the public but enough to be convincing. He hadn't even spoken a single word, so how in damnation had he managed to end up on a Section? *Christ, I'm in the shit now,* he thought, *I'll never get out in time.* A speck of uncertainty was growing ever bigger in the pit of his stomach. Mark was shivering slightly as the cold sweat of anxiety was intensifying. His control over events had been spectacularly eradicated.

# Chapter 9

## The Court of Dr Sharman

One way or another, I made it through the rest of the ward round, which took all morning and half of lunchtime, and I tried hard not to contradict Dr Sharman, but it is not in my nature to let the bully win. Underneath my expressionless exterior, I was furious. I don't get bullied. I hate bullies, I thought, as I was reminded of my endless battles at school, which explained my consequent incendiary reactions to any sort of injustice, either perceived or real.

Remain calm and do the right thing, I advised myself. As soon as I'd had that thought, it immediately occurred to me that I had tried to do the right thing once already, resulting in Jesus being placed on a Section 3 of the Mental Health Act. That fact alone meant he could end up in hospital for up to six months of his innocent life.

I was confusing our patient with the unlikely possibility that he was as saintly as the real Jesus. Nevertheless, it was not imaginable for me to collude with Dr Sharman's approach to care. The Charming One continued in a vindictive vein throughout the ward round that day. I noticed that he seemed hell-bent on increasing each and every patient's medication, and as a result, drug charts were being re-written left right and centre. It was becoming obvious that we nurses would be dishing out medication like Smarties, but 'twas ever thus.

Several of my colleagues were either intimidated by the doctors, or sadly chose a submissive approach, identifying themselves with the old-fashioned idea of the 'doctor's handmaiden'. Despite this, there were enough of us on Pargiter Ward who bucked the trend, and were not afraid to do the right thing. I confess, that on occasion, we even had to resort to professional subterfuge.

A number of the patients on the ward had recently been struggling with nasty side effects, mostly because, in my opinion, Dr Sharman had been heavy handed with the doses of medication he chose to make use of. One poor man was so restless that we became increasingly concerned for his wellbeing. It made him profoundly miserable.

Through deliberate deceitful means, we were able to avoid administering his most recent increase in dose, because Emma claimed not to be able to read the prescription on the drug chart, and Dr Siddiqui had, as an oversight, forgotten to re-write it. This gave a reprieve of several days, allowing me to raise the problem in ward round on that Tuesday.

I approached this in a cautious manner with Dr Sharman. He appeared to listen to the complaint, and I was optimistic that he would at the least reduce the dose or change the medication for another. However, he had me in his sights, and my efforts backfired, yet again.

'You appear to believe you are the expert today, Nurse Morris. Let me remind you that there has been a remarkable improvement in this man's symptoms, entirely because of the medication, and we will be sending him on home leave at the weekend. So tell his wife to collect him on Friday evening, and we will discharge him on Monday, assuming all goes well. I'll remove his Section when he returns after the weekend.'

That was power play. Nothing else.

The patient appeared bewildered, not least because he didn't actually have a wife. He lived alone. Nevertheless, he was pleased with the result and later told me before he left for his weekend leave, that if he hadn't had the glimmer of hope in the shape of discharge on the horizon, that suicide was beginning to look like an option worth consideration. He was in any event, planning to stop taking the medication as soon as possible after his discharge. In the meantime he would play along with whatever Dr Sharman wanted, in order to be released from his Section.

'This medication, it's unbearable,' he stated categorically, and I didn't disagree with him. I even documented the remarks in his case file in the confident knowledge that no doctor would bother reading my notes. They rarely did.

Before long it was Greg's turn to be seen in ward round. Dr Sharman could not be persuaded to leave his throne to assess Greg in a smaller room. For a brief while we held on to the vain hope that Dr Sharman would consider this as an act of kindness. No, instead, the nursing staff had to carefully escort Greg to the large office, crammed with intimidating professionals, and do our best to manage the resultant distress. As he entered the room, Greg was muttering and searching around with wild eyes. Fortunately he had Margaret specialing him again, who talked gently and consistently to keep him as calm as she could. Charming had no such professional subtlety in his repertoire, and he went straight for the psychiatric jugular.

'He doesn't seem to be taking his medication properly. Spitting it out, aren't you, young man? Yes. Let's sort out injections, please, Dr Siddiqui. Clopixol. Don't bother with a test dose. No need to bother with that. Straight in with 400mgs weekly, as of today.'

I was dismayed that none of his entourage tried to guide their consultant towards acceptable clinical practice. Not one of them mentioned the fact that Greg had already been prescribed liquid medication to improve his level of concordance with treatment. Neither did any of the passive gutless group of doctors propose an increase in the dose that Greg was currently taking, to see if that would improve the situation.

'Sorry, Dr Sharman, you did say after a test dose he would be starting on 400mgs Clopixol weekly injections?'

'No, Nurse Morris. There you go again. I'm the prescribing doctor, and I have a PhD in Psychopharmacology on my CV, and I made it abundantly clear that there is no requirement for a test dose because the patient has already been trialled on antipsychotics orally, young lady.' He informed me of this in a fine patronising manner. Short of patting me on the head, he couldn't have done a better job.

'Yes, I understand that, but what if he has a reaction to this different drug?'

'Nurse Morris, pay attention, if you will, to your nursing duties, and desist from challenging my treatment plans. It is not your place to do so.' He snarled at me. 'And frankly if there is one more interruption from you today, I will ensure that you are transferred forthwith to another ward, or preferably another hospital, and furthermore, I shall be speaking to your senior manager about your dreadful attitude.'

\* \* \*

That told me.
  Bully.
  Bastard.

\* \* \*

Poor Greg, I thought. I knew from experience that he would have to be physically restrained for an injection to be administered, which was bad enough, but there was also no way of telling how significant the side effects would be from the whacking great dose he had been prescribed. I felt tears stinging my eyes, but I managed to keep it together, determined that Charming was not given the satisfaction of seeing the results of his bullying.

# Chapter 10

## Making Sense

That first ward round seemed to take up hours of everyone's time. After his turn, and to make the most of the experience, Mark joined the group of patients and relatives who were waiting to face their nerve-wracking ward round appointment. He witnessed the fall-out as each of them emerged afterwards.

He watched in fascination as each patient returned, listening carefully in order to glean what he could about the decisions made in the inner sanctum of that large room. Mark saw the young man who had been in the side room, being escorted by the nice lady called Margaret, who often spent time reading to her patient to relax him. She appeared to be crying when they exited the ward round room only minutes later. Mark was desperate to know why. *What the hell happened there?*

One man had real trouble sitting and waiting his turn. He was restless, and when he did sit for any length of time, his legs wiggled up and down endlessly. His pelvis appeared to be gyrating like that of Elvis in his prime, but quite involuntarily and without the music. He was describing to anyone who would listen, that this went on 'day and night. It never stops and I can't go on much longer. I'd rather be dead than this.' Mark could not fail to notice the amount of desperation in the man's voice. *Is that what I'm supposed to take? Tablets that make you want to prefer death?* Mark shivered at the thought.

In an unexpected turn of events, when the same man returned to give the outcome of his ward round appointment, he was remarkably cheerful.

'The news is good,' he said, rubbing his hands together with joyful expectation. 'I can go on weekend leave, and then I'm for a discharge meeting on Monday, and after that I'm out of here. The good news is that I now have a wife! I didn't have one before I went in to see Dr Sharman, but he decided that I should have one, and that the nurses need to phone her up, whoever she is, and get her to collect me on Friday. I hope she's a looker, with really big boobs! What a great weekend this could be, if only that were true.'

Raucous laughter resounded around the dayroom, and everyone joined in the humorous chatter resulting from this happy announcement. Mark had no idea if the man was still mentally unwell, or whether what he had said was reflective of the true facts. Either way, it was entertaining, and to everyone's relief the man's despair had been temporarily alleviated.

Throughout that day, as well as watching the goings on in the ward, Mark spent time around the other patients whenever he had the chance. A tall fresh-faced young lady, who turned out to be an occupational therapist, had approached him in the afternoon. She advised him that there were activities and groups that took place on the ground floor in the OT department each day 'apart from the weekends.' However, because he was not speaking, they would suggest that he joined the art sessions, which would commence again in the morning. 'I'll collect you and introduce you to the rest of the group personally,' she offered. 'What's your name again?'

*Nice try!* Mark remained silent, appreciating her attempt and nodding politely, but not disclosing anything verbally. He was actually cheered by the news that there were ways in which he could fill his days. Being mute was extremely restrictive for his mind, which was yearning for him to ask lots of questions. Maybe he could hold out one more day, but until then he had to resort to helping out with jigsaw puzzles, crosswords, and being a listening ear.

He was pleasantly surprised by what he had learnt by the end of the day, not only about the patients, but also about the staff team. It was obvious that the regular patients on the ward were distrustful and wary of Dr Sharman. Most disliked him intensely and inevitably compared him to the last consultant, Dr B.

'Dr B was a real gent,' said an elderly gentleman named Rodney. 'He had a heart. Not like this new one. He's an out-and-out bastard. I stopped the tablets because they're shit, the ones he gave me, what ... four months or so ago. I wouldn't give them to my worst enemy. What did he do? Put me on them again, only a bigger dose. I know which ones work for me, but I forget to take the ruddy things sometimes,' Rodney explained, 'but that bastard doesn't listen. Doesn't care. He's a shit.'

Mark pondered the 'Catch 22' situation that Rodney was in. If he didn't take the tablets he would become ill again, whatever that entailed, and end up in hospital. However, if Rodney took the tablets prescribed for him, he had a miserable existence. Mark wondered how many people were failing to get back on with their ordinary lives and who were resigned to relapse for the same reason. This could mean not coping, ending up on the streets, or returning to hospital on a regular basis for more of the same.

* * *

Contemplating those depressing possibilities, Mark experienced yet more stirrings of uncertainty about the situation that he had placed himself in.

# Chapter 11

## Stuck on a Section

After ward round, I had to break the news to Jesus Trainman about the implications for Section 3. The final recommendation on the paperwork had been completed by Dr Bastard Sharman, and I had a responsibility to inform Mr Trainman what this meant, because even though his real name did not appear on the pink recommendation form, it was still legal to detain someone under the Mental Health Act without knowing his or her true identity. It happened quite often. In the previous three years, we had two ladies both convinced they were the Queen of England, and a male middle-aged Princess Diana. Not all at the same time, fortunately.

Jesus Trainman could be *'detained for treatment for a period of up to six months,'* so I carefully explained the *'Right to Appeal'* information, and left Mr Trainman with a copy of the required leaflet to peruse. He seemed to have a wry smile on his face, which I could not fathom. Then I slunk off for a good cry in the staff toilets. It had been an awful day so far.

'He's done what?' Emma exclaimed, as she came onto the ward for the late shift. I was then on my way to the medical secretaries' offices on the ground floor to deliver the Section papers, and to make a copy for the ward records. I didn't have much time in hand to chat.

'You heard me. Honestly that man is a complete bastard!' I shouted over my right shoulder as I departed.

The lady in the Mental Health Act office, Harriet Morris, no relation, always seemed kind and helpful. She scrutinised the Section information on the forms, and cast her eye over the recommendations written the previous day. She ensured that she had the second recommendation from another approved doctor, in this case Dr Sharman.

'Oh, that's helpful. Dr Sharman seems to think Mr Trainman is a known patient. What a shame that he can't remember this chap's name. Still, perhaps he knew him from his last hospital. He'll remember sooner or later. We can request the old hospital's records then, can't we, dear?' She smiled in my direction, before going about the business of filing and recording the information.

For whatever reason, I did not question a word she had said, even though I was bewildered by her comments. Something was awry with the paperwork, so when I asked to take a copy of the Section papers, all of them, I deliberately took two copies of Dr Sharman's Section 3 recommendation. I put one of those in my pocket, with a plan to take my time and have enough privacy to read what was written, away from the busy ward environment. Once I had completed the simple task of photocopying paperwork, I returned to the ward and filed the rest of the papers as I was supposed to.

'Jesus no more has psychosis than I have,' I said to Emma. 'How can we justify administering Haloperidol, for goodness sake? It's wrong. Anyway the drug chart has been written, leaving us to consider morally and ethically what to do about it.'

'You have got to be kidding. We can't withhold treatment, Monica Moronica! And …' added Emma, 'what if Charming is right?' She wagged her finger in my direction. Duly reprimanded, I simply grinned back at my good friend and colleague. She was right of course.

Although it was actually nearer to teatime, I made it home for a well-deserved, late lunch. I chatted to my big fat cat, Boris, so named because he bore a striking resemblance to the Russian President Boris Yeltsin, and I told him about my 'amazing, supersize crap day.' I ruminated endlessly about the events of the ward round and Dr Sharman's fine display of bullying tactics.

I remember thinking that a man had not upset me this much since my most recent and long-term boyfriend, Ben, had decided to leave me for another woman.

He had found himself a young blonde airhead from the office. In all probability he wouldn't have noticed that there was a space in her head where a brain should have been. Although a good six months had passed, he would have been unable to look beyond her enormous tits, to discover a personality inside, if there was one.

According to Ben, he was proud of me for the great job that I did in the NHS for 'those sorts of patients', but he couldn't cope with the fact that I always had to be right about everything. I didn't think that was fair, and I threw his belongings into the street in an act of childish revenge. Not that I was bitter. Even if I wasn't wholly content and fulfilled in my life, I was at least free from the incessant wittering about football, which I hated anyway.

Emma was beginning to despair of me. After Ben had unceremoniously moved out, I had settled into a routine of social avoidance. After work, I liked nothing more than to vegetate in front of the telly. I hadn't taken up any new activities or joined a club as Emma had suggested. In fact I was licking my emotional wounds, having been distraught when Ben left, because I had honestly thought we were heading for marriage and children. When I eventually gave myself enough time to review my doomed relationship, I had concluded that Ben had lacked an understanding of how important my career was to me. If I had been honest with myself at the time, I should have declined additional shifts and spent time with Ben. Weekend and late shifts were bad enough in themselves for playing havoc with any routine, but they had all but destroyed a joint social life. What remained, was my focus on being a good nurse, in the hope that it would fill the gaping hole that Ben had left me to contend with.

These days it was me and Boris the cat, in our new compact and bijou flat, and that evening I was planning to crack open a lovely bottle of wine as I was on a late shift the next day. I consoled myself with the fact that I deserved wine. It was a necessity, not a luxury, as was the bar of chocolate waiting for me in the fridge. I also anticipated being able to flick on the TV and catch up with an episode of Cheers or Roseanne. Something mind-numbingly uncomplicated but uplifting was in order. However, before dulling my senses with wine, I decided to use what little brainpower I had left, to examine the words on the Section 3 recommendation paper written by Dr Sharman earlier. The copy I had in my pocket was crumpled, but the words were clear to read.

The first part had pre-printed options where the person completing the form confirmed their qualification as a Section 12 approved doctor. The form also required opinion and evidence as to why they were making the recommendation for detention under a particular Section.

Dr Sharman had completed the required parts of the form, and indicated that he already knew the patient. That was strange. He went on to state the following, '... *and has a diagnosis of schizophrenia. He is currently exhibiting clear signs of relapse in the form of grandiose delusions of a religious nature, paranoid delusions, and is responding to unseen stimuli. His presentation is of a nature and degree which warrants recommencement of treatment via detention in hospital, which cannot be achieved by any other means as he presents a risk to himself, his own health, and as a risk to the public. He has declined an informal hospital admission.'*

The document was signed with Dr Sharman's usual flourish, '*Dr Giles Sharman*', and was timed and dated.

I was stunned and confused by what I had read. I checked the name on the paper, and it stated Mr Trainman (*real name unknown*) and yet Dr Sharman had written that this was a known patient with a diagnosis.

If that was the case then how does he know him?

Does he really know him from his previous hospital?

Why doesn't he know his name?

And if Charming is acquainted with him, but does not know his name, then how can he know that he has an established diagnosis?

What was old Charming thinking, because obviously his recommendation would be markedly different from the approved social worker's, and from Dr Siddiqui's, written only the day before?

I needed to find out who reviewed these Section papers and checked their validity, apart from staff in the Mental Health Act office at Hollberry Hospital Psychiatric Unit. The recommendation for Mr Trainman was worse than a bit half-hearted or sloppy. It was a deliberate set of false statements written to validate Dr Charming Sharman's decision to place a man on Section 3 out of spite. I was no expert on the law, and particularly vague about Section 4. I didn't think I had ever come across its use. Either way, what Charming had written was a lie, blatant lies.

As a result of this torturous mystery, I had a sleepless night, despite the wine. Most of the wee small hours were spent dreaming up various ghastly punishments and murderous endings for Dr Sharman. A few of my ideas were really inventive, and others were a respectful reinvention of Roald Dahl's Tales of the Unexpected, with Sharman as the victim in each case.

My favourite was the tale in which the murder weapon is a frozen leg of lamb, which is then fed to the police who are sent to investigate. Genius though that idea was, I couldn't remember how the body of the victim was hidden or disposed of, and I wondered how I would hatch a plot that would put old Charming in my vicinity while I was holding a frozen leg of lamb. He tended to avoid me as if I deeply offended him in some way.

# Chapter 12

### Appealing

Mark saw nothing of Monica until the afternoon of the following day, by which time he had been given prescribed medication. In the morning, on the first occasion, he had used his tongue to divert the tablets into his cheek to avoid swallowing them. Despite the endless rehearsals at home, this had been trickier than anticipated. He was nervous and this hampered him significantly. Mark had also been ignorant of the fact that the whole process was overseen by the administrating staff nurse, from within a medication room, through a hatch. That particular nurse watched his every move. He was also keenly observed by one of the healthcare assistants who was standing within feet of him. The set-up ensured that everyone who was prescribed medication, arrived to receive it. In his head, Mark was struggling with a constant replay of the 'medication time' scene from the unforgettable film 'One Flew Over the Cuckoo's Nest'. *That's me, stuck in the loony bin, God knows how long for.*

Despite this pessimistic review of his circumstances, Mark was fascinated by the thoroughness of the ward teamwork. His name 'Mr Trainman' was checked against the drug chart, and the nurse who did not resemble Nurse Ratched from the film, confirmed what was written down as the prescription. Mark found her to be thoughtful and gentle in her approach as she went out of the way to explain what the medication was, and what possible side effects there might be from taking the tablets.

*Why hadn't the consultant been this thorough and informative when he prescribed it in the first place?* Mark wondered.

The staff nurse then told Mark when his next dose would be due. Having thoroughly assured herself that full advice had been given, she encouraged him to take the tablets in front of her, before she then signed the drug chart. Mark followed the instructions, then left the area promptly, ensuring that he spat the tablets into his hand, well out of sight of anyone. He also made sure that he did not head immediately towards a toilet, convinced that would arouse suspicion. He repeated the same process again after supper when his second dose was due.

Having been downstairs in the art group for part of the morning, he looked forward to more activities in the afternoon of the next day. Being occupied was a far better way to pass the time than remaining on the ward where the clocks ran painfully slowly. Monica had sent a message to the OT department requesting to see Mark on the ward as soon as the relaxation group had finished.

Feeling suitably relaxed, he found her in the ward office. All in all he had quite enjoyed the freedom of the OT department, and his second day in a mental hospital was so far proving to be much less stressful than his first.

\* \* \*

I would love to say that I managed to warn Jesus not to take the medication, or that I persuaded the doctors to change their minds about prescribing any, but that did not happen. By the time I next saw Jesus, he had already been given two doses of medication, and appeared slower in his movements. Not as overly sedated as I had feared.

He seemed pleased to see me. Relieved even. I had arranged to catch up with him personally in order to help hasten his right to appeal against his Section. I suppose it was my way of trying to right a wrong. Maybe he wasn't sedated, just relaxed.

No, he wasn't. There was something wrong. Jesus took a seat opposite me in the small office, and when his bright blue eyes caught mine, they betrayed a certain degree of trepidation on his part, I thought. He then passed me a piece of paper with the words, '*My name is Mark. Please help me*', written on it in spidery scrawling handwriting.

I must have appeared shocked because he put his finger to his lips to indicate for me to keep quiet. While my brain computed the possibilities contained within this brief but poignant written request, I hesitated in my response. Was he trying to tell me that he was struggling with a real mental health problem? Unlikely. Was he trying to get me on side to collude with a plan to escape from the ward? Possibly. Had he realised that he could be in all sorts of trouble because he was on Section 3? More than likely.

I decided to accept the words on the paper at face value, and as usual to do the right thing. 'You need to appeal to the hospital managers and the formal appeal tribunal, then they will listen to your case and decide if you should remain detained in hospital under the Mental Health Act.'

He nodded and I therefore continued.

'When you appeal it's best to have a solicitor to represent you, and they can be the most helpful people in these circumstances.' Which was true. 'I have a list of solicitors here. I can contact one for you, if you give me your consent.'

Jesus Trainman, now known to be called Mark, looked down the list and shrugged with a questioning expression on his face.

'These people have been recommended by other patients,' I said pointing about halfway down the list. 'They seem to be thorough and work really hard to challenge any detention. Section, detention, formal admissions are all the same thing by the way. Do you want me to phone for you and explain the situation? You may need to write down relevant information for them though.'

Mr Mark Trainman shook his head at the offer of pen and paper, which I found annoyingly obstructive. However, I had his permission, via a clear nod, to contact solicitors and this was good news all round because I had steered him towards a local firm that I had become familiar with in the past three years or so.

Huntley and Greaves were well respected, and one of their younger partners, Richard, son of Huntley senior, was often seen at the hospital, and he was the firm's expert in the Mental Health Act. He was a fine competitive adversary in any tribunal hearing, and we both seemed to relish our written and verbal sparring rounds, where he would attempt to pick the tiniest hole in my nursing report. Richard would use any error or contradiction in support of his argument against the detention of his client, whoever it was. In turn I would try to write the tightest of reports giving him no scope for debate. As a result, it was usually the consultant psychiatrists who took the brunt of a grilling from the tribunal, thinking their reports were beyond criticism, and yet they were generally found wanting. At times they were made to squirm in their seats when they failed miserably to answer the questions either from the tribunal or the solicitor. Those were my favourite moments, where I could shine purely by doing my job well.

I phoned the offices of Huntley and Greaves where I spoke to Cheryl, the most efficient of administrators. She knew who I was immediately, and guessed that I was asking for representation for an appeal against a Section. She was amused by the information I gave when she asked for the 'Name of the client please, Monica.'

'Mr Trainman.'

'First name?'

'Sorry, we don't know yet,' I lied. 'He doesn't speak and he hasn't given us any written information either, but he may well give details to Richard in confidence,' I prompted.

'Oh yes, this one sounds right up Richard's street. He's busy this afternoon, but I'll get a message to him, and hopefully he'll make arrangements to visit the ward tomorrow if he can. It's still Pargiter Ward, Monica, isn't it?'

'Yes, Cheryl. Thanks a lot. Could you see to it that Richard asks for me to be available because I'm the mystery gentleman's named nurse, and I need to ensure that Richard has the relevant details? This is potentially tricky, and I can't explain over the phone. Sorry.'

'That's okay. No problem. Will do. Speak to you soon. Bye now.'

That was excellent news. It had occurred to me that Richard might have been on paternity leave, and I couldn't for the life of me remember what he'd said about when the baby was due. I trusted Richard's judgement, and planned to give him the ins and outs of Dr Sharman's unfathomable decision-making in this case. I was convinced that there was something fishy about the decision to use Section 3, and about what was written on the Section paper. Relieved that Richard was available to represent him, I went to find Mr Trainman to give him the update.

I chose to keep referring to him as Mr Trainman in case I slipped up and called him Mark. I still don't know why I was keeping this so secret. On reflection, I think it was intuitive on my part not to reveal his name to anyone at that particular time, as I had been considering the possibility that Mr Trainman could be taking advantage of me for his own ends, whatever they were.

He had been consistent in his presentation the whole time he had been on the ward. Not once had he spoken to anyone, nor had he become restless agitated, or angry. Indeed he stuck out because he behaved more like a seasoned member of staff, spending much of his time sitting with the other patients on the ward listening to them or silently joining in with cards or games. He even helped with the giant blackboard crossword puzzle that we'd put in the main lounge for everyone to have a go at solving.

I was puzzled myself. Who was he and what was he doing here?

Why did he simply not tell the charming Dr Sharman his name and who he was? He would stand a good chance of being discharged on the basis that Dr Sharman could claim that the treatment had worked its magic. Mind you if I was he, I might worry that whatever I told Dr Sharman he would assume that I was delusional and would keep me locked up and treated for the hell of it.

Why was Mr Trainman choosing not to speak? If it was a trauma related reaction then where was the rest of the evidence for distress? What's he hiding and why was he not demanding to be let out?

Emma had her own Sherlock Holmes versus Moriarty theory and maybe she was correct. Was it the case that our Jesus lookalike was a bigger and more devious psychopath than Dr Sharman himself, and was in fact a cold-blooded killer? Was I now implicated in colluding with him? If so, I could lose my job and my registration if I was not careful.

The ward alarm had sounded briefly, a few seconds after I had finished on the phone to Cheryl at Huntley and Greaves, but by the time I arrived on scene, order had been restored. A minor skirmish had erupted between two of the male patients. One had apparently stolen the other one's Toblerone chocolate bar, and the accusations had resulted in a physical push me pull you. The nearest staff member to the kerfuffle had needed brief backup to settle the argument, but this did not take long and no damage was done, other than to the Toblerone itself which received a battering when used in self-defence. The incident became affectionately known as the First Battle of the Chocolate Wars. There were indeed a number of such battles over the ensuing days, and they invariably involved the same two people and bars of chocolate.

I eventually found Mr Trainman, who looked for all intents and purposes to be secretively making copious notes using his bedside locker as a table. He had pulled the curtains around his bed space, and appeared as if he was not expecting to be disturbed as he sat on the edge of the mattress. The dormitory door was slightly ajar, and as I made my usual silent approach, I caught a glimpse of him through a gap in the curtains, writing furiously. I watched noiselessly for several minutes before deciding to knock the dormitory door and call out, 'Mr Trainman? Are you about?'

That was a bit thoughtless of me, because he hadn't replied to anyone since his arrival on Pargiter Ward, but I needed a reason to approach the bed space and pull back the curtains to check his whereabouts. In those few seconds, he had miraculously made the notes disappear, and was sitting on the edge of his bed pretending to read a tatty old magazine. I knew he had heard me calling him. He was mute, not deaf.

I couldn't quite work out where he had rapidly hidden the notes he was making, but I was certain that I would be searching for them when I had the opportunity.

'Oh hello, there you are. I've come to let you know that I've called the solicitors and they are arranging for one of the partners called Richard Huntley to act on your behalf at your appeal. He's usually really thorough and his secretary hopes he can be here to see you tomorrow. If not, then definitely on Friday. It can take a week or two for appeal tribunal hearings to be set up, so try to be patient. Oops, pardon the pun!' I have a way with words. I had also seriously underestimated. It often took more than three weeks for a tribunal to be arranged.

'This is the NHS,' I reminded Mr Trainman, with a note of apology in my voice,' and the legal wheels of the Mental Health Act do turn quite slowly, I'm afraid. Perhaps you can join more of the groups downstairs to keep you occupied. They do a creative writing session which you may like,' I added, for my own amusement.

Mr Trainman looked deflated, but nodded to confirm he had understood and agreed. That was a standard response to the news that the Mental Health Act Commission was lacking in urgency. On the whole, we had disappointment as a reaction, with a general look of deflation, or lots of tears and wailing, or the destructive violent response, all of which I found understandable.

* * *

*Two weeks! Two whole weeks!* Mark screamed inside. He couldn't wait that long. What was he supposed to do in the meantime? Fester? Still it could have been worse. Could it? He had to firmly convince himself that he could easily manage two more weeks if the end result was to be worth the effort.

# Chapter 13

### A Little Clue

I was missing my good friend and colleague, Emma, who was away for a couple of days with her boyfriend Jake. The two of them had gone mud wrestling or dyke jumping, or an activity equally as ridiculous, I can't remember exactly. She breezed back onto the ward on the Friday, bursting with renewed energy, and I couldn't wait to update her with the latest.

'We have part of a name,' I proudly announced when she enquired about progress with Jesus Trainman. 'I say that, but I don't mean we, I mean me, because I haven't told anyone else yet.'

'Why not, you twerp?' Emma asked with a bemused look on her face.

'I don't know exactly,' I replied, subdued. 'I'm a bit wary of how Charming will react, and also I'm not sure about Jesus. Something is decidedly not right, but not in a mental way. More in an unsettling, dodgy, underhand way.'

'Good God, you sound like me, and you're usually the sensible one. Why don't you show Charming the note and let events take their course? What's the worst that can happen?'

'That's my point, Em. At the moment, I don't seem to be able to predict what could be the worst thing. Poor Greg has ended up chemically coshed by injection, looking like a zombie. Everyone else is relieved because he doesn't need close obs anymore and the doctors are calling that an improvement, would you believe. If I tell Charming that we have a note saying 'my name is Mark, please help me,' he will more than likely see it as irrefutable evidence that Jesus is psychotic.'

'Yes, but he thinks that anyway, and the man is already being treated with medication and on a Section 3, so it can't do any harm to have a first name.'

When I told Emma about the issue with the Section papers, she went straight to the shelves and pulled out the ward file containing the copies of every Section paper for patients on Pargiter Ward. Judging by her expression, she was as dumbfounded as I was when she read what Dr Charming Sharman had written on Mr Trainman's Section 3 recommendation.

'He can't write that, surely? He doesn't know him, does he? That settles it,' she announced. 'You give Charming the note, and if he knows Jesus, he should simply recall his full name once he's given the first part of the riddle.'

'Good plan. How far away is the next ward round? Or ... I tell you what, shall I phone his secretary? Yes, that's a better idea. I can tell him over the phone, that way he can't see my facial expressions. You stay here so you can hear what he says.'

Phoning through to Charming's office, I secretly prayed that he would be far too busy to take a call. I explained to Lucy, his secretary, why I was contacting, and she seemed delighted that I had news. How such a nice person could work for such an awful man was beyond me, but she never said a bad word about him.

'Hang on, Monica. I'll see if he's free.' She then put me through.

'Giles Sharman,' he announced in his usual dismissive tone.

'Hello Dr Sharman, it's Nurse Morris from Pargiter Ward. I have a first name for you for our mystery man. Mr Trainman. His name is Mark.'

'Is that it? Anything else of any use?'

'Sorry ...' I stammered a bit. 'I, I thought if you had the first name it may ring a few bells with you and you might recall his full name.'

'How the hell would I do that? ESP or a Jedi mind trick perhaps? I have never met the fellow before. See if you can do a bit better than that, Nurse Morris, before you disturb me again.'

'Yes, ssssssorry,' I stammered once more.

He hung up abruptly.

Emma and I looked at each other for a while in silence, before Emma filled the void with a relevant observation. 'Jedi mind trick … Star Wars fan then. Amazing. I never would have imagined that.'

'No, indeed …'

'I fail to understand old Charming. He wrote a lie, a total fabrication to place a man on a Section 3. Why would a Section 2 not have been sufficient punishment?'

Emma was digging around trying to pick stubborn particles of mud, grit and greenery from her left ear with her little finger. As she continued to do so, she regaled me with stories of her muddy exploits from the past two days and then announced that she had heard about an event called the World Bog Snorkelling Championships which she was going to enter next summer. I confess that I had no idea what she was babbling on about.

It was around that time that dear Richard Huntley, solicitor extraordinaire, arrived on the ward. He had promised to try to make it that day, and it was a relief to see him. Emma volunteered to sort out various ward and patient requirements, giving me time to direct Richard to his initial consultation with Mr Trainman. I informed him that we now had a first name for his client. With a quizzical look in my direction, he confirmed that he was already aware of this. How he knew that piece of information or where he had obtained it was a mystery, as only myself, Emma, and Dr Sharman knew this. I had only disclosed the fact a matter of minutes previously. I didn't have time to pursue this with Richard who was keener to meet his new client than he was to chat with me. To be fair, that was his job.

* * *

Mark Trainman was pleased to meet Richard, judging by his expression, and I offered them the use of a small office nearby while I went to collect ward notes, a drug chart, and for good measure, took them both, hot drinks. Richard had arrived armed with lots of spare paper and pens, and I hoped that Mark Trainman would open up to Richard; otherwise it would be an awkward first meeting.

* * *

I left them to it, and risked an exploration of Mr Trainman's bed space in the dormitory during his absence. As it happened, Gina the cleaner was in the room tidying and neatening up the odd bed, even though she was not supposed to. Patients were encouraged to make their own beds, but more often than not we stepped in. I for one couldn't cope with unmade beds in a hospital ward. Gina's presence was usefully convenient for me. It meant that I could pretend to be doing the same. I looked as if I were helping her and while I did so I had a proper rummage to find the papers I had seen Mark Trainman feverishly hiding earlier.

Found them.

'Bugger! What the hell is this? You have to be kidding.' What did it all mean? I was fairly certain that I was looking at shorthand. Now that is mad, I thought. It could be, I don't know if it is mad or not, it's gibberish to me. Bloody marvellous!

* * *

I couldn't take the risk of leaving the ward to find a photocopier, as I would undoubtedly be caught with the papers in my hands. So I placed them carefully back where I had found them, predictably under the mattress.

I hoped Richard was having more luck.

# Chapter 14

## Some Weeks Earlier

Mark walked slowly but purposefully towards the back of a large imposing office block in central London, making his way along the narrow service road. He could smell and taste the pollution in the air. Nasty. He had taken the train from his parents' home in Suffolk with reservations about whether to take on another assignment so soon. He was less battle weary, and had enjoyed the food and relaxation over the past four weeks, but wasn't even sure he wanted to stay in the UK for much longer.

'Hello, mate. Long time no see … excellent tan by the way. Been somewhere nice?' A slim neatly dressed young man looked Mark up and down, mocking his choice of business attire. Mark couldn't care less how he dressed, and as usual he wore a pair of well-worn Levi jeans, his beloved leather sandals, and a scruffy t-shirt. He was clean-shaven, and his long dark hair was tied back in a ponytail. He had his battered trusty old camera in a brown leather case slung over one shoulder by its long strap. Despite the modern attire, and having shaved, he still looked like everyone's idea of Jesus; something he was well aware of. Mark secretly enjoyed the expressions of surprise on people's faces or double-takes from passers by. It made him smile.

'Hello, Charlie. How are you?' Mark said as he crossed the road to catch up with his younger colleague. He knew that Charlie was being facetious in his comment about his tan, because Mark spent most of his life in the Middle East.

'I take it we're both headed in the same direction. What's this about, do you know? It's a bit cloak and dagger.'

'Not a damn clue,' shrugged Charlie. Mark liked Charlie immensely, he always had. Charlie was a lovable tear-away who had never escaped his reputation as a womaniser. For good reason. Mark wished that he had Charlie's confidence when it came to the opposite sex.

'How's your love life these days?' asked Charlie, picking up on Mark's weak spot. 'As barren as the deserts you spend your time in, I would guess. You always look like you're in need of a good shag. Cut your hair. That'll help.'

'How will that help?' replied Mark, inadvertently giving away the fact that Charlie was correct about his lack of a love life.

'Jesus: did he have a wonderful love life? No. You look like Jesus, and so women will avoid you. Stands to reason. You're not enough of a caveman. You're too nice. Women like their affairs to be rough, treacherous, uncertain.'

'Do they now?' Mark thanked Charlie for his valuable advice, and decided to ignore it. Mark had had girlfriends in the past, but they soon became fed up with his disappearing acts when he went on assignment. One-night stands weren't an acceptable alternative.

'I thought you were still shacked up with the lovely Penny Arnott?'

'No. She had a better offer. She was in Hong Kong a few weeks ago, in your neck of the woods, I believe. She's free, if you're interested.' Mark tried to convince Charlie that this was a nonchalant comment, laden with masculine bravado, and with no emotion attached. In reality, it was painful for Mark to even say Penny's name out loud. He had been viciously wounded when she had packed her bags.

'Crackin'. I'll look her up. She still working for Reuters?'

Mark nodded in response. He ended the unbearable conversation.

* * *

Mark and Charlie made their way through the rear doors via intercom to reception, and said hello to the security man inside, both wafting their passes in his direction. They then went upstairs, bypassing the noisy smoke-filled newsroom, and headed straight to a large and airy meeting room next door to the editor's office. Although freelance, both Mark and Charlie did a lot of work for the Albion Group of newspapers, covering foreign assignments, usually at times of political unrest. That was most of the time, and could be anywhere in the world.

Mark had made the Middle East his home for years, much to the detriment of any real social life, but he loved his job and wouldn't have settled for anything less exciting. It was the thrill of the chase and the final exhilaration of a journalistic coup that kept him returning for more, like an addict. He had clocked up more time in war-zones than most of the armed forces that he came across, and although he always appeared the epitome of the unflappable war correspondent, the last few years had begun to take their toll. He had dreadful trouble sleeping. He was feeling tired, and at the same time jittery from the caffeine that day. Mark used strong coffee to keep him more alert. He owned a t-shirt that said '*Be alert ... your country needs lerts*,' which tickled his sense of humour, and he wished he had worn it that morning as it might have helped to fight his fuzzy-headed fatigue.

'This is a sort of reunion then,' remarked Charlie. 'I've spotted at least three other journalists that I know well. See, there's Jock Mackenzie, and there's Linda. I don't recognise that posh bloke in the flashy whistle standing near the projector, do you?'

'No, I don't think I've seen him before. Blimey that is an expensive looking suit. What do you think? Lawyer? There's a serious air about him.'

They sauntered across the room, scouting around as they helped themselves to a cup of cardboard coffee from a machine. Mark turned his nose up at the watery offering in his cup. He sipped; it was better than nothing. Carrying their coffees, Charlie led the way as they went over to speak to Linda, a middle-aged battle-axe of a woman with a wicked sense of humour. She had been writing for years in various political columns, and had a scathing wit. Hilariously no one in the general population knew what she looked like nowadays. The papers always published a photograph at the top of her articles that she had professionally commissioned some time in the 1960s.

Putting their cups of coffee down for them on a table, she gave both young men a motherly hug, which judging by Charlie's face was more familiar than he would have liked. His whole head disappeared into her ample breasts, and he came up gasping for air. 'Yes, lovely to see you too, Linda,' he croaked, stepping back and out of her reach. She gazed lustfully up at Mark, who was much taller than his companion.

'Come here, my Laurence of Arabia. Let's have a look at those lovely blue eyes. A hug would be in order for you too,' rasped Linda in her well-established smoker's voice.

Mark allowed himself to be crushed to Linda's bosom, because it was easier than trying to avoid the inevitable tongue lashing if he didn't. He knew that Linda was convinced he was gay, simply because unlike most other foreign correspondents, he did not smoke and only drank in moderation. Healthy living was an alien concept to most in the newsroom at The Daily Albion.

Unlike the papers owned by Rupert Murdoch, The Albion Group had not gone to Wapping, although they had moved to more modern premises and embraced the newer printing technologies. As previously, they also continued to be well respected for the quality and accuracy of their copy. The old days of spending most of their working hours in the pubs around Fleet Street had long gone for most news reporters, apart from die-hards like Linda of course. Journalistically she would, at that time, have had her daggers out for the likes of the Prime Minister John Major, but he was so bland and boring that she had taken every opportunity to prickle about Bill Clinton, who was more deliciously vulnerable to a scandal.

The writers of the outstanding satirical Spitting Image TV series, often picked up on the barbed and outrageous observations Linda made in her columns, and she was even occasionally mentioned by name on the programme. She made no secret of the fact that she was glad that her notoriety attracted no more than a name-mention, as to have a Spitting Image puppet made of her would reveal how much she had aged. A puppet in her image would also evidence her surrender to middle-age spread, and would inevitably exaggerate the uncomfortable level of menopausal sweatiness she experienced. The writers of that series took no prisoners.

'What's this all about then, boys?' asked Linda, once she had calmed down.

'No idea, sorry,' replied Mark, 'but I think we're about to find out.'

At that moment, the editor John Starkey walked through the door, accompanied by a number of people of varying shapes and sizes, and the room came to attention.

'Please, ladies and gentlemen, take a seat, and we shall reveal your next job, if you choose to take up the opportunity of a lifetime.'

*This sounds promising*, Mark said to himself, while earnestly hoping that he was not about to be sent to Bosnia by way of a change from the Middle East.

The editor then introduced the guests he had seated next to him: a handful of medical researchers, a professor, and a lawyer who turned out to be the man who had been standing next to the overhead projector when Charlie and Mark had arrived. Starkey then asked for the eight journalists present to make use of the paper and pens in front of them to take shorthand notes if they wished, because as he pointed out to them, 'there will be no printed copies of the following presentations.'

The journalists looked around, and picked up the pens in front of them in anticipation, raising the occasional eyebrow to each other.

'I'm sorry that this appears somewhat hush-hush, but as you will soon hear we need to keep this assignment plan under the media radar until such time as you have all completed your individual tasks. This will make more sense once Professor Hugo here, has given you the details of what we are endeavouring to achieve.'

Mark didn't know what to make of the announcement. There were no real clues forthcoming.

# Chapter 15

## The Rosenhan Experiment Explained

P rofessor Hugo was introduced again as a medical researcher, and he stood at the head of the table making use of the overhead projector to show a handful of acetate slides during his presentation. The researchers were from the University of London, as was neatly depicted on the overhead screen in a diagram for the audience to see. *No help there*, thought Mark, eager for them to get to the punch-line. *What the hell is it that they actually want from us?*

Professor Hugo Greenaway, who became affectionately known as 'Prof Hugo', began a rather lengthy but enthusiastic explanation. Mark was struck by how the professor was the epitome of the mad scientist. He had wild wiry unkempt hair that preferred to remain vertical, underneath which there existed a cherubic rosy-cheeked face. Prof Hugo was straight out of the 1940s. He wore a short-sleeved shirt overlaid by an unfashionable knitted tank top, which he had paired with oversized corduroy trousers in a ghastly caramel colour. Added to this were round horn-rimmed glasses and brown brogues on his feet. His shoes were screaming out for the attention of polish. He was immediately likeable.

'Ladies and gentleman, thank you for coming today. You are about to enter the world of psychiatry together. I realise that this is not necessarily your field of expertise, but you have been asked to come along because you have certain skills and attributes that we believe are required for the assignment we would like you to undertake on behalf of the paper, and for the

Research Institute. I therefore will try to set the scene to make this a lot clearer to you.'

As he spoke there was an audible gasp from the people in the room who were meeting Prof Hugo for the first time. He had a most unusual voice, and even though he must have been familiar with lecturing to hundreds of postgraduate students, he stuttered his way through.

Mark was stunned. He'd never heard anything quite like it. Prof Hugo had a helium voice and nervous style. The tone was so high and squeaky that everyone hung on each word, in astonishment. Around the table, the journalists had forgotten to take notes and were, it seemed, temporarily immobilised by the performance of the man in front of them.

Journalists are notoriously competitive, and once over the initial shock, this introduction had them leaning forward on their marks, and at the ready. All apart from Mark who sat back in his chair, not too enthused.

Prof Hugo went on. 'There is currently a wave of antipsychiatry protests amongst those who have experienced mental health care. Mental patients, the insane, the mad, the bad, and the sad, call them what you will. Those that write about the experience in protest, often refer to themselves as "survivors of the mental health system". We at the institute want to get a better idea what the underlying facts are, because our qualitative research so far, has led us to believe that there is validity in the first-hand accounts. What we are hearing seems to identify an abuse of power by consultant psychiatrists in controlling this vulnerable part of society.'

Mark was disappointed. *Is that it? Researching dodgy psychiatric institutions. They'll never let us in. They never have.* Mark felt unusually deflated by the news that the assignment was going to be so tame. He tried to tune back in to what Professor Hugo was saying but had lost interest. He distracted himself by doodling, and allowed the professor's squeaky words to drift by.

'We think this misuse of power, abuse if you will, has been occurring since the time of the large asylums in this country.

When we say abuse, we really mean abuse, and we wish not only to research but to expose this abuse at the same time, if it exists.'

The professor paused as if to gather his thoughts for a few moments, and then he tried to continue, but lost his grip on the acetate films that he was trying to place on the overhead projector. As a result, he fumbled and grabbed at the slides, which behaved as if they were slippery eels, slithering gently to the floor, defying his every attempt to catch them.

'Oh dear. Oh dear. Now where was I?'

He repeated these words on each occasion that this mishandling of slides happened during his presentation. The audience, including Mark, made mammoth efforts to control and stifle the uproarious laughter that threatened to erupt each time this comedy sketch took place. By the end of the presentation, Mark's ribs were aching with the exertion of trying not to laugh, and he was sure his fellow journalists were in the same predicament. Most were holding onto themselves with arms held across their midriffs, lips were being bitten and tears were rolling unhindered down cheeks by way of release.

'Ah yes.' The antipsychiatry movement. They seem to be made up of these so called survivor patients of mental health services, but also of psychologists, social commentators and indeed psychiatrists. They, as a group or groups, assert that our psychiatric facilities are bulging at the seams with people who either shouldn't be there, or for whom medication is not the answer.

'It appears that people are abandoning their drug treatments, and in most cases, but not all, they are becoming unwell again and therefore needing readmission to psychiatric wards. This has created pressure and apparent indignity and suffering. In effect we may in the UK have exchanged large asylums for lots of smaller oppressive ones. Let me explain in more detail how we believe we can demonstrate this one way or the other.'

Prof Hugo had the room's attention, although not purely because of the content of the information. Most of the journalists were watching his every entertaining move, and their faces were lit up, like those of children at a circus.

'In the 1970s in the USA there was a famous experiment carried out by a psychologist who was also a university professor by the name of David Rosenhan. He set out to determine how valid psychiatric diagnoses were. At that time there was, and still is, a lot of criticism of how the mentally ill were diagnosed and treated, so Rosenhan set up an experiment to test this, by sending pretend patients into various psychiatric hospitals across a number of states in America. The pretend patients were instructed to report that they were hearing voices in order to gain admission to those hospitals if possible.'

Linda interrupted. 'If this one-flew-over-the-cuckoo's-nest research has been done before, why are we considering doing this again? It's hardly newsworthy to repeat it.' Mark agreed. As funny as the presentation was, he was not on board with the proposed assignment.

'I appreciate your question, and I hope that things will become clear, as I go through the detail. There will be ample time for questions once I have set the scene, as it were.'

Prof Hugo held Linda's gaze briefly as he floundered for a few seconds fiddling with his notes, and there was a considerable delay before he proceeded. 'Where was I? Oh yes. In the 1970s. The Rosenhan Experiment. Which was famous by the way. Now then, when the pretend patients arrived unannounced at the various hospitals, they reported that they were hearing voices. Have I said that bit yet?

'Anyway, they had to describe their voice-hearing experiences in the same way. They told the psychiatrists in each case that they had unclear voices, which said the words "hollow", "empty", and "thud". There were twelve of these pretend patients, and they gained admission to hospitals across the USA. No other psychiatric symptoms were reported or described by them in any way, and they gave false names and fake information as to their occupation and such like. Are you with me so far?'

Prof Hugo outlined that the pretend patients in this experiment were instructed to behave normally after they were admitted, and they were also instructed to report to staff that they were no longer experiencing any hallucinations. So in effect, the pretend patients had only reported hallucinations for a brief period of time, and these voice-hearing reports, on their own, would not necessarily indicate the presence of a mental illness.

'However, in each case they were all given a diagnosis of a mental illness, and they were all prescribed medication. Most surprisingly each one of them had to admit to having a mental illness and agree to continue on prescribed medication before they could secure their discharges from the hospitals.

'I emphasise again that … that,' stuttered Prof Hugo, 'this was in every case. Professor Rosenhan had taken part in the experiment himself, you know. He was stuck in hospital for weeks.'

According to Prof Hugo, while the pretend patients were in the hospitals, no one had challenged them or even identified them as imposters. 'I need to make it clear that the pretend patients did not actually take the medication; they pretended to do so, and flushed it down the toilet, taking care not to get caught. And the contact the patients had with doctors, who, remember, are the professionals in control of decisions, was for an average of six point eight minutes per day, shocking, when you think about it.'

Now the professor informed the listening audience that, while these were alarming outcomes in themselves, there was actually a second and more surprising part to Rosenhan's experiment. One of the hospitals where the first part of the experiment had taken place, was offended by the initial research findings, and Rosenhan was challenged to send further pseudo-patients. The hospital in question believed that their staff would be able to detect any imposter. A timescale was agreed during which 193 new patients were seen. Of these, the staff at this particular hospital identified forty-one as potential pretend patients, with nineteen being suspected as such by a psychiatrist and at least one other member of staff.

'That seems pretty impressive, doesn't it?' challenged Prof Hugo who was at last getting to grips with the use of the overhead projector. 'But ladies and gentlemen, how many pretend patients had Rosenhan sent to that hospital?'

There was a long pause. Mark was interested enough to listen intently for the answer.

'None. Not one!' announced the professor proudly. 'Rosenhan then, would you believe, wholeheartedly upset the psychiatric profession by concluding in his research that they, the psychiatrists that is, could not distinguish the sane from the insane in their hospitals. Much of the psychiatric profession was outraged when he published the full findings. So then where does this lead us?'

Mark perked up. *Finally, we get to the point!*

'Well,' revealed the professor, 'we are aiming to repeat a version of part one of the experiment. It would be anticipated that things have improved and moved forward since the 1970s, but as I said earlier, the evidence we have to-date does not seem to indicate that this is the case.

'We have approached you, the journalists around the table, because of your backgrounds and reputation. Most of you have careers in which you have had to give factual accounts, where you have borne witness to extraordinary events, and you have the capacity to file clear thoughtful and accurate reports in the middle of turmoil. This should therefore be easy for you. However, you may need to call on your personal resources, as we are making one or two changes to the Rosenhan experiment.'

Prof Hugo paused again, carefully observing each of the journalists around the room. 'Any immediate questions?'

Mark was still in a state of mild disbelief. He had spent the last few months in the Lebanon, in Israel, and in Palestine. He had been in Gaza at the beginning of July when Yasser Arafat returned after twenty-seven years in exile. After which there were real hopes that the Middle East would settle down with the political scenery looking rosier. Mark had anticipated being less busy as a result, however he was not expecting his next assignment to be this. It could be a really nice change, he thought, to spend a few days in a nut house, or conversely he could be bored witless. He had one simple question at that point.

'If the hospitals in this country are bursting at the seams, just how are we going to get ourselves admitted without being bonkers for real? Let's face it, if we behave normally and get discharged, then this is not going to be very fruitful for either the paper as far as copy, or for your research,' Mark offered.

The prof nodded, appreciating the question. 'That is a consideration, and if the results indicate an improvement in care and treatment, then we have to question the whole anti psychiatry movement and its political motives. But you do raise a good point about the potential challenge of achieving admission. This brings me neatly onto the different approach we will be using in comparison to Rosenhan. We are going to base our experiment on behaviour rather than voice hearing or reported symptoms of any kind. This effectively negates the criticism that Rosenhan received. After publication of his findings it was proposed by the world of psychiatry, that because the pretend patients in his experiment had actually described mental illness symptoms, this created enormous bias towards diagnosis of a mental illness.

'So ... you are all going to devise a plan for admission based on bizarre or irrational behaviour in order to gain admission if you can. Additionally you will remain silent, mute, or at least wordless for the first few days. The plan is that you will then return to normal behaviour but not speak to the doctors or staff initially. The project can then be managed in the same way as the Rosenhan team by giving false names and occupations, but not admitting to any symptoms or feelings or behaviour that you do not normally experience.'

*Bloody hell*, thought Mark, *We're going in. Undercover. How on earth is that going to work?*

'Once you have settled in, you should be able to access a telephone to contact one of us who are leading the research project to confirm your admission. That will be, John Starkey,

Lewis James who you will meet shortly, and myself. There will be no need to make any written reports until the end of the experiment. However, you need to be aware that any one of you could end up under a Section of the Mental Health Act, which is why we have invited our local neighbourhood lawyer, Lewis here, to clarify this possibility.

'That's enough talking and listening for now. Let's take a break and have a coffee, a cup of tea, a cigarette break, or whatever you need. Please remember not to discuss this in public areas. We will be asking for complete silence. Have a good chat with each other though, and be back round the table in twenty minutes, if that is okay?'

The room remained silent and still for a couple of seconds before Charlie piped up. 'How's Linda going to manage without her fags and gin in a hospital? That's a bit cruel.'

Linda was lightening-quick with her riposte. 'There speaks Charlie who spends his entire working life in the Foreign Correspondents' Club in Hong Kong, drinking, smoking and extracting stories from people who actually do the job they are paid for. Or, when he's back in dear old Blighty, he can be found shagging their wives for the same reason. Perhaps you should pretend you feel guilty about this and want to jump from a bridge, a high one.'

Charlie smiled cockily, and returned the compliment using fairly ripe language that made Linda laugh and then cough. Much to Mark's irritation, she lit up her fifteenth cigarette of the day.

With the room buzzing from the noise of chattering excitement, everyone could let out the laughter that they had been painfully holding onto for so long.

Mark remained reflective. He had been struck by what Prof Hugo had insinuated. He had seen people with incredible resilience in war zones, but also witnessed the demise of many who cracked under the strain, including a handful of his colleagues in recent years. He wondered about Charlie, who, on the face of it, appeared charming and full of his usual flirtatious energy and childish enthusiasm, but who was going to great pains to avoid active frontline war zone journalism. Linda's comment about him leeching information from other journalists had been remarkably truthful. Mark could see why Charlie needed to absent himself from the on-the-ground reporter role, because the truth of it was that most of them didn't survive long. Many returned to a desk job or ended up drug and alcohol fuelled shadows of their former selves. Of course he had also lost a few close colleagues altogether, as the death toll amongst foreign war correspondents was notoriously high given the nature of their work. Mark found himself on one hand relieved that he was not off to Bosnia, and on the other, tempted and intrigued by this experiment and assignment. He wasn't too worried about the risks. What was the worst that could happen? He'd get found out and thrown out of hospital, which would hardly come as a surprise, because he was well aware that psychiatric wards were generally no-go areas for journalists. Still, it would be a free hotel bed for a few nights, in the company of other interesting guests. Maybe it was time to retire from the Middle East front line for a while at least. For now, he wanted to get a lungful or two of fresh air away from Linda and her foul cigarette smoke.

He stepped into the polluted London air.

# Chapter 16

## The Sharp-dressed Lawyer Speaks

The serious-looking lawyer, not previously recognised by either Charlie or Mark, stood back from the head of the table. He waited for the assembled group to settle again and sit with pens at the ready for round two.

He had lost the serious expression, and was smiling and relaxed. Before speaking, he gave a broad grin exhibiting a fine set of even white teeth. Tall and dark featured, he was sharply dressed in an obviously costly suit, which fitted perfectly. John Starkey, wearer of the crumpled suit look, and the editor of the Daily Albion, introduced this smiling man as Lewis James, 'a barrister with a specialism covering mental health law and civil rights.'

It turned out that Lewis James was not a serious character.

'Hello to you lovely journalistic sensation-seekers, and research boffins. Yes, I am Lewis James.' His clear and resonant mellow voice with a noticeable Northern accent echoed around the room. Mark found that it was not easy to work out whether this was a Yorkshire or Lancashire accent, but it was intriguing and rather unexpected. The man himself looked too London-executive posh, for a down-to-earth northerner. The effect was curiously incongruous.

Lewis James did a passable impression of Tommy Cooper. 'Lewis James, James Lewis … just like that, shushuum. Please try not to get the names the wrong way round, as you may have need of my services in the coming weeks, and it is important that you have my name and my contact number indelibly etched on your brains and in your memories. Although you may find it hard to believe, I originally worked as a mental health nurse. Yes indeed, that was years ago, and it may explain why I don't sound like a barrister, or sometimes behave like one. I'm also married to a consultant psychiatrist.

'Aha, I see I have your attention. Yes, she's a wonderful woman and a dedicated doctor, so I'm taking a tidy risk by joining this research project as legal advisor. Now then, because I cannot discuss this with my wife in any shape or form, things could become awkward. I'm sure she will suspect that I'm up to no good, as she's remarkably perceptive. Having said that, confidentiality rules okay in our house, and she's used to me not being able to discuss important cases. So I'm safe enough for now. I suppose it depends how long you and I are going to carry on this clandestine relationship.'

Lewis James meandered around as he spoke, carefully catching the eye of each of those seated around the table, occasionally tugging at his cuffs and flashing his pearly white teeth as he did so.

'I'm here to dispel and debunk a few myths, and also to guide you through the "shoulds" and "coulds" of this project. By that I mean, what should happen to you when you attempt your admission to hospital, and then also to help look at what could happen to you, in order for us to consider necessary contingencies.'

Mark was relieved to hear that here, at last, was a man in the know. This idea for research was all well and good, but he was damn sure that no one else in the room actually had experience of what it was like inside a psychiatric ward.

Sensibly, Lewis began with the basics, and he outlined that once each of the volunteers had decided on a suitable false identity – including a plan for admission and back-story – they would be temporarily registered with an out of area GP. In fact they would be as far away from their home territory as was reasonable, to avoid bumping into someone they knew, or who knew them.

'When and how you give information about your false selves and your temporary GPs is up to you, but as you will be newly registered as temporary patients, the GP practice will have no past history to give to the hospitals when they ring for background information about you.'

One of the journalists by the name of Jock, a ferret of a man with a strong Scottish accent, put his hand in the air, and was invited to ask his question with a nod and a wave from Lewis James. 'Aye, what aboot an address? Surely we will need one to register?'

'Correct, yes, you will be given one of those too. The road names and postcode will exist but the house number will not. In effect my friends, you will become a finely tuned group of undercover agents by the time you enter the hospital environment.'

'Now you're talking,' muttered Mark. At last there seemed to be evidence of organisation. Mark stopped doodling, and instead gave his full attention to what was being said.

Lewis James clarified that the research project would be confined to English hospitals only.

'Scottish mental health law is different,' Lewis explained. 'We did consider Wales but they speak Welsh far too often, so we thought better of that idea. Anyway, what should happen is, whichever your route in, you will more than likely end up being assessed by an on-call doctor. You have been asked to remain silent or at least wordless, but I would suggest that you make the odd noise, or hum or wail. Whatever you do, your behaviour must be a cause for concern enough to warrant an admission. If you get it right, then you may succeed in raising anxieties purely by the method you choose to get you to the point of assessment. For example, the idea of jumping off a bridge is pretty good, as long as you don't actually launch yourself into the Thames.'

Lewis James had quickly picked up on the reference made by Linda to Charlie about jumping from a bridge, and he became more animated as his descriptions went on.

'Now then, let's imagine your admission raises an unhealthy amount of concern, and that a decision is made to assess you under the Mental Health Act. Don't worry. Remember that the medical staff and the approved social workers are trained to carry out this role, and they have to act in the interests of you as the patient, and the wider public. If this does happen, you will only be placed under a Section 2, which allows for assessment where necessary for up to twenty-eight days. I repeat: up to twenty-eight days. It doesn't mean you'll be in for a whole month. A Section 2 is used because you do not have an established diagnosis, and even if you do in real life, you now have a false name, so they don't know if you are already a little bonkers. Which, quite frankly, you must be to sit here at least considering whether or not to take part in this outrageously adventurous experiment.' He laughed.

'Anyway, I must impress on you to be careful not to overdo the acting, as you may attract too much attention which would result in treatment being administered early on in proceedings, and there may be consideration of the use of an injection. You must avoid this. Remember, as the prof said, you will be expected not to swallow any medication given to you. Unless you have a headache or need a sleeping tablet in which case, please make sure you know what you are being given. Here is my top tip. If a nurse or doctor offers you "something to help you relax", this may not be a sleeping tablet. Always politely decline. However, if you have been prescribed treatment with tablets, then you must pretend to take them. Please don't get caught hiding or disposing of medication otherwise, again, you may be required to take liquids or be given an injection. Simply become model citizens, and show the staff how you have recovered from whatever took you there in the first place.'

Mark realised that this was far from being a tame assignment. Injections meant needles and he hated needles. He'd rather risk humiliation by chatting up a girl and being rejected, than have an injection.

Lewis James then returned to his favourite subject of the law. 'If you are placed under a Section, you must appeal at the earliest opportunity. You should be given the details about your rights if you are placed under Section, but no one automatically appeals for you. If you do unexpectedly end up on a Section 3, which is highly unlikely unless you have done something stupid, then appeal immediately. This is why we insist that, as soon as you are admitted, you show no further strange or bizarre behaviour. If you are already odd or bizarre then frankly you are on your own.'

There was a ripple of laughter around the room at this comment.

'The team on the ward in these hospitals are there to look after you and help you, and we are only interested in the skill and ability of those staff to assess and identify mental illness, and only to treat if this is necessary. They are also under pressure for beds to be freed up, so if you are not requiring care and treatment then your discharges should be relatively swift. We anticipate two weeks maximum, and that would only be if things did not go as well as planned.'

Linda raised her hand. She had been remarkably contained, and appeared to be focussing on every word and gesture from Lewis James. Mark assumed that she had become transfixed by his matinee idol good looks.

'Could I ask about the patients we will be on the ward with, and will we have our own rooms, and could you explain the usual arrangements for use of the bathroom and toilets and such like?'

'Ah! Yes, lovely lady,' Lewis replied. Charlie and Mark looked at each other, and tried not to allow themselves a chuckle at the thought of Linda being described as lovely. 'These are indeed most important points. Let's look first at the practicalities. Not all hospitals are the same, but in general there are a mixture of single rooms and small dormitories. Many places are well appointed, and others a little tired looking, shall we say. There is usually access to a payphone so you can contact John Starkey, Prof Hugo, or myself. We advise taking a couple of ten pence pieces with you, but you should not take wallets or purses full of money. Only have with you a minimal amount of cash for necessities. Nor should you have any of your own ID in your possession. I'm sure that is an obvious point, but worth saying nevertheless.

'Now then, other information: those of you who are tobacco addicts may be relieved to hear that psychiatric wards have a smoking room, which should be home from home for those of you who are normally based in newsrooms, if the one here is anything to go by.

'The bathrooms are basic and adequate, but be aware, there is the facility for staff to unlock the doors from the outside, and if patients require special close observation because of a suicide risk, then the member of staff will need to be present within the bathroom and the toilet. I know, not nice.

'I reiterate, please do not over-act, and be your usual selves once admitted, and your privacy will be assured.'

Stopping and looking at them all again, pausing for a while, he then said in a slow and measured manner, 'The patients in acute psychiatric wards are there because they are not well. They require care and treatment in the same way that anyone would if admitted into a general hospital ward. They come from various walks of life, and will have different stories to tell. I said at the beginning that I would dispel some myths … here goes. Despite what sensationalist journalism would have us believe …'

Lewis gave a knowing look around the table before continuing. 'Most mentally ill people are not, I repeat not, violent and dangerous. They may behave through fear in an aggressive or hostile manner because they genuinely believe they are at risk of harm.'

Lewis went on, 'If my food were to start tasting bitter, for example, I might think I was being poisoned, but who wants to poison me? Actually in my case there are several possibilities … but you get my drift. The vast majority of patients who you'll meet on the wards, will be obviously mentally unwell, but remember, these are people like you or me, who deserve to be treated with respect and dignity. So I ask you, when you write about your experiences, please maintain the confidentiality of the other patients. As in the case of any other interview you hold, you may be confident about asking permission to report their story. However, if you think that person does not understand the implications, then be professional and don't identify them.

'On one important note: please remember that it is an offence under the law in this country to aid a person who is detained under Section in absconding. I'm saying this because you may feel sorry for one of the other patients, and they may be desperate to leave, but you must not collude or collaborate. It's illegal.

'Also, please give respect to the staff members who are trying to do a stressful job in difficult circumstances.

'Let's face it, journalists do not get this opportunity often, if at all, because you are not usually invited to the mad hatter's tea party. This time you are going to be at the party, but don't enjoy yourselves too much. Are there any more questions?'

'Yes. Could you explain a bit more about possible treatments, and things like electric shocks, and how we would avoid that if it was prescribed,' an anxious female researcher asked.

'Indeed. No need to worry so much. You will not be offered ECT. This is for extreme cases of intractable depression, and rarely in cases of acute schizophrenia. So please do not fret about that as a possibility, this isn't "One Flew Over the Cuckoo's Nest",' said Lewis James, looking deliberately at Linda, who smiled in response, without the need to say a word.

'Possible treatment with medication can range from antidepressants to antipsychotics, but again, you will not swallow these tablets, as we discussed earlier. By the way, you should not allow your fellow patients to know you are disposing of tablets.

'Other treatments ... psychology and such-like is rarely available on the hospital wards, but you will usually attend activities, group sessions, art and occupational therapy of some kind, to fill your days.'

'What's the issue with a Section 3?' Charlie asked earnestly.

Lewis was more than happy to go into detail. 'A Section 3 carries with it a number of wider implications. If you are subject to this particular Section of the Mental Health Act, then you can be treated for up to six months and if necessary it can be renewed for a further six months. That's a long time out of anyone's life, especially for a medical treatment. It deprives people of their liberty when, let's face it, they are not on the whole, criminals. The consultant psychiatrists are in a powerful position: to be able to grant periods of leave, to approve discharge from a Section, and to renew Sections.

'Section 3 is usually applied to those individuals who have a known diagnosis of a severe mental illness such as schizophrenia for example. Wider implications include granting of visas for foreign travel. These may be restricted if you have been detained on a Section 3 at any time.'

'Oh shit,' remarked Charlie. 'Not such good news for foreign correspondents then.'

'That's why, young man, I have made it clear that should this happen to you, you need to appeal immediately and inform me. Remember these Sections should not end up appearing on any documentation that applies directly to you. As we have already discussed, you will have a false identity so it is therefore not possible to add a Section 3 to your own CV. But they are legal forms of detention at the time they are in place, and you would have to comply with the requirements imposed.'

'Ah, right. Got you, finally.' Charlie admitted that he was not necessarily keeping up with the specifics. Mark was relieved that Charlie had asked this question. He too had become confused as to the differences between Section 2 and Section 3. Now it was clear. Don't get Sectioned.

'But,' added Lewis for dramatic effect, 'you would have to be unlucky to come across a consultant who would put you on or keep you under a Section. In the worst-case scenario if you did, you could be forced to accept injectable medication, and that can be mightily unpleasant. I was going to say that nobody has ever been known to die from psychiatric medication being injected ... but that is not strictly true.'

'Isn't it?' Mark queried. 'How bad is that stuff?'

'It's rather like any medication. You could potentially have an allergic response to it. However there are some unpleasant side effects that can be experienced with antipsychotics specifically.'

'I think it is really important that we are told about these,' insisted Linda. 'After all, you instruct that we spit out tablets or at least that we do not swallow them, but what if we do accidentally, or they give us liquid or an injection. I think we deserve to be told what to expect in the event that we are better at swallowing than spitting stuff out.'

Charlie choked on his coffee at this comment, which was laden with innuendo, but he did not look in Linda's direction. A few of the other journalists, who knew Linda of old, looked down at the table, stifling any wayward titters.

'Fair enough,' Lewis agreed, ignoring the comedy moment. He then produced a printed acetate sheet, and placed it on the projector. Mark looked at the list of long and unfamiliar words as Lewis defined them, one by one. When he had finished, his audience appeared to be in a state of slight shock.

'Good God, according to your descriptions, the risk is that if we take this stuff, we could end up as a shuffling, dribbling, restless but stiff zombie incapable of thinking or sex or even ... possibly dead. That sounds utterly desperate,' remarked Linda accompanied by nods from her fellow experimenters around the table.

Lewis was quick to respond.

'In most cases people only experience a moderate level of sedation, and if they're unlucky enough to get these other side effects then there are medications to counteract the problem. As we said, don't swallow them, don't over-act, and you will be fine.'

# Chapter 17

## Plans

The group chatted animatedly, which Lewis took as his cue to initiate a planning session for their attempted admissions to psychiatric hospitals across the country.

'Can I suggest,' he offered, 'that you get yourselves together, and generate ideas about your back-stories and your plans to attempt admission. Feel free to make your suggestions as wild as you like, but remember that as extreme as your imagination may be, I doubt you will top what actually takes place in the reality of the psychiatric admission ward.'

The noise level in the room rose over the next hour or so as the researchers, the journalists, and the experiment lead team entered into debating all sorts of weird and fanciful plans, a number of which they ran with, and others that were scribbled down, crossed out, and thrown in the bin. They soon realised that they needed to avoid anything involving violence or potential harm to themselves.

\* \* \*

Linda devised what she said was a sure-fire plan. Her plot would involve dressing in a crown and robe and deliberately laying in the middle of a road, on a pedestrian crossing so that she didn't get run over. If her outfit was accurate enough, and she gave regal waves to drivers and pedestrians as she lay on the zebra crossing, it would be plainly evident that she was indeed mad.

She identified that the ensuing traffic chaos would result in a rapid response from the police at least. 'If I'm in luck, I should bag myself a policeman and a fireman or two. There's something incredibly kinky and sexually dynamic about fire fighters,' she said. 'Red hot.'

\* \* \*

Charlie stuck with the bridge idea, but thought that adding a tutu or dressing up as a gorilla would give him more of an air of insanity. This addition to the basic plan was not well received, and Charlie was asked to reconsider.

After a while and a gentle brainstorming of ideas from around the table, Charlie came up with an improved proposal. His newest offering involved behaving as if he thought he was being followed or threatened, and had therefore run to the bridge to leap into a river in a desperate attempt to escape his non-existent persecutors. This received full approval from the group.

\* \* \*

Jock went for a Monty Python-inspired plan which involved repeating the sound 'Nee' at every opportunity, while pretending to ride a horse via the use of two coconut shells being banged together, skipping through a market or shopping centre. He was already planning embellishments to this idea, such as rearing up at certain people or lampposts for added effect.

\* \* \*

The ideas were reviewed and debated vociferously amongst the groups. Important points such as ensuring they were sober at the time, were agreed. This was particularly relevant in the case of the more theatrical of suggestions, because there was a distinct possibility that if there was so much as a whiff of alcohol, the individual could easily be taken to police cells, and charged with drunk and disorderly conduct.

A handful of ideas were positively received. One of the researchers, Andy, turned out to be a keen amateur actor, and he devised a plan to present himself at hospital asking, via a written letter, to be given a scan of his brain. His story was that he was being monitored by the Russian KGB, and had been implanted with microchips in his ears. He was requesting for these to be located and surgically removed. He would inform the recipient of the letter that he was unable to speak because he was being recorded and would request replies to be whispered or preferably written down for him to read.

Lewis James gave the young man a round of applause. 'Bravo young research boffin, this is a workable plan likely to guarantee a psychiatric assessment. I wonder though, how you are going to explain your beliefs once admitted to a ward?'

After a discussion, during which the whole group debated whether the contents of the letter would be seen as describing symptoms, and thus introducing bias, they modified the details. Then there was a light bulb moment from the young researcher Andy, who announced, 'Perhaps I could say I found an insect in my ear, and had misinterpreted the noises it was making.'

'Genius!' replied a highly excited Lewis James. 'More like this please and we shall have a high success rate.'

At first Mark had struggled to find the right inspiration, until one of the research team pointed out what was staring everyone else in the face.

'What you need are five loaves, a few fish, and to gather a large crowd of hungry followers, while looking all Jesus-like and doing other such miracles.'

'Of course.' Mark berated himself for his lack of imagination. 'It's so bloody obvious.'

He asked if he could be allocated to a hospital somewhere near a train station. In his mind he was trying to imagine how on earth he was going to draw enough attention to himself and use his Jesus looks to his advantage.

'The difficulty is gaining enough attention if you are going for a religious performance,' confirmed Lewis James. 'The great British public is, on the whole remarkably tolerant, extremely polite and mostly avoidant of confrontation. They will usually gently ignore the odd bit of religious fervour. However, your idea of a train station is sound, but you will need to make a bigger splash than just walking about as if you are praying. You can't speak remember, at least not in understandable English.'

Mark realised that he was in a fortunate position. His father was a retired high-ranking member of the Foreign Office, which resulted in Mark being privileged to have lived in far-flung countries, often for years at a time. His mother was of 'Persian ancestry' and she proudly announced this whenever asked where she was from. His parents had met, fallen madly in love, and run the gauntlet of disapproval from both their families in order to marry. This was not quite as romantically testing as it first appeared, because Mark's mother came from a Christian family who lived in the Sultanate of Oman. After their initial misgivings, the whole family had been immensely supportive and loving. Mark, courtesy of his parents, had the benefit of first-hand experience of living in Oman, Turkey, Cyprus, and across the Middle East, learning the customs and gaining an understanding of the different cultures as he grew up. Most usefully he learnt the languages, including various Arab dialects. Helpfully his mother's family imparted wisdom and knowledge about the history of that part of the world that no westerner could ever hope to comprehend.

Mark confirmed his mastery of languages to Lewis James, and suggested that a scrambled version of a Middle Eastern type Esperanto might be a useful tool. He and Lewis both thought it was too much of a risk to make use of one foreign language. No matter how obscure, there was always a slim chance that someone in the vicinity of Mark's planned station platform performance would understand him. Having pondered the possibilities, they finally hit on nudity as the incitement to an arrest by police. Then, with any luck, he would be referred for a psychiatric assessment.

'I may well get a mention in the local newspapers with that one,' Mark identified with a wide grin. 'Morning rush hour, what a sight for those poor unsuspecting souls! I think I need to at least keep my sandals on, otherwise I'll only have one orifice left available to me in which to hide my loose change for the payphone, perish the thought.'

Mark worked through the finer details of his plan with Lewis giving guidance. They were enjoying the creativity of the task almost as much as the banter back and forth across the room. The journalists were each insisting competitively that their own plan was the best and most certain to succeed.

# Chapter 18

## An Unexpected Turn of Events

Mark needed advice. He knew that he should call either Lewis James the barrister or John Starkey his editor, but if he did that, he would have to begin speaking in order to request use of the ward telephone. If he did speak at that stage would that be wise?

There was a slim possibility of removing the two ten pence pieces that he had sewn into the strap of his sandals, and sneaking into the payphone booth if he could find a moment when it was left unlocked. This was highly unlikely. The staff team was meticulous when it came to safety and locking doors. Mark had watched their every move. Each member of staff carried master door keys at all times, along with a black tubular alarm that they had hanging from their belts. They were constantly watchful as to the whereabouts of each other and the patients in their care.

Inconspicuously they used hand signals and looks or nods to indicate to each other what needed observing or attending to. This impressed Mark, as it was not something he had foreseen as being part of maintaining a calm secure ward. He had been subconsciously influenced by the belief that the staff would be wearing white coats and rushing around with straight jackets, desperate to restrain and incarcerate wailing patients. *Wrong again*, Mark thought.

It looked as if he was going to have to continue pretending to take medication, and Mark fleetingly debated whether or not he should actually take the tablets in order to describe the experience.

He was well aware that this would be more honest in terms of observational journalism, but he had no idea if Haloperidol or whatever it was, would be one of those tablets that would give him horrible side effects, so he thought better of that experiment for the time being.

Elsewhere, his potential for newsworthy copy had also improved dramatically. His run-in with Dr Sharman had been far from boring or predictable, which hinted that the research team might be onto a story worth investigating after all. What if his other journalist colleagues were having the same sort of experiences and dilemmas? What if they weren't?

The more Mark analysed the situation, the more he realised that as a patient he was almost powerless, and therefore reliant on the staff to act in an understanding and caring manner. He needed to request an appeal, which the journalists and researchers on the project had been advised to do by Lewis James. He would need help to do this. A difficult task for a mute patient.

Why was it that the patient had to request an appeal? Most people in this situation would, or should, be acutely mentally unwell and therefore, mused Mark, they would not necessarily be capable of realising that they needed to appeal. He had been horribly misunderstood so far, and he hadn't even spoken to anyone, so without appealing against the Section, he could be stuck there for months.

When he had written the note, '*My name is Mark. Please help me*', Mark had predicted that this would nudge Monica into an interesting reaction resulting in him being miraculously persuaded to speak. Not so easy.

However, when he gave the note to her, she delivered results without prompting, in as much as she steered him to an appeal. Mark was not in the least bothered by her obvious guidance towards a particular firm of solicitors. With these things in place, he hoped he could at last open the lines of communication to the research team and John Starkey at the Daily Albion. What he needed to know from them was: should he keep to his false identity, backstory, and occupation? These important facts so far remained unknown to all. Or, alternatively could he disclose to his solicitor the real reason he was on the ward and use his real identity? Mark didn't know what to do for the best.

When Monica had gone to make arrangements with Huntley and Greaves the solicitors, Mark had headed back to the large dayroom to see if there was anything worth watching on the TV. He hoped against hope that he could catch a glimpse of the news, or a decent current affairs programme. He felt excluded from the outside world already, despite having been in hospital for less than three days.

Much to his annoyance, Mark had found the TV stuck on the usual rubbish: an American comedy series, which undoubtedly would be followed by a coma-inducing late afternoon quiz show for morons. No one was sitting watching the TV screen. There were only a handful of patients in the dayroom, but they were either asleep or, as in the case of one lady, entertaining herself by smiling and laughing in response to whatever her voices were saying to her. *She's away with the fairies*, thought Mark, continuing to pass by the door.

When he turned the corner of the corridor, he heard a bit of a rumpus happening in the opposite direction and as he swivelled around to look at the goings on, he spied that the door to the telephone booth was slightly ajar. The alarms on the ward then sounded loudly making him jump out of his skin, and which also resulted in the available staff rushing to support whoever was in need of assistance. The main ward doors were locked to ensure that no potential opportunist escapee could sneak out. The commotion at the other end of the ward afforded Mark chance to get to the payphone unseen. He had no way of estimating how long he would have to take advantage of this opportunity, but he decided to risk it. He would take the chance that someone might see him.

He deftly released the ten pence pieces from his sandals, and dialled the number for John Starkey, who he was sure would be in his office at this time of day. He struck lucky. Pushing the first coin into the slot when the pips sounded, he spoke directly to John, shouting over the sound of the alarms. 'I haven't got much time,' he explained. 'I'll keep it brief but I may have to cut you off in a hurry.'

The unfamiliar sound of his own voice had startled Mark somewhat, but he was relieved that it still functioned. He confirmed with John what hospital he was in, and that he had been put on a Section 3.

'Did you do something stupid?'

'Never mind, but no. Take this down. I have appealed against the Section as instructed. Huntley and Greaves Solicitors are going to represent me. A solicitor named Richard Huntley. Ask Lewis James to contact me through them, please. I don't know their number. Got it? Huntley and Greaves in Hollberry. Got to go. I'm okay though.'

Mark put down the phone, and slid unnoticed from the phone booth, leaving the door as he had found it. His heart was pounding with tension at the possibility of being caught and he realised that he had been holding his breath for so long that he was almost gasping for air.

The alarm was suddenly silenced, and the ward smoothly resumed its usual peaceful atmosphere, as if nothing had happened. Mark, ignorant as to what the fuss had been about, was later brought up to speed by one of his fellow patients. There had been 'a proper punch up, like a war ...' over a bar of chocolate. Mark secretly wished all wars were as benign as that one.

Once he had left the phone booth unnoticed, he casually meandered to his bed space in the dormitory to make notes. Mostly his notes were about the pros and cons of revealing his true identity. He was so absorbed in this that he did not hear Monica approaching, and he didn't know how long she had been at the dormitory door when she called out, 'Mr Trainman, are you about?'

She wasn't stupid, and Mark knew that was a deliberate ploy. Faster than a magician, he made his pages of writing disappear under the mattress. Even so, he was convinced that she had seen him. He only hoped that she could not read shorthand.

# Chapter 19

## To Be or Not to Be the Real Mark, That is the Question

Before he was admitted, and well ahead of his planned naked platform performance, Mark had worked hard on his cover backstory. He had decided to call himself Mark 'El Amin' because ironically it means 'the truth' in Arabic.

He was looking forward to revealing how he was a PhD student studying Middle Eastern politics, undertaking a thesis investigating the role and function of kidnapping westerners as the means of political negotiation. These were things he was comfortably acquainted with, and he was rather proud of how neatly he would fit his new persona. Mark El Amin the eternal student, as opposed to Mark Randall, the battle-weary and dispossessed foreign correspondent.

He had initially devised, what he considered to be, a valid story for his bizarre behaviour on the day he was picked up naked from Hollberry railway station. Originally he had planned to convince mental health professionals that he had been abroad, and picked up 'a virus of some kind', which had resulted in a fever. Bizarre behaviour accounted for. His aim was to explain away his muteness by asserting that he was confused and disorientated, and had elected to remain silent until he had worked out where he was, and what was happening to him.

However, Monica had blown his cover story wide open on the day of his admission, when she had efficiently taken his temperature with a new fangled paper stick that she put under his arm. He hadn't realised that it was a thermometer until it was too late.

This was not a disaster however, as Mark then had time to rethink his cover story during the long hours that he lay awake on that first night. In doing so, he had arrived at a more plausible reason as to why he had behaved so oddly on the station platform. He had 'gone to the toilet on the train', he would tell the psychiatrists, and there had banged his head when the train juddered violently to a halt. Thus he had experienced a temporary aberration brought about by concussion. Perfect.

There was a hitch in the projected timing of Mark's plans. According to Monica, his appeal could take weeks to set up. A lot could happen in two weeks and a consultant who had little capacity for care was deciding Mark's immediate future. But, rather than wallow in frustration, Mark consoled himself that his situation would make for a good story. Unexpectedly, he had a lot to write about.

There was one other potential storyline that Mark had stumbled upon, courtesy of his fellow patients. He was certain that the staff on the ward had no inkling of it. Although Mark was not wholly sure of the validity of the information, it had a ring of truth about it, and he was determined to follow this up.

One of the Chocolate War combatants known as Welsh Phil, was a cheerful character on the ward, genuinely popular with the staff and other patients alike. He disclosed a few tantalising morsels of intriguing interest, shortly before Mark was to meet with his appointed solicitor, Richard Huntley. Phil was a large Welshman with a nose that was a living testament to his past boxing prowess. He was in the smaller dayroom where he was regaling a select group of patients with the dramatic details of the first battle of the Chocolate Wars. Mark sat immediately behind Phil, unobtrusively observing the scene.

'Poor old Dopey Dan has convinced himself that my chocolate is poisoned,' Phil said, turning around to Mark to explain. 'I keep a stash in my locker, see. Can't manage without it.'

He turned back and faced the interested gathering in the room. 'So there he is, Dopey Dan, trying to take my Toblerone so

I couldn't eat it and get poisoned, which if you think about it is quite thoughtful of him. But see, I wanted to keep my Toblerone. I like Toblerone and I won't share it with anyone. I have in fact been known to eat it in bed in the dark under the covers, so I don't have to share it.' He continued, 'Anyway I had to hit him with it in the end, to get him off me, silly idiot.'

Phil then went on to make several remarks about Dr Sharman that had everyone leaning forward to hear. Mark had his radar on.

It turned out that Phil was sure that the details of the first battle of the Chocolate Wars were going to be reported in the next ward round, and he seemed worried about the consequences. 'That bastard is not going to let me get away with things lightly, I'm certain of that,' he said as he then rationalised this fear.

According to Phil, he had previously been admitted to Farley Hill Hospital back in the late 1980s. He explained to the group of patients who were still listening intently, 'As you probably know, I'm a manic-depressive. They call it "bipolar" nowadays. I'm not always ill, see, and I've only had a couple of big trips to hospital. I get magnificently manic, now and again but mostly I'm fine or depressed. Being depressed is a lot worse. Anyway, back in 1987, I had stolen a lorry, huge great artic it was. I was convinced I had a big fight set up with Joe Bugner. Boxer. Used to be famous. Anyhow, I was pulled over on the motorway for weaving in and out of the traffic. The other drivers were slowing me down, see? It's a long story, but I ended up in Farley Hill. Nice-looking place, fabulous grounds to walk in, but he was there, Dr Sharman, and I was in there for months! He left before me, mind, and there was a proper scandal. I don't know what exactly, but the staff were whispering all sorts. A couple of patients had been taken to the general hospital seriously ill, collapsed, see?'

Phil went on in a conspiratorial manner. 'It was years ago now, but I'm sure it's him. Same arrogant bastard. I shall do my time, take my medication and go, when I get let out. That was looking like next week, but I may have blown my chances now, thanks to Dopey Dan.

'I advise you to keep your heads down and keep taking the tablets. If he catches you or thinks you're not taking your meds, out comes the needle and the land of the zombie shuffle awaits, just like it has for poor Greg.' Right on cue, Greg shuffled past the open doorway.

Phil then turned once more to Mark and said pointedly, 'You probably won't need to worry too much, being the son of God, and not having much wrong with you. You should be out of here soon, I reckon. Still, keep your head down mind. You are dealing with Lucifer himself here.' Phil laughed as if joking, but Mark was fairly sure he had been rumbled as far as not having a mental illness went.

Phil's story sounded a bit melodramatic to Mark but, as tired as he was from lack of sleep and no access to proper coffee, he wanted to know more about Dr Sharman's past. He had to find an excuse to start speaking in order to get hold of the information he needed, but he required the advice of Lewis James first and foremost about which Mark he should be: Randall or El Amin.

# Chapter 20

## When Mark Met Richard

Lewis James was telephoning the offices of Huntley and Greaves, and had at last succeeded in getting through. He had tried to call three times in the last hour, only to be greeted with an engaged tone. This was at least a sign of a popular law firm.

'Huntley and Greaves, how may I help?' asked the efficient Cheryl as she picked up the telephone that Friday morning.

'Ah good morning, my name is James Lewis, and I would like to speak to the partner due to represent a young man by the name of Mark El Amin at a pending mental health tribunal.'

Lewis had been surprised to hear from John Starkey that any of the group taking part in the research project had been legally detained in hospital, let alone on a Section 3, but he was glad that Mark had made contact to let them know.

He had supposed that Mark was using his agreed false identity, and Lewis had therefore asked for him using his assumed name. Lewis, joining in the undercover approach, decided that he was going to pretend to be the El Amin family solicitor, James Lewis, on behalf of Mark's pretend parents who lived abroad. He was unexpectedly wrong-footed when Cheryl replied, 'I'm sorry Mr Lewis, but we don't have a client of that name. Can I ask what your role is and why you are contacting us?'

Lewis gave his cover story, and also gave the details of the ward name.

'I think the best thing for me to do, Mr Lewis, is to put the details of your request through to Richard Huntley, who would be the most likely partner to be dealing with this type of case, and ask him to contact you directly, if that's alright.'

The conversation had given Lewis enough time to gather his wits and take a fair guess that Mark had remained mute, and so far had not disclosed his name. Awkward. 'Thank you very much. That would be ideal. This young man's parents have been phoning around local hospitals trying to locate their son who has been missing for a number of days. They were told there was a man fitting his description on Pargiter Ward, but it sounds like that may have been a false hope. Unfortunately, as they live in Australia, it falls to me to follow up in person.'

'I'll ask Mr Huntley to call you as soon as he can. It would be better to discuss these matters with him.'

'Of course,' said Lewis. 'I completely understand. Thanks for your help.' Realising that he would not be getting past the immovable Cheryl, Lewis admitted defeat. He gave Cheryl his London office, home, and mobile telephone numbers.

* * *

Cheryl phoned internally through to Richard to tell him about the call. 'He didn't sound like he was a posh London lawyer,' she said. 'But then again, he probably isn't one. His story sounded dubious. I think he was fishing for information.'

'Thanks, Cheryl. I think I'll wait before I get back in touch with this so-called family solicitor. I'd like to hear from our new client, Mr Trainman, if he decides to speak to me. Could he be Mark El Amin? Interesting.'

* * *

Sitting opposite Mark in the small office on Pargiter Ward was his newly appointed solicitor. They both waited while Monica popped in and out, delivering hot drinks, and the relevant case notes and charts.

Mark took the time to make a rapid first impression assessment of Richard. He was smartly dressed as expected, appeared efficient, and had been careful to ensure that he had the notes he needed before he formally introduced himself to Mark, and added, 'I've brought a pen and paper with me as I understand you prefer not to speak at the moment.'

Mark was struck by the firm authoritative manner of Richard's opening statement. 'That is not strictly true,' responded Mark. Richard smiled knowingly, and sat back in the well-worn office chair. The office door had a window in the top half, and across this was a curtain, partially pulled back. From the outside, it revealed Richard sitting at the desk, however, Mark, sitting opposite, was obscured from the view of any passer-by. No one would see him speaking.

To Mark's surprise, Richard's first question was, 'Is your name Mark El Amin by any chance?'

It was Mark's turn to smile and give a short snort of a laugh through his nostrils. He realised that Lewis James had been in touch with Huntley and Greaves, and helpfully he was now fully aware that he needed to stick firmly to his false identity and cover story. 'How did you find that out?'

Richard explained, in brief, that Mark's parents had been searching for him, and the family solicitor, a Mr James Lewis, had contacted Richard's office. Richard said he had wanted to check the validity of this story with Mark before responding to the call from Mr Lewis in London. 'You should perhaps call him yourself to put your parents' minds at rest, especially living so far away.'

Mark paused, nodded, and 'ummed', playing for time before replying. He was surprised that his cover story included parents, and where did they live, Scotland? How far away is far away?

Richard unknowingly came to his rescue. 'I don't suppose you have enough money on you to call Australia, and I'm almost sure the ward can't run to permission for a call. It would be cheaper and more sensible to ask your family solicitor to update them with the news that you have been found alive and well. Are you well?'

'Yes, apart from being stuck in here, I'm fine, thanks. I shouldn't be in here.'

When Richard smirked at this turn of phrase, Mark realised that he must have heard that comment many times. Mark wagered that most of Richard's clients would try to convince him that they shouldn't be in Pargiter Ward.

'Tell me if you would, how you ended up here,' invited Richard, 'and please excuse me if I write down the specifics – they can be more important sometimes. I need a chronology of events, if you can run to that.'

Mark could, and did. He had his cover story at the ready and Richard nodded sagely as he wrote down the details. A couple of times he asked for clarification, but on the whole he allowed Mark to talk through the chronology of events unhindered by interruptions. Mark reassured himself that he had done an excellent job of passing himself off as an eternal student.

Once finished, Richard looked at Mark intently and asked, 'Why haven't you told the staff or the consultant what you have just told me?'

'It's like a bad dream,' Mark said. 'I feel alright now, but I didn't know what to do for the best, so I waited until I had the opportunity to speak to you, someone independent.'

He tried to hold Richard's gaze, conscious that Richard was sceptical about his version of events. Mark knew that as a solicitor, Richard was used to not being told the truth, and Mark had noticed him cross-checking a couple of facts before deciding to scan through the formal hospital admission paperwork. There were a lot of papers in front of Richard, requiring careful consideration. On the desk was a Section 3 recommendation form and Mark spied the name Dr Giles Sharman next to a swirl of a signature. Richard picked up the form and scrutinised it for several seconds.

Mark remained positive that Richard would prove to be as thorough as Monica had led him to believe, but despite this optimistic view, he shifted in his seat uncomfortably. *This man knows his stuff*, Mark realised as he watched Richard taking in the facts.

Richard read through the words written on the Section paper by Dr Sharman, and as he did so Mark noticed a couple of significant changes in Richard's facial expression. As Richard's eyebrows shot upwards, he said, 'Oh, I see you already have a diagnosis of schizophrenia.' Richard looked up expectantly at Mark from the sheet of paper he was holding.

Mark was visibly shocked by this revelation. 'Do I? Since when?'

'I was about to ask you the same question. According to the information in front of me, you are known to mental health services and have a diagnosis of schizophrenia, and this admission was due to a relapse. What medication were you on before?' Richard asked. Mark knew he was hunting for the truth.

'I wasn't,' replied Mark who was feeling uncomfortable. There had been a mistake made somewhere along the line. 'I don't have a mental illness. I don't have a diagnosis of any mental illness, and I have never been on medication for a mental illness, until this week that is.'

'Leave this with me,' Richard said looking puzzled. 'I wonder if there has been a mix-up.'

'There must have been. I truly don't have any diagnosis. Actually …' Mark said, hesitating, 'I need to know whatever you find, and I want to be able to trust you. I will talk to the nurse and tell her what I've told you. If I have to, I'll even speak in ward round to Dr Sharman, but I have to say that when I saw him, in fact the only time I have seen him so far, that man was convinced that I have psychosis. I hadn't even spoken and he accused me of being paranoid. Perhaps, when he hears what I have to say, he will remove this bloody Section. Then, hopefully, I can be discharged.' Mark realised that in part he was fooling himself with his own optimism.

Richard agreed that it would be more sensible for Mark to communicate openly, and in the meantime he would continue with preparation of reports, 'I'll carry on, in case it goes ahead,' he confirmed with a conciliatory grin.

Mark liked Richard from the word go. He approved of his directness and sharp intellect. Richard didn't patronise him, and Mark felt guilty for having to deceive him. Following his first meeting with Richard, he was of the opinion that progress had definitely been made.

He had a spring in his step as he left the office and experienced overwhelming relief at being able to speak at last. Mark was looking forward to asking questions, and to be able to interrogate and research!

Most of all, Mark could look forward to the next ward round with Dr Sharman. He would make everyone realise what a pompous self-serving arse the man was, by making the dear doctor retract his diagnosis, and stop prescribing medication that wasn't needed. Then Mark could go home, and once he had done the background checks about this Dr Sharman scandal rumour, he could write the story.

*I need to call Lewis, and perhaps he can ask my pretend parents to organise sending me some decent clothes, I can't go home looking like this*, he said to himself.

He bumped straight into Monica as he turned the corner on his way back to the dormitory to update his shorthand notes.

# Chapter 21

### He Speaks!

'Oh crikey! I'm sorry,' I exclaimed, patting Mark on the shoulder by way of apology for bumping into him as I rounded the corner. 'Hope you got on okay with Mr Huntley.' I carried on down the corridor, not expecting a reply.

'Yes. Thank you,' Mark answered. I nearly toppled over in surprise. I turned and gave the biggest most genuine of smiles. 'That's great to hear, Mark,' was the best I could manage in reply.

He nodded and went on his way, grinning. He had a lovely soft voice, Mr Mark Jesus Trainman. This was turning out to be a good day.

I had been marching down the corridor to deal with Dan, who had begun to cause another problem with Welsh Phil and his stash of chocolate. I needed to get to the bottom of this before another skirmish became a full-scale battle. I was so taken aback by Mark speaking, that I nearly forgot why I was dashing around the corner.

However I arrived at the scene in good time to hear Dan pleading with Phil not to eat any more chocolate because it would kill him.

'No Dan, it won't kill me. It is not poisoned, I promise,' said Phil, trying to allay Dan's fears. Dan was telling him that he had been reliably informed 'by them' that cyanide had been put in one of the bars of chocolate, and it was like Russian Roulette as to when Phil would die. Dan was adamant. He was crying, genuinely in fear for Phil's life.

I felt like a bit of a fool. All this time I had assumed Dan was trying to steal Phil's chocolate, because he wanted chocolate, and for no other reason. I should have known better than that, especially after working on an acute ward for so long.

If I had more time to spend with the patients and less sorting out paperwork or finding staff to cover shifts, I would have been on top of this situation long ago, I told myself. How could I have been so half-hearted in carrying out my duties? Poor Dan had been distressed and upset for days. I hated to admit it, but I had let the mystery of the lovely-looking Jesus distract me from the needs of the other patients on the ward and I was extremely disappointed with myself.

Once the immediate situation with Phil and Dan was resolved, I spent a fair bit of time with Dan. Only then did it become obvious that his delusional belief about Phil's chocolate being poisoned was firmly fixed. There may have been a benefit in moving Dan or Phil into a side room, I thought, but I also suspected that the respite would be short lived. Still, at least Phil could have a rest at night, I concluded. So I arranged this with one of the healthcare assistants to sort out.

In the goldfish bowl office, I quickly perused Dan's drug chart. The other patients called him 'Dopey Dan' in reference to the amount of cannabis he had been using leading up to his admission, which undoubtedly had contributed to his paranoia, and his eventual departure from reality. According to his drug chart, he was not on any antipsychotic medication. I searched in vain for a second chart in case one had been recently written. It made no sense to me that a man with distressing delusional beliefs was not on any medication, and so I referred to the case notes. Records from Dan's first ward round, following his admission about four weeks previously, stated that it had been Dr Sharman's view that, '*This patient presents with an entirely drug-induced state. Spontaneous resolution likely within four to five days.*'

I found the next ward review entry, which said the same thing in not so many words, and so it continued for each Monday ward round up to the most recent review. That one inferred that Dan was making a steady recovery, and would be ready for discharge the following week, once he had been on trial home leave. I found no record of home leave being agreed or arranged. As I usually covered Tuesday ward rounds, I must have missed the significance of the pattern. Was I not listening properly in handover meetings? This was another blow to my usual high standards. I was slipping dangerously close to incompetency.

In an attempt to redeem myself, and out of frustration, I examined the nursing reports, which to be frank, could have been describing a different person from the one seen by the psychiatrists. Every one of the nursing entries in the notes, without fail, identified on-going distress, delusional beliefs, made specific reference to paranoia, and to fears about others being poisoned. Dan had received no treatment for acute psychotic symptoms. Disgraceful.

I was not Dan's named nurse on the ward. It was one of the night staff who had taken that role, which always made nursing representation less effective in ward rounds. Knowing this, I went on a personal mission, to look up the care plan review details and discover the truth behind Dan's lack of progress. Sadly the reviews did not reveal much of use, as the records were sketchy at best. Going through the main notes, however, I picked out at least one phone call a week from the named nurse to one of the doctors requesting a review of the treatment plan, which only consisted of a dose of night sedation and Lactulose for constipation.

'What good is that for delusions?' I asked myself out loud. 'What's the matter with Dr Sharman? He seems to be making it up as he goes along! In fact he's so full of shit, that maybe he should take a laxative. It might cure his delusion that he's a psychiatrist.'

Maybe he is making it up, I convinced myself as I reached for the phone to contact the on-call doctor and make my request, politely but firmly, for active treatment of Dan's psychosis.

Dr Siddiqui was on-call again. He was always on call it seemed. I explained the situation, and made my request for commencement of antipsychotic medication. 'Perhaps one of the newer medications and a small dose to start with. It may help him sleep as well,' I ventured.

'No, I don't think so,' he replied. 'Dr Sharman is clear that symptoms will remit now that the gentleman concerned is no longer under the influence of the cannabis.'

'They haven't remitted, Doctor, and they have become decidedly worse recently. In fact, we have had a number of incidents recorded that have been as a direct result of his delusions. Of course it may be the case that Dan has been self-medicating with cannabis, to manage underlying mental health problems.' I said, dragging up the best argument I could muster at short notice.

'Hmm … Dr Sharman will see him in ward round next Monday or Tuesday and he can review the situation then, I think,' came the vague reply down the telephone line. I would have happily strangled the man with the flex if he had been in the vicinity, and I was astounded at his lack of compassion. Was he actually suggesting that the whole situation was not even discussed until the following week? It was Friday, and there was a whole weekend to get through when the Chocolate War could easily escalate to include other foodstuffs, and other people.

'Dr Siddiqui, I can't write that in the case notes, can I? After all, it would look as if you were refusing to assess or treat a patient in distress, wouldn't it? I'm sure you don't mean that to happen.' Argue that point, I thought.

'Oh, no, of course not,' he inevitably responded. 'I'll come up in a couple of minutes when I have spoken to Dr Sharman about what to do in this man's case.'

'Why do you need to ask him first?' I challenged, careful not to sound too forceful. 'He may give you a hard time if you haven't at least spoken to the patient and reviewed the notes before you ask his opinion. He can be touchy about that sort of thing can't he?' I played yet another fine card with that suggestion.

'Okay, I'll come there first.'

I put the phone down, and ran my fingers through my scalp. As I lifted two clumps of hair towards the ceiling, shouting 'aaaargh' to no one in particular, Richard Huntley came to the ward office door, and laughed at my obvious despair.

'Sorry,' I muttered. 'And there was I, thinking that the day was getting better. How can I help, assuming you need help with something?'

'You're always helpful, Monica. Our mystery man decided to speak to me …'

'Yes, I bumped into him a moment ago. It was a bit of a shock.'

'And,' continued Richard, 'I'm sure you can straighten out the queries I have in the case of Mr Trainman as was. Mark. He is, by the way, called Mark El Amin; you may want to make a note. Firstly, I need to know if has he been told of his diagnosis, either verbally or in writing or both?'

I slumped in my chair in a rather exaggerated fashion as I motioned for Richard to take a seat. 'I don't think either apply. There's nothing in his ward notes to confirm a diagnosis given by Dr Sharman, but when he was admitted, Mark had a working diagnosis or query around a drug induced episode, made by Dr Siddiqui.'

That was the truth as far as I knew. 'However,' I said, 'I couldn't help noticing that the Section 3 recommendation outlined that he was a known patient and had a diagnosis of schizophrenia, which didn't make any sense …'

I then went on to explain to Richard, in confidence, that I had followed this up with Dr Sharman, who had denied previously knowing the patient. I found myself asking Richard for help. Not for myself, but for Mark, who I was sure did not have a mental illness. 'He might have had a bit of a weird moment, and it could have been drugs, who knows, but he's not displaying anything indicating psychosis. Nothing. His sleep is terrible, mind you, and he gets night terrors, but that's pretty much it.'

I shared my fears with Richard that Mark might be using the ward as a place to hide, and that I wasn't sure why he was here. 'Some of the patients are questioning this too,' I added. 'Still, we shall soon know more, now that he's speaking.'

Richard was pragmatic about the whole thing. He planned to do what he usually did, and that was to scrutinise the records, cross reference the facts, prepare himself, and give the ward team and Doctor Sharman a hard time at the appeal hearing.

As a result of my wobbly emotional state, I then let slip an awful comment, 'Perhaps you could check to see if he is a real doctor while you're at it …'

When Richard looked at me expecting me to be smiling as if I had made a joke, he didn't see a smile. He saw tears in my eyes, and a slight quiver run across my lower lip. I bit my lip and turned away from him sharply, ending the conversation as I stood up. 'Never mind. Just thinking out loud.'

As I said that, Dr Siddiqui popped his head round the door. I handed him Dan's notes, and informed him rather abruptly that I would be with him in a minute.

'Sorry Richard, you had other questions you wanted to ask,' I said, trying to get a grip on my emotions, and wondering if my hormones were playing up.

'No, don't worry for now. I shall no doubt work them out for myself. I may be a bit longer, so is it okay with you to use that office for the next hour or so?'

'Of course, it's no problem.'

I left Richard to it, and after a while forgot he was there. My next task was to escort Dr Siddiqui to see Dopey Dan. Even he could not deny that the poor man needed proper medication to help him. My efforts were finally rewarded after I had almost exhausted myself persuading Dr Siddiqui to act on his own accord. When he wrote out the drug chart, I made sure it was taken immediately to the hospital pharmacy, so that we could get Dan started on treatment without further delay. I had even managed to ensure he was not prescribed Haloperidol or Droperidol for a change. Hurrah!

Don't get me wrong, I didn't object to their use entirely, indeed they worked well for the most disturbed patients, but in my view, they were not the drugs of choice as a long-term treatment. Goodness me, I wouldn't want to experience those side effects, I thought.

I sat in the goldfish bowl office to write up the relevant patient notes, and it was only at that point in the shift that Emma and I were reunited. She scooted into the office, full of beans.

'I hear Jesus is talking,' she said brightly.

'Yes,' I replied, somewhat astounded. 'Where did you hear that?'

'The patients, silly. Welsh Phil and the dodgy duo are sitting in the small dayroom, chatting away with him like they are good buddies.'

'The dodgy duo?'

'Yes, you know, Tweedle Dumb and Tweedle Dee.'

'Emma!' I chastised her for being so disrespectful to two rather round gentlemen who happened to look similar, and who had become inseparable on the ward. They were both on the road to recovery from depression, and this had much to do with their newfound friendship.

'You okay?' she asked me.

I didn't bore her with the full details of how my day had gone since I had seen her last, but she was intuitive and canny.

'I guess that Dr Sharman and his lies have hit a raw nerve with you,' she said. She was correct in her assumption. My sense of injustice was jumping up and down inside my head screaming for action.

'I have been doing a bit of sleuthing on your behalf today,' Emma announced as she busied herself putting files away. 'Janet and I had a bit of a shave-a-thon. One or two of the men were looking decidedly scruffy so we opened the Pargiter Ward bath and barbers emporium. We had been sorting out the leftover toiletries in the clinic room, and it seemed a waste not to do something with what was there. We gave the majority to the patients who don't have any family to bring stuff in for them, and we lined the men up for showers and baths. Then Janet, who it turns out is a wizard with a safety razor, gave them a shave. Only the ones that needed it the most. I tell you, Greg was as chuffed as chuffed could be. He hasn't had the motivation to wash properly since Charming put him on that injection. It's cruel at that dose. Oh, and Jesus came along too, right at last knockings. He had been on the telephone. Where did he get the change for the phone, did you give it to him?'

I shook my head.

'Anyway he sounds lovely when he talks, and he looks even better now he's had a shave. Still looks like Jesus though. He doesn't look like a Mark. I'm going to struggle to call him by his real name.'

'What has that to do with sleuthing?' I asked eventually, when Emma drew breath.

'Oh yes. Janet was shaving Welsh Phil, which was a task and a half because as you know he can't stop talking at the best of times.'

Pot, kettle, black, I thought.

'Anyway, he was saying that he thinks he knows Dr Sharman from Farley Hill Hospital back in 1980 blah-di-blah. He was sure there was some sort of scandal. Phil has told this same story to a number of the patients and there are rumblings about exactly what this scandal may be. This could become a bigger problem, because, let's face it, Mon, most of the patients are jumpy about ward round as it is, but especially Phil because of the Chocolate Wars.'

* * *

'Oh, that's not Phil's fault. Dan is splendidly paranoid, and thinks someone is poisoning Phil's chocolate stash, so he keeps trying to protect Phil by taking the bloody chocolate. God, you couldn't make it up! Anyway, as mad as it sounds, you will be pleased to hear that it is being sorted as we speak. He wasn't on any meds you know. Dan. Bloody hell, Em, I had even begun to wonder if Charming is a real doctor, but if Phil knows him from previously, then he must be. I feel a bit of a prat right now.'

Actually, it was more than that, I experienced a horrible sinking feeling when recalling what I had said to Richard Huntley about my belief that Dr Sharman might not even be qualified.

\* \* \*

'Don't beat yourself up. I haven't finished my sleuthing yet,' Emma said. 'My sister Laura used to work at Farley Hill in the eighties before she had kids. I'll give her a ring and see if she remembers him. I hope the scandal is juicy. A sex scandal. Bound to be!'

\* \* \*

We had to stop talking and concentrate, as we needed to get ourselves back on track with the requirements of the ward, and its endless routines. Emma had drawn the short straw for ward round on Tuesday instead of me, and she was not looking forward to it. We agreed to help each other with the preparations on Monday, but before that, Emma and I had the weekend to plan for. Unusually we both had time off together, which meant that we could chat away to our hearts' content for hours. Emma had also badgered me until I agreed to go with her to the rugby club in town, after work on Saturday. The match would be almost over by the time we arrived, but I had promised I would go along for a drink, and to address my social avoidance by actually talking to the opposite sex.

Emma was trying her level best to set me up with Max Davis. He was nice enough, but too sure of himself and bit of a caveman. I was more excited by the prospect of a trip to the cinema on Sunday afternoon to see Forrest Gump. After which I would slurp wine in front of the telly on Sunday night. Lovely.

# Chapter 22

### True Colours

My new social life awaited me, with only Saturday morning to get through. That was no great hardship, as weekends tended to be genteel affairs on the ward. The majority of the patients were on home leave, and there were no activities downstairs in the OT department. Moreover, no doctors would be appearing on the ward unless requested. Visitors came and went in a steady stream, often bringing long-awaited items of fresh clothing and food. Patients, if they were permitted to do so, could have leave to walk in the hospital grounds or go out to lunch with their loved ones and friends. For others, it was unfortunately a long boring drag through to Monday when the chaos of the ward rounds started again.

I would usually buy newspapers on the way in to work when I was on shift at the weekends, and that week I had badgered and cajoled the local newsagents into donating unsold magazines, and out-of-date local and national newspapers to us at the hospital. These contributions went down splendidly with staff and patients alike, and especially with Mark, I noticed. He practically devoured every morsel of information in the papers and the magazines as if he were ravenously hungry.

'You alright, Mark?' I enquired gently.

'Yes, good thanks. I was feeling excommunicated from the outside world,' he explained. 'I never knew I would miss the news so much.'

He seemed genuinely engrossed, and went straight back to reading everything I had delivered that morning. He had a valid point about feeling disengaged from the world outside the hospital, and I made a note to request daily papers for the ward from the management. I had a sneaking suspicion that the staff would end up buying these, but it would be worth asking anyway.

A short while after lunch on that Saturday, I asked Mark if I could speak to him. I think he knew what was coming. I wanted him to give me the ins and outs of how he ended up in hospital, his family history, his background, his medical history, the whole lot. I asked him standard questions about sleep, appetite, mood, memory, concentration, thoughts, beliefs, and I delved into whether he had ever had any unusual experiences. A usual bill of fare, for psychiatric assessment purposes.

It was a fascinating assessment process as it turned out. Mark, as far as I could determine, had no psychosis, past or present, but he did seem to have other problems. His sleep was very poor indeed and he had more than night terrors. He had flashbacks but could not, or would not, detail these in relation to specific traumatic events. He had low-level anxiety, and his mood was not as good as it could have been at times. Despite his willingness to divulge information, I still felt that parts of what he said did not represent the full truth.

I was wholly unconvinced by the story that he had banged his head in the train toilet compartment before leaping naked onto the platform, but it did serve to remind me that I had requested a CT scan for Dr Siddiqui several days previously, and an appointment had not been forthcoming. It was a bit late, as the request had been as a result of Mark being mute on admission. Not that I could work out why it was still required. I'm not a doctor.

I am a thorough nurse, however, and therefore I wrote up the comprehensive assessment report and filed it in the notes to help the team to fill in the blanks about Mark. It would aid Emma with her ward round feedback to Dr Sharman. Come Tuesday, I was not confident as to how well Charming would react, as undoubtedly he was going to feel embarrassed about getting this case so wrong, and I was going to prove my point.

'Bloody hell.' I recalled my ex-boyfriend's detailed character assassination. 'Ben was spot on.' I did like to be right all the time. I hated being criticised, and I was most uncomfortable with being wrong. But if I'm wrong I will say so, as much as it hurt. I hoped vehemently that the whispers about Dr Sharman being involved in a scandal were wrong, because otherwise we would have a disruptive set of patients primed to fire off in the direction of the staff, if the rumours turned out to be true … whatever they were.

* * *

Monday had come around too quickly, and I was not in the mood for work. I had enjoyed my time off far more than was good for me and my liver was making an aching complaint that day. Emma and I had both raved on almost endlessly about Forrest Gump – what a brilliant film! I was pondering the fabulous phrase 'Life is like a box of chocolates, you never know what you're going to get' as I walked from the lockers and on to the ward in good time for handover. As it turned out, that phrase was prophetic.

The ward seemed its usual shambolic ward-round-day self, and I was gearing up for sorting out the vast number of pharmacy orders and leave arrangements for the majority of the day, and after that I would be preparing for the next day's ward round with Emma, as I had promised. We were both waiting in eager anticipation for her sister Laura to get in contact. Frustratingly, we had to console ourselves with leaving a message on her answerphone machine because she was away for the weekend with her husband and children. Emma's parents had informed Emma of this fact only after we had established that no one was at Laura's home to answer our calls. We had no choice other than to wait for Laura to call back. Meantime the rumours about Dr Sharman's past continued amongst the patients. Most staff seemed oblivious, thank goodness, or chose to assume it was fantasy on the part of one of the patients.

I did a whirlwind tour of the ward and checked the allocations board, which outlined who was in what bed where, and by virtue of coloured magnetic labels, the board denoted what Section of the Mental Health Act, that person was on, if any. Simple, but effective.

Charlotte had drawn the short straw for managing the ward round that Monday morning, and she appeared to be deflated in her mood when she walked into handover. She used the word 'crushed' to describe how she felt. Nevertheless she bravely gave us the lowdown, not only on the general issues for each patient on the ward, but the outcomes from the ward round itself. She did not succeed in completing this before succumbing to tears. She explained that Dr Sharman had been in a thunderous mood, complained about his coffee, and had only agreed to keep to the discharge plan for Rodney Wells if he accepted that he had to take his medication in injectable form. Apparently, Sue, his CPN, who he had worked with for the last four years, had been present and even she had said that this was an unnecessary action. She had already purchased a pill dispenser box with the days of the week on it for him, to help Rodney remember to take his tablets.

Secretly, a lot of my ward colleagues aspired to become CPNs when they sought to move on in their nursing careers. Working as a community psychiatric nurse was stressful but it had its compensations. The CPNs always appeared smartly dressed and confident as they carried their big diaries and leather briefcases.

'Sue was assertive,' said Charlotte, 'and well organised for the discharge. She and Rodney had plans. Sue had arranged reminders for Rodney on his fridge and bathroom mirrors and she even promised that his medication could be reviewed if it didn't suit him. She'd already made a follow-up appointment for him to be seen by a community psychiatrist in six weeks' time. Rodney was pleased with this plan, although I suspect he was also simply relieved to be getting off the ward. He was desperate to go home.'

At this, Charlotte had begun to cry. She described through her tears and the odd nose-wipe, how Dr Sharman had become more than furious with Sue the CPN. He had ranted and raged, even accusing her of undermining his authority and professional decision-making. Sue the CPN, according to Charlotte, had been dumbfounded, but had then retaliated by informing Dr Sharman that she was not expecting to be spoken to in such a manner.

'He said, "In that case I suggest you wait outside" and demanded that she leave the room,' said Charlotte. She then cried and sniffled for a while longer before controlling herself again. 'Rodney begged and pleaded with Dr Sharman, he was distraught,' Charlotte sobbed. 'Dr Sharman wouldn't rescind his Section unless Rodney had an injection. He was crying when we gave it to him. We were all crying. It was terrible.'

Those in the room listening to Charlotte were silent, and only occasionally did we look at each other for confirmation of how we were responding to this news. Once Charlotte had finished her feedback, we talked all at once.

'Poor Rodney; such a nice man. He wasn't even that bad at remembering his meds,' one of us said quietly.

'I think we have to raise this again with Gordon,' someone said, referring to the senior unit manager Gordon Bygraves.

I reminded everyone that we had tried to raise objections several times in the last six months, and the result was always a curt denial of any problem, and a deaf ear or blind eye being turned to any facts presented. 'It was not well received.'

'What about the Medical Director?'

'Who's the current Medical Director?'

'We have to do something. How about we put our concerns in writing?'

'What about a Union Rep? Could they do anything?'

The suggestions came in thick and fast, but in the end no one took up the challenge of putting pen to paper. Vance, one of the healthcare assistants suggested that he could speak to a Union Rep for advice, and to test the water. His offer was accepted, and we agreed that, in the meantime, we had to be brave and raise concerns with Dr Sharman directly, documenting any disagreement in the nursing notes for evidence.

At that moment, Gordon Bygraves' secretary put her head around the door, and announced that she was looking for me.

'I'm sorry to interrupt. Monica, could you come with me please.'

There was no hint at what was about to happen. Life is like a box of chocolates.

I followed Gordon Bygraves' neat secretary to his spacious office on the ground floor, which held not only Gordon himself within, but also Dr Giles Sharman and the lovely lady from the Mental Health Act department, Harriet Morris, no relation.

'Please come in, Nurse Morris,' requested a serious looking Gordon. I took his stern expression as a forewarning that something ominous was about to come my way. The three senior NHS staff figures of Gordon, Harriet and Dr Sharman sat in stylish office chairs, which they had placed strategically in a rough semicircle, while I stood inside the door in front of them, rather like a naughty schoolgirl summoned to the headmaster's office.

'We have an unprecedented situation on our hands, Nurse Morris, but fortunately we have Dr Sharman to thank for arriving at a swift resolution.'

I still didn't know what was coming.

There was then a lengthy discussion about a discrepancy on Mark El Amin's Section papers, and an attempt at explaining in a convoluted way, that the hospital had found it necessary to seek advice from the Mental Health Act Commission itself on the best way forward. I was perplexed as I stood in front of them trying to follow the conversation.

Harriet sighed and tried to simplify the main points for me, as obviously, judging from my confused expression, she realised that I was at a loss as to why this had anything to do with me.

'The thing is, Monica, Dr Sharman has been most magnanimous in his support for you. He appreciates that you did not intentionally supply him with the incorrect application form in ward round last Tuesday. He completed the Form 11, and we are aware that it should have been a Form 4 for a Section 2. This is not as dire as it seems as the signatures and information, and importantly the times, are correct.'

Quite frankly, standing there with my mouth gaping I must have looked like a frog trying to catch a fly. I was incredulous. What were they talking about?

Dr Giles Sharman, appearing self-assured and more than a little arrogant, gave a wide smirk and leant forward. He then took up the narrative. 'Yes, please don't let this worry you. We know, that you think what you did, was correct at the time. We have taken steps to rectify the situation because we have to resubmit the recommendations anyway in the light of the information which you kindly sent through to Harriet on Friday: that we now have a name for our mysterious patient.' He then sighed. 'However, the hospital managers may take an extremely dim view of your actions in regard to Mark El Amin's appeal request.'

'I don't understand,' I said, managing at last to make a connection between my brain and my mouth.

'No, we do appreciate that, which is why we have asked to see you, Monica,' smiled an imperious Dr Sharman as he tilted his head and raised one eyebrow at me.

Monica? He never called me Monica. This charm offensive was most disconcerting, and to make matters worse, in the Twilight Zone of Gordon Bygraves' office, both Gordon and Harriet were hanging on his every word, with the occasional pitying glance in my direction. It was bad enough that Sharman loved himself so much, let alone everyone else swooning over the man.

'Let me explain,' he condescendingly offered. 'You put in a request for an appeal on behalf of Mr Trainman as he was known at the time. An appeal against Section 3, when in fact he was detained under Section 2, or would have been if I had noticed that you had given me the incorrect recommendation form. I do hold my hands up here everyone, to be clear … I should have noticed this at the time. However it is common knowledge that a patient initially detained under emergency Section 4 should be transferred onto Section 2 by the completion of the second medical recommendation. Not onto a Section 3.'

'I didn't know that,' I whispered.

In my head I was still trying to work out what on earth was going on. Mark had been admitted under a Section 4. Dr Charming Sharman had definitely transferred Mark onto Section 3 the next day. He had said it out loud, and I didn't even recall that I had sorted out the recommendation form for him during that ward round the previous Tuesday.

I still had a photocopy of that form in my flat.

I didn't question the version of events as told by Dr Sharman. I stood there, stumped.

'Not to worry. There has been a second assessment under the Mental Health Act this morning, which was highly informative. It appears our man is now talking unhindered. It is a shame Monica, that you didn't let me know that he had been in full verbal communication with ward staff since Friday. Nor did you inform me that you had submitted appeal paperwork on the patient's behalf, last Wednesday I believe? Tell me how did you do that when, at the time he remained mute?'

'He wrote a note,' I replied.

'Yes, he did,' Dr Sharman said, looking reminiscent of a grinning shark about to launch an attack. 'But that note, which you neatly and efficiently filed in the patient notes, did not make any reference to a request for an appeal against his Section, did it? And to put yourself in an even more precarious position, you contacted the solicitors on his behalf. Did you choose them for him too? I'm not suggesting coercion, you understand, but the Mental Health Act Commission may see it that way. They won't actually, you will be pleased to hear ... because Harriet has not yet sent that appeal request.'

Oh my God. What's going on? I thought as I experienced a dreadful heavy sinking feeling with cold and jelly-like legs into the bargain. That request should have been posted straight away. I daren't ask why it had been delayed.

'That was an unfortunate oversight,' Dr Sharman said, helpfully answering my unspoken question.

I didn't believe him.

'Now that our patient is officially on Section 3, he can re-appeal as of today.' He grinned at the two managers next to him. 'Our most pressing issue is to ensure that the patient is properly treated, and I shall see him in ward round tomorrow. I suggest that you re-read him his rights under the Act, using the correct leaflet, Monica, please. The same one you mistakenly used on the last occasion, and you will not need to apologise for the confusion. He has already been told that the reassessment had to take place this morning because he had disclosed to us his true identity. I believe we also have a GP identified, and that his parents have been looking for him. They live in Australia, so they are not in a position to see him but there is a family friend that we have details for, I believe.

'Don't worry, Monica. As I said, I'm sure it won't be long before the appeal can be set up, and your misdemeanours will soon be forgotten. At least we did not get so far as wasting solicitors expensive time ...'

He generated a sickly grimace, which seemed to linger in suspended animation on his face, and yet it was not the sort of smile that was ever reflected in his eyes. I allowed myself a small shiver in response.

Oh shit, I thought, as it occurred to me in one thud of apprehension, that they obviously had no inkling that Richard Huntley had already been to the ward. He had scrutinised the notes, and what's more he was on a mission about unlawful Section papers.

In that moment, I couldn't remember if I had written anything in the notes about Richard's visit to the ward on Friday. I frantically searched my memory library and was able to reassure myself that, no I hadn't written anything because Richard still had the notes with him in the small office at the end of the day. I didn't even see him leave; therefore another nurse must have put the notes away.

Did that nurse write in the notes that Richard had been to the ward to see Mark El Amin?

I was brought back from my fraught recollections of Friday, to the painful present by Gordon Bygraves who was speaking to me intently.

'… so we shall say no more about this, to anyone, Monica. As far as those of us in this room are concerned, the matter is dealt with. Your thanks should go to Giles and to Harriet for being so observant. We could have found ourselves in extremely hot water, but we are lucky to have such an eminent consultant on the team. Our bed situation is much improved and we have patients being discharged relatively swiftly. What with the National Psychopharmacology Conference coming up in London shortly, we shall be making a name for ourselves as a centre of excellence, certainly in respect of the quality of care and treatment …'

Gordon Bygraves rambled on.

Fleetingly I had wondered what eminent consultant he was talking about, but as he was still gazing lovingly towards Dr Giles Sharman, there was little doubt, and I again felt nauseous.

'Thank you,' I muttered as I turned to leave the office with my mind in a whirl and my stomach churning. I was attempting to come to terms with the realisation that Dr Charming Sharman had put himself in an unassailable position in the eyes of the hospital managers, meaning that nurses making a further complaint against him could easily be discredited.

# Chapter 23

## A Disappearance

Once back on the ward, my first priority was to check the nursing notes to see if there was any reference to Richard Huntley being on the ward on Friday.

No. Nothing. Good.

My second priority was to phone Huntley and Greaves, and speak to Richard. I found a moment to use the small office, the same one that Richard had used on Friday. I succeeded in getting through to Cheryl without delay, and she was happy to put my call straight through. I didn't know how to broach the subject with him other than to be truthful.

'Richard, I'm so sorry to bother you. I'm not sure that I should be making this call, but there is an issue with Mark El Amin's Section paperwork.'

'You're not kidding!' came the reply. 'It's hard to fathom why he was put on a Section 4, let alone a Section 3, which should have been a Section 2 by the way, but the main point is, that the information contained in that recommendation is a work of fiction as far as I can see. I too am not sure that I should be telling you this, but I believe the detention of your patient to be invalid, and therefore illegal.'

'Richard,' I was gabbling desperately, 'did you know Mark was re-assessed under the Mental Health Act again today? And he's on Section 3. Again. Apparently I gave Dr Sharman the wrong form last week, even though I didn't, and Mark should have been on a Section 2. I didn't know that. Although I don't think I've done anything wrong, earlier I was given a right royal bollocking for what I'm sure I didn't do, and for requesting an appeal against Section 3 on Mark's behalf. But it hasn't been sent to the commission and it's my fault, and what's more, the managers don't know that you have already been to see Mark and that you have seen his notes and his Section papers, well, old Section papers ... God this is such a mess and I don't understand any of it.'

'Good grief! Monica, slow down!'

I duly obeyed, and went through step-by-step, slowly, what had occurred that morning. Richard arranged to come to the ward without delay to see Mark, explain the issues, and to do so while making out that he was accessing the notes and meeting Mark for the first time. He had convinced himself that I was being made a scapegoat for hospital cock-ups, and he said so. However he needed facts prior to acting.

I was supposed to be seeing Mark to advise him as to his rights, again, but I had to give myself time to think before I made my next move. Mark had been assessed for Section 3 again that morning and had been successfully detained under the Mental Health Act. How on earth could that have happened? He didn't appear to have any mental illness, so what did they find that I had not? I went back to the notes, but there was nothing of any help in there, only brief confirmation of the outcome of the assessment that morning.

Section Papers. Copies. Where were they? No. Not in the ward copy file.

In fact there were no copies of any Section papers pertaining to Mark to be found on the ward. Not even in his notes, where the previous ones should have been filed as historical information.

After I had a slight brainwave, I phoned down to Harriet Morris on the pretext that I needed to see the information on the recommendations before I could read through Mark's rights with him again. 'After all I don't want to get it wrong this time,' I said to her, almost believing myself.

I was stewing away, convinced that I had done nothing wrong the last time I read Mark's rights to him, and I was appalled that

I had been accused of 'misdemeanours'. Nothing I had actually done was that bad. Not in my book.

Harriet, being a genuinely kind individual, albeit easily influenced, agreed to get copies of the latest Section papers to me immediately, and she assured me that she had no idea where the old ones had been filed … 'Sorry.'

It was a good half an hour later that Harriet brought the most recent Section paper copies to the ward for filing, and as she was leaving again, she met face to face with Richard Huntley on his way in to see his 'new client'. She chatted amicably with him for a short while. They knew each other professionally because it was Harriet's job to organise the practicalities of the tribunal hearings held in the hospital. She would normally confirm with solicitors their access requirements to patient case notes and to Section papers. I had undermined standard procedure in Mark's case and was beginning to regret the fact.

Harriet ended her brief chat with Richard 'No problem, I'm glad to be of help.' She shot me a glance, but I wasn't confident that I knew what her body language was saying. 'I'm sure Monica can sort out whatever you need,' she said as she smiled at Richard pleasantly and headed for the lifts. It turned out that Richard had the foresight to call her before leaving his office to request access to the notes for Mark. Harriet would never know that he had already done so. Clever man.

Richard then turned to me and said carefully, in hushed tones, 'Monica, just give me the notes and the copy Section papers and then leave me to it. Whatever happens in future do not get involved in trying to help me. Keep to your usual nursing boundaries and I'll do the necessary. I think you may be putting yourself in a tenuous position, career-wise, if you are seen to feed information to me. Thanks, and in other words, I'll take it from here. Don't worry.'

The more people around me said the words 'don't worry' the more I worried. Emma caught sight of me as I went in search of the patient rights leaflets, and her first words were, 'You look worried, or is it a hangover?'

I had forgotten about my hangover. I was a bit shaky, but that was nervous energy, anger, anxiety, and self-pity rolled into one. I had allowed myself to be bullied spectacularly that morning in Gordon Bygraves' office.

'What happened with Gordon this morning?' Emma asked, innocently.

'Oh God, Emma ... It's such a long story, but in short, I've been shafted to save Charming. And Mark Jesus Trainman El Amin is still on a Section 3, even though he does not have a mental illness that warrants any admission to hospital. Will that do for starters?'

'Sounds like a normal Monday,' Emma replied. 'Did you hear that Mark had a visitor yesterday? He now has clothes that fit him properly. Let me tell you, "fit" is the word. Oh my. A pair of Levi's maketh the man!' she exclaimed, revisiting her lustful side briefly. 'Nice chap by all accounts; the visitor. Margaret was on duty and she reckons he looked like Cary Grant. You remember him. North by Northwest, that Hitchcock film. Margaret was gushing and girlie about him ... so it sounds as if you missed out again!'

I wasn't actually listening to what Emma was saying, because I was going over and over in my mind the inaccuracies of the conversations in Gordon Bygraves' office downstairs. Then I tried to analyse what Richard had said. All of which was self-defeating, so I made the decision to keep my head down for now, and get on with my job instead.

Leaflets. Where was the one I needed?

When I found the right one, I went in search of Mark, who it turned out, was downstairs in one of the groups again. I left a message with the OT department asking for Mark to find me when he was able. No rush. He wasn't going anywhere for now, and besides which, he had heard his '*Rights to Appeal*' information the first time around.

When I returned to the office Emma collared me again.

'Mon, I forgot to tell you. Laura phoned me late last night. About "you-know-who" and the scandal thing.' She was speaking in code, as staff members were popping in and out of the office in quick succession.

'She was of no use,' Emma said. 'She remembers there being a problem with a drugs trial, and a couple of the patients who were rushed to a general hospital for treatment, but nobody seemed to be blamed at the time. Dr Sharman apparently left to take up a research post somewhere.

'It was said to be coincidence that the patients who became ill were on his ward. That was the official line at the time.'

'Is that it?' I asked, disappointed.

# Chapter 24

## News from Around the Country

'Lewis! Thank God. Bloody marvellous!' Mark could not have been more pleased to see Lewis James stroll onto the ward on Sunday. He had not realised who it was at first, as Lewis was casually dressed, and not suited and booted, barrister style, as if for work.

As he warmly shook Lewis's hand, grinning widely, Mark took in the smart designer polo shirt – Ralph Lauren, and not one of those snide ones from the market. He envied the dark blue Levi jeans that his visitor was wearing, and as Lewis then smoothly placed his sunglasses on top of his head, Mark spotted the Ray-Ban logo and smiled inwardly.

'You look like a tramp,' came the brutally honest observation from Lewis as he patted Mark's back. He couldn't fail to have noticed the baggy second-hand clothes hanging from Mark's slim frame. The two men had developed a good bond of friendship since their first meeting at the offices of the Daily Albion weeks earlier, and Mark was genuinely appreciative of the manly hug he received. 'Is there a place we can talk in private around here?' Lewis asked. 'Or shall we go out and get a coffee?'

'God, I'd love to,' replied Mark, sighing wistfully at the thought of a freshly ground coffee. He could almost smell the magical aroma. Breaking the unhappy news to Lewis that he didn't have any permission to leave the ward, accompanied or otherwise, they were forced to settle for a mug of rubbish NHS ward coffee. It was the cheap stuff that comes in giant tins, and has no flavour. Mellow was not the word, although insipid was closer to an accurate description.

'Cor, bugger me, Mark, this is crap. How do you put up with it?'

'No choice, mate. I'm sodding-well stuck in here. A Section 3 in case you didn't know.'

As it was a Sunday, the ward was almost empty of other patients, giving the pair sole use of the small dayroom, which was not only vacant, but also strangely silent. Unusually, the TV had not yet been switched on. Not a soul walked by or interrupted for the next hour or so.

'Six days in hospital so far, and none of that time has been particularly taxing, just frustrating,' Mark confirmed. 'In fact, I'm learning to appreciate the change of pace in life. Granted, being stuck in here is not pleasant, but I'll miss Creative Writing for Beginners, when I leave.'

'You have to be joking! Really? Creative Writing? Now that's ironic. Well done.'

'Don't take the piss. It's therapeutic. No pressure and no deadlines to contend with. Creative writing has turned out to be a huge amount of fun, actually. It was a Godsend when I was still mute.'

Lewis, had news to impart. He explained to Mark that when he had been in contact with Richard Huntley the solicitor, it had been necessary for him to rustle up a cover story of his own.

'Ah. So you became James Lewis, family solicitor, not to be confused with Lewis James barrister. Of course! … ingenious. No one would ever guess,' Mark said sarcastically, 'and, by the way, thanks for giving me parents in Australia, nice touch. Did they send me clothes?' Mark asked with a nod in the general direction of a carrier bag placed by Lewis's feet.

'Oh yes, sorry, young man. Nearly forgot. I have clothes and tasty snacks and money for you. Mostly loose change for the phone. I've also treated you to a toothbrush, in fact a whole wash kit. You sounded so desperate for basic bathroom essentials.'

'I was desperate. I've had to wash and make do with other people's left over toiletries, would you believe? Quite degrading, even for a scruffy oik like me. Apparently there's no money in the NHS to have such items supplied by the hospital, so if you arrive on the ward in the clothes you are standing up in, that is all you have. In my case it was a pair of sandals. They gave me these groovy lost property clothes to wear, and that is all I have. Not even any pants! Mind you, I look a lot cleaner than I did. The staff gave me a trim up of the old facial hair on Friday, which I think I can now call "designer Jesus stubble".'

Mark was pulling out clothes from the bagful that Lewis had provided and nodding appreciatively at the quality. 'Oh these are nice,' he said as he found a brand new pair of Levi jeans. 'You even bought the right size, you clever bugger.'

Lewis steered Mark back to the business in hand. He let Mark know that he had received a phone call back from Richard Huntley on Friday, quite some time after Mark had seen him on the ward for the first time.

'It was fairly late on in the evening when he called me,' said Lewis, 'but I'm glad he phoned. I like the man. He tells me he has your full consent to discuss your detention, your appeal, your treatment, and everything in fact, with me. You put this in writing for him I take it?'

'Yes. Spot on. I needed him to be able to tell you everything.' Mark was having a good rummage through the bag of most-welcome gifts from Lewis.

'It was a good plan, because that man seems to have stumbled upon a possible illegal detention in your case, and he was planning to check out the facts before challenging this through the Mental Health Act Commission. I agreed to discuss with you how we should best proceed. My advice would be that we let Richard Huntley pursue this as he suggests. It will make a great story for you, and the research team will be thrilled.

'If that's okay with you, I'll catch up with Richard on Monday or Tuesday, and let's see how we go with your next ward round.

It would be good if you can be off this Section of yours either way. We can still expose the illegal detention of course.'

'I'm more worried that nasty piece of work, Dr Sharman, will put me in a position where I have to take medication, like it or not,' Mark said. He then proceeded to inform Lewis about what he had witnessed, and about the rumours amongst the patients that Dr Sharman was the subject of scandal. Mark hinted that Lewis could perhaps arrange to set the research team a task to investigate this angle.

'I'll have one hell of a story then,' Mark announced. 'Detained illegally by a psychiatrist who was involved in scandal. Gold dust. By the way, how are the others getting on? Did they all get admitted? Is there anyone else, apart from me, under a Section?'

Lewis had tales to tell in respect of Mark's journalist colleagues and the researchers who had agreed to take part in the experiment.

Linda, the heavy smoking battle-axe gossip columnist, had done a fine job of ensuring that she was picked up by the police, dressed as the Queen in full regalia and waving to her subjects. She was taken to the local police station and thence to a psychiatric hospital in Shropshire. Her antics had made the local papers. She had demanded that passers-by should curtsey and kneel before her. 'She knighted one or two, right there in the street with the traffic stopped and jams backing up for a good mile or two,' Lewis chortled.

'I'm disappointed,' Mark said. 'I scoured the local papers, and there was not a single mention of any naked Messiah on the station in any of them. No CCTV pictures, nothing, and let me tell you, I put on one hell of a performance.' Mark pouted childishly.

Lewis, like any good parent, ignored him and continued with the update. The reports coming in were that Linda had taken to being in an acute psychiatric ward like a duck to water. Seemingly, she had sounded cheerful on the phone when she spoke to John Starkey, her editor at the Daily Albion, who was worried at first. 'Cheerful' is not a word used to describe Linda, not by anyone, and John Starkey thought she had finally cracked. But then it came to light that she had accepted Lorazepam from the nurses and loved the effect so much, that she was angling to get hold of at least one tablet on a daily basis.

Lewis had to explain to Mark that Lorazepam was, 'a benzodiazepine, addictive stuff that is, a bit like Valium. It makes you relaxed and carefree.'

Mark struggled to imagine this, and grinned at the disturbingly unfamiliar thought of a cheerful, relaxed, and carefree Linda. 'Blimey.'

According to Lewis she had 'plenty of fags with her' and had even been out to the local pub with a couple of the other patients. She was heading rapidly for discharge home. The reports he received were second-hand 'via Prof Hugo at the Institute.' The arrangement was that Prof Hugo, Lewis, and John Starkey had divided the intrepid experimenters up between them and were keeping an eye on a specific number each. If possible, they were pretending to be visitors to get face-to-face access in order to double-check on everyone's welfare, apart from that of Jock Mackenzie, the Scottish journalist.

'Jock made a right fool of himself,' Lewis disclosed, laughing as he told Mark the sad tale of Jock, who had insisted on carrying out his Monty Python-inspired admission attempt. He had entered a large indoor market in Derby dressed as a medieval knight of old, saying 'Nee' loudly, and galloping along using two coconut shells for the sound effects. This was exactly as he had described a few weeks previously in the offices of The Daily Albion. However, it turned out that the good people of Derby were so amused by him, they assumed he was a professional entertainer, a clown, or collecting for charity. An elderly couple had thrown money at him, as well as applauding. The police didn't bother to show up because not one soul reported anything untoward, and Jock eventually made his way to the hotel where he had stayed the previous night. He checked back in, exhausted by his own efforts.

Mark found this hilarious. Once he had stopped laughing, he then asked about Andy the researcher with the genius idea. 'The one who planned to pretend he thought he had microchips implanted in his ears and was being monitored by the KGB,' he reminded Lewis.

'Oh, yes. He's in. Under a Section 2 for the first couple of days, but as he was so well behaved, the consultant there took the decision to revoke his Section, and he's an informal patient now. I'm not sure they fell for the story that he had found an insect in his ear, because he's been given a diagnosis. Something along the lines of an acute and transient psychotic episode, I think. They've prescribed medication too, I'm sure.' That diagnosis sounded complicated to Mark.

'Charlie. What about my mate Charlie?' Mark asked, genuinely concerned as to how well his friend was coping with being cooped up and undercover.

'Oh, he did a great job!' reported Lewis. 'His jump-off-a-bridge idea worked a treat, but the poor man is way up in Newcastle and struggling with the accent I reckon. The other patients call him "the cockney", and despite this, he's well liked by the girls. But I'm not sure even he can handle those Northern lasses. He's already been warned that the hospital is not the place for physical relationships.'

Mark gave Lewis a querying look.

'He was caught shagging in the toilets.'

'Why am I not surprised?'

''fraid so. A mixed-sex ward for Charlie may be a double-edged sword. While there are no discharge plans yet, he may get himself thrown out if he keeps getting caught in compromising positions. Anyway, he spoke to John too, and seems okay in himself, although he was not sleeping well, so he has joined Linda in the Lorazepam Appreciation Society. Are you on anything?'

'No. I'm supposed to be taking Haloperidol ten milligrams twice a day, but I have refined the knack of poking it into my cheek with my tongue and I simply palm it and flush it down the loo much later on. The nurses are fooled by my tiredness, I'm knackered most of the time anyway, but my fellow patients are not buying it. They know, because I can't produce the other side effects they have. The restlessness, I can't keep it up. I forget. I can't do the stiffness either.

'Most of them don't think I should be in here, they know that I'm a fraud, an interloper, an imposter. Apparently it works in the same way that gay men can tell another gay man. They simply know I'm not mentally ill. As the saying goes in here, it takes a mad man to know a mad man.'

\* \* \*

'I think they're right,' Lewis confirmed. 'Personally, I think you're all mad for agreeing to this little jaunt. You do realise we're going to have a hell of a job getting you out of here within two weeks, don't you?'

'Mmmmm. I do.'

# Chapter 25

## An Unpleasant Smell

Not dwelling on his own incarceration, Mark wanted to know from Lewis about the rest of the research, and how many fellow experimenters were in hospital in total. Most importantly, he was keen to find out if anyone had been discharged yet. He wanted to be the first one to get his stories into print.

'The rest are all in, apart from Jock. We had a bit of a surprise in one case, although we should have taken account of the possibility. One of the young researchers, India? Indira? Is that her name? Yes, I think that's right … she had no trouble in getting herself admitted, but there was no bed in her target hospital. So she's ended up miles away, and would you believe in her hometown! So far, no one she knows has seen her or recognised her, but it's a bit touch and go. None of the experimenters has been discharged yet. What we are finding though, is that the hospitals are quite different from each other, judging from the reports coming in, so it's luck of the draw as to what experiences people will contribute to the wider picture. How are you coping with being here? It's a bit drab looking, isn't it?'

Lewis scanned around at the plain painted walls of the room as if to make a point. 'To be frank, I'm none too impressed by the green walls and green lino everywhere. And that smell of stale smoke adds a special tinge of neglect to the overall ambience of the place, don't you think?'

'Yes it's a bit drab, but the nurses and most of the other patients are an interesting bunch of people,' Mark replied. 'I can't complain about the way they have treated me on the whole, and they are good at what they do, the nurses. A few are a bit half-hearted, and a number of the night staff enjoy a good sleep, I have to say. Mind you, it depends which of the staff nurses are on duty. Most are great … caring and thorough, and they check that everyone is safe and sound.'

* * *

'And, I have a named nurse,' Mark said, sounding really proud of the fact. 'I had no idea what one was when I first arrived, but she seems to take responsibility for what happens while I'm here.

'You know, Lewis, until now, I hadn't given this enough thought, but these patients in here, are incredibly vulnerable. We, the patients that is, rely on the nurses to do the right thing to help us, to guide us through the routines, the treatments, getting access to clothing, food, telephoning the outside world, and I suspect they take inventive steps to lessen the impact of the treatments.'

'What do you mean?'

Mark went on a bit of a rant. 'Lewis, I have to tell you, there is a dictatorship at play here. A drug dictatorship.' Mark explained. 'Dr Sharman, the consultant, is a raving psychopath. He's a nasty, vindictive, arrogant arse. The patients are petrified of what he'll do next. That includes me. Can they go home? Can they see their families? Can they go out? What medication will he make them take?

'The patients have no choice, because those choices have been taken away from them. We don't have much of our dignity preserved in here. Would you fancy having to sleep in a dormitory or having someone hand you your razor, or check up on you in the bath, or deciding if you can or cannot leave the building? Bloody degrading. Shocking, Lewis, demeaning. You know, I've been toying with the idea of taking one of those Haloperidol tablets, so that I can actually experience what real patients are having to go through.'

'I'm not sure that's a wise move, sunshine.'

'Yeah, well. What strikes me is that most of the patients know that they need to take medication of one sort or another, simply because they get ill again if they don't. They plainly don't want to take the cheap zombie shit ones Dr Giles Sharman is insisting they have. Oh sorry, Lewis! What a prat I am. I realise that you know this. I forgot, you used to be a psychiatric nurse.'

'That's okay. It's good to hear your views. It's why you are on this trip, after all.' Lewis pulled out a pad and pen. 'I need to write that consultant's name down and get Prof Hugo's researchers on to seeking out his background information. Having said that, I may be able to find out much faster than anyone else.' Lewis looked at Mark with a conspiratorial smirk.

'I've chaired quite a few conduct hearings at Medical Practitioners Tribunals, and it's actually relatively easy to look up information relating to any doctor registered to practice medicine in this country. If this was a scandal, then I'm fairly sure it would've raised enough concern to go to a hearing. What did you say was the name of the hospital he worked at before?' asked Lewis with his pen poised mid air.

'If my memory serves me right, the name of the hospital was, Farley Hill, and it was 1987 when big Phil was there.' Mark replied. Not that Lewis had any idea who Big Phil was or that he was Mark's closest informant on the ward.

Mark continued. 'Dr Sharman was somewhere else between practicing there, and coming to this hospital. I'm in the dark as to where that might have been, but I'll see if I can find out from the patients. Dr Sharman has only been here for the last six months or so. The patients don't rate the man. His predecessor, a Dr B, was more popular and the patients continue to talk in glowing terms about him. I don't know what the B stands for … an unpronounceable surname, I'm told. He was well liked, so I think it's been a bit of a shock for everyone here to meet an entirely different character, but it also means that not all consultant psychiatrists are bad.'

'My wife will be delighted to hear that.'

'Shit. Sorry. Big foot in mouth moment.'

Once Mark had finished sheepishly apologising for his mistake and inadvertent insult, he continued to ask for Lewis's help. 'If you can dig up some dirt about Dr Sharman, I would appreciate knowing anything you uncover. I'm dying to understand who or what type of person we are dealing with here. He's making people's lives a misery. Bloody tyrant! I was ignorant to the fact that one man could abuse so much power. It's a revelation to me how he gets away with it.

'I say that … I have seen him challenged by Monica, my named nurse, and I think she was badly burned at the ward round last Tuesday. She came out looking like she'd been through a mangle. Dr Sharman loves that position of power, and he loves himself. His suits are flashier than yours, and he checks himself out in any reflective surface he walks past, vain twat!'

'Thanks for that insight,' remarked Lewis with a slight laugh. 'Joking aside, you could be in a risky position here. If you are required to take the medication and you refuse … you are, on paper, detained under a Section 3, and steps would usually be taken to ensure treatment, if you get my drift.' Lewis then demonstrated a syringe being plunged toward his own right buttock, enlightening Mark as to the true meaning of his words. 'Perhaps enforce would be a more accurate word,' Lewis said, nodding. 'I'm sceptical as to this consultant's modus operandi, and I cannot for the life of me fathom how you have been placed on, and remain on, a Section.

'I think, Mark, that you need to have an exit strategy lined up. If you get an opportunity, it may actually be safer for you to take your leave and go AWOL. Richard Huntley and I can deal with the legal side. Having said that, I will have to tell him the truth about the research experiment, if we get to that point. I'd rather do that, than leave you here at the mercy of … I don't know what to say …' Lewis struggled and failed to find the right words. 'If you're right, then this man could well be psychopathic, and if that's the case then all the patients and most of the staff are potentially at risk, of bullying at least. At worst: harmful abuse. We do need to gather the evidence my boy, so get gathering and stop messing about chatting up named nurses.'

Mark was surprised that Lewis had picked up about his growing interest in Monica. He couldn't help it; he really liked her. It was easier when he had been mute. He didn't have to worry about what to say, or how to engage her in a conversation. "Do you come here often?" would be an irrelevant clumsy chat-up line. It had been perfectly natural to watch her as she worked, and she was so easy in her manner that he didn't feel shy around her as he normally would in the vicinity of an attractive woman. *Get a grip, man*, he had told himself. This was no time, and certainly no place to be taking a fancy to a woman. *Bum*, thought Mark. *Why here? Why now?*

Lewis looked thoughtfully down at the note pad that he still had in his hand, and asked, 'Mark, have you got any written reports yet?'

'Of course, but they're in shorthand.'

'That doesn't matter, unless it's your own made up version.'

'No. But it's Teeline as opposed to Pitman. Most good secretaries can read it, especially if they are over fifty,' Mark said with all seriousness.

'Can you let me have what you've got so far, in the event that you lose it, or can't get it out with you? I'll have it typed up. Here, take the rest of this pad and interview whosoever you can about this dodgy consultant. I smell something most unpleasant,' Lewis concluded.

Mark eagerly made his way to the dormitory to collect his series of scribbled chronological diaries.

When he handed them over to Lewis for safekeeping and translation into typed format, Lewis was made to promise faithfully not to hand them in for editing. Mark wanted to write the full story himself. 'Oi, you just remember these are aide memoires, not finished articles! So don't bugger about with them.'

Lewis rolled them up carefully inside a newspaper, confirming that he would indeed keep his promise to Mark. He strolled out of the ward saying a smiling cheery farewell to the staff and patients that he passed as he left through the double doors towards the lifts and stairwell.

Mark became temporarily downhearted when Lewis left to catch his train back to London, but at the same time, he felt more reassured that he was being kept an eye on by the research team.

# Chapter 26

## Sectioned Again

Mark's feeling of optimism was short-lived. Straight after breakfast the next day, he was taken to see Dr Sharman, Dr Siddiqui, and the beige square lady social worker, Mrs Anna Brown. As a result he experienced an overwhelming sense of déjà vu as he sat down in front of them.

'Crikey, what have I done to deserve such attention?' Mark greeted them with a polite grin. Assuming that their mistake had been realised, he was expecting their announcement that he was no longer under a Section.

The group did not smile in return. Dr Sharman, who approached the meeting with a professional but amiable air, took the lead role. His whole attitude was most unlike the man that Mark had seen in action during the ward round the previous Tuesday. This friendly version of the consultant psychiatrist unnerved Mark. He listened attentively as Dr Sharman explained. 'The hospital have now confirmed your name, address, and other details, which we were previously were unaware of. Therefore we are obliged to review your status under the Mental Health Act.'

This seemed to Mark, to be a reasonable explanation, on the surface. However, knowing that Richard Huntley had revealed a discrepancy in the Section paperwork, he was immediately suspicious of Dr Sharman's justification for yet another assessment under the Mental Health Act. He'd had one in A+E the previous week, another in ward round the day after that, and now he was being subjected to another assessment.

*Never mind*, he thought, *let's see where this is going. If all is well, I could be a free man very shortly.* He nodded to Dr Sharman, who proceeded to ask a series of relatively superficial questions about Mark's mental health. Mark was content to oblige with carefully considered answers. 'Look, I shouldn't be kept in hospital. There's no need, you see. My mental health is fine now. I'm feeling a bit embarrassed about all the fuss actually. I must have hit my head when the train pulled into the station. I don't even remember what happened exactly,' Mark assured the three assessors who maintained poker faces.

Dr Sharman asked him about whether he had ever heard voices when there was nobody around. Mark, in the same way that he had when Monica asked the same questions, denied any such experiences. 'No, never have. Nothing unusual.'

'Do you ever see, feel, or smell unusual things?' he was asked and again he gave a factual answer.

'No, never,' he lied, determined not to mention the flashbacks. Mark had said roughly the same to Monica when she had assessed him.

Then there appeared from nowhere, an inner voice that popped into Mark's head. Not an hallucination, no, this was the voice that we experience when we realise that we may have done something wrong, or thoughtlessly uttered words without due consideration for the consequences. The little voice, like our conscience, niggles and nags, rebuking us for not using the brains we were born with.

Mark's inner voice treated him to a proper scolding for his stupidity, and as result, he became incredibly irritated with himself for being so open with Monica. Monica had told him that in her opinion he did not have psychosis, but the man in front of him was determined to prove that he did. Mark recognised far too late that he had freely given Dr Sharman the ammunition needed to keep him detained in hospital. It was in the notes that Monica had written. Dr Sharman had her report in his hands.

'It says here that you have night terrors and have reported experiencing flashbacks. Would this report be inaccurate?'

'No. I mean yes. I mean, I do get flashbacks, but I'm not psychotic.'

Mark tried in vain to close the metaphorical door on the stable from where the verbal horse had bolted. 'I lived in the Middle East when I was a child and our family was caught up in the fighting. I witnessed terrifying acts of terrorism, so I have flashbacks sometimes, but I know what they are and I have learnt to live with them.'

Mark prayed that this background information would result in a better level of understanding, by Dr Sharman in particular, and with any luck there would be a change of mind about the Section. He would agree to stay in hospital as an informal patient, if offered the chance, and Mark didn't even mind if they wanted to put him on different tablets; he wasn't taking the ones they were already giving him.

The poker faces remained in place, as Dr Sharman continued. 'We believe you are suffering from schizophrenia.'

'So I heard,' Mark countered. 'Although I'm not sure how you came to that conclusion. I don't have schizophrenia.'

'You are to continue your treatment, and when you are better you can be discharged to get back to your usual life ... what is it? Oh yes, studying for a PhD. It appears your specialist subject continues to be the Middle East according to this.' Dr Sharman was again reading from Monica's assessment report. He chose to ignore Mark's challenge. 'I have made it abundantly clear that you remain under a Section of the Mental Health Act. Therefore you must comply with the treatment plans that I have determined. I will increase the dose of your Haloperidol and you will soon be on the mend.'

Mark shook his head, baffled. *What is the pompous psycho-pillock getting out of this?* 'Dr Sharman, I don't have schizophrenia, and I'm not suffering from anything other than a bit of insomnia. I therefore object to having to take any increase in the dose of the tablets you are prescribing, as quite clearly I can't be on the mend from something which is not broken in the first place, namely my sanity. I don't see what there is to gain from keeping me here on a Section.' Mark was firm but polite. Assertive. *Stick that in your po-face!* He thought.

'I'm afraid these decisions are out of your hands, Mr El Amin,' came the riposte from Dr Sharman. 'You have the right to appeal, and we shall take this up again in ward round. Am I seeing you today or tomorrow?' Dr Sharman asked, seemingly unaware of the upset he had caused.

Dr Siddiqui answered the question on Mark's behalf, and then the trio of mental health professionals dismissed Mark to think about the consequences of all that had been said in the previous ten minutes or so. As far as Mark was concerned, he had made no progress.

'Still on Section 3 ... still in hospital ... still pissed off,' he concluded aloud.

He was determined to make the most of his difficult circumstances rather than cave in to self-pity, so Mark set himself a target. This week he would be on a special assignment to find out what more Welsh Phil might know about Dr Sharman's past. Mark hoped that Lewis would be getting the wheels in motion from the outside too, in order for the scandal to be revealed in all its glory, and the sooner the better. 'That bastard deserves to be exposed for what he is. Stand by, Dr Sharman. The pen is mightier than the medication. I'm on a mission now, so bollocks to you,' Mark muttered, striding down the corridor.

\* \* \*

He headed to morning groups on the ground floor, with his new smaller notepad and a pen tucked in the back pocket of his clean Levi jeans. Meanwhile, Dr Sharman, Dr Siddiqui, and Mrs Brown completed the paperwork for the most recent of Mark's detentions. Section 3. Dr Sharman wrote almost exactly what he had done previously.

Dr Siddiqui, on the other hand, wrote a vague description, which tallied with what Dr Sharman had concluded. He was too scared not to.

Mrs Anna Brown, beige and square, was clearly just along for the ride, having left her backbone at home again. She did not question one single point that was discussed or written down. She merely confirmed with Mark, when she found him downstairs in Creative Writing for Beginners, that he was now on Section 3.

He was mildly amused.

He'd been on Section 3 before so there was nothing new in what she was telling him, as far as he knew.

'I have a duty to inform your nearest relatives.'

'Good luck with that,' Mark said, knowing that his pretend parents were in Australia and could not be contacted.

With a sinking feeling, Mark realised that the whole system was shambolic.

# Chapter 27

## Backed into a Corner

As Emma escorted Mark into the large room for his second ward round, Dr Sharman was preening himself for the umpteenth time so far that day. Mark noticed how weary Emma had appeared. He thought perhaps the day was taking its toll on her usual chirpy good humour as ward round had dragged on past lunchtime, yet again. Mark could tell that Dr Sharman was holding court, when he heard the consultant detail the rationale behind his earlier decisions, and by going to extreme lengths to describe the pharmacological actions of the medication he had prescribed.

Mark slowly crossed the room and took his seat, and as he settled into the upright uncomfortable chair, he found that he was now party to the great man discussing 'this interesting case' with his acolytes. Pleased to hear that he was considered to be an interesting case, Mark listened carefully to every word. He also took out his pen and writing pad, and wrote down verbatim all that was said, without Dr Sharman even noticing. The noble consultant was far too full of his own importance to look at the patient to whom he was referring, and he pontificated on the subject for several minutes.

'… was reassessed yesterday under the Mental Health Act 1983, and he's now on a Section 3 as a result. He reported on-going auditory and olfactory hallucinations. The voices were in the third person, commanding in nature and this in itself is an indicator for schizophrenia. He displays no insight into his illness …'

*What the hell is the idiot talking about? I never said anything about hearing voices*, thought Mark.

'… and predictably because of the lack of insight he's not in agreement with remaining in hospital informally …'

*I wasn't even offered the choice*, Mark recalled.

'… is declining treatment …'

*If I don't have schizophrenia then I don't need treating for it do I!* Mark thought as he shifted forward in his seat tightening the grip on his pen.

'… and we have the significant chain of events that led to him being admitted. The risk to the public must take precedence here gentlemen.'

*What's that then? The risk of being prayed for, in a made-up language, or the risk of seeing a man the way nature intended. What a complete twat.*

Dr Sharman topped off his observations and personal opinions with the following words to his entourage: 'We must, as you will no doubt come to appreciate as you progress with your careers, we must ensure that we manage any level of hostility, aggressive behaviour and agitation, and ensure we are treating accordingly. Therefore I increased this man's medication yesterday,' he said looking at the drug chart and not at Mark. Mark was not perturbed by the increase in his dose, as he was still not swallowing any of the tablets, and thus it was irrelevant to him how much it was increased by.

'However …' Dr Sharman said, while pausing for effect, as was his want. 'I have realised that the requirement here is for more active management, shall we say. Therefore I propose to make use of Droperidol liquid instead. Five milligrams twice a day. Commencing this evening please Nurse Foster with a one off dose of ten milligrams. I take it we have stock?'

Mark saw Emma's stunned expression, and realised that he was in for trouble. Emma nodded. Then she shook her head and said, 'Actually I'm not sure without checking.'

* * *

'I have no doubt that the hospital pharmacy will oblige if necessary,' Dr Sharman responded, with a supercilious grin.

Mark coughed. 'Would you mind explaining to me what your intentions are regarding my treatment, Doctor,' he said, through gritted teeth. 'I'm quite happy to continue taking the tablets.' Mark's mind was whirring away with the possible steps that he might have to take, to avoid accepting the liquid cosh. He had heard enough about it from his fellow patients to know that Droperidol was Haloperidol's evil twin sister.

The really ugly one.

Mark had debated with himself for over a week about whether he should take one tablet of Haloperidol, as an experiment. Now it seemed, he was going to be forced into becoming a human guinea pig, like it or not. The alternative was an injection. *Shit.* He had to be quite careful what he said next.

Dr Sharman was astonishingly brusque in his reply to Mark's request for an explanation. 'I believe I clarified to you yesterday that you are required to take medication as I decide to prescribe. You will improve and then you can go home.'

'Can I at least have an hours' escorted leave, Doctor?' asked Mark in as innocent a voice as he could manage. 'I need to get out of the hospital for fresh air, I have been here for over a week, and the exercise would be good for me.'

This was the only thing Mark could think of. He had to find a way of absconding. This was getting too risky. Story or no story, he would go with what information he had already. There was plenty that would keep the public on the edge of their seats when they read about this.

*Buggeration, this is tense*, Mark thought.

Dr Giles Sharman glanced briefly at his entourage and then back at Mark and said patronisingly, 'And I came up on the down boat, did I? Mr El Amin, if I were to give you leave, the day after you have been placed on a Section 3, and in the full knowledge that you do not wish to accept treatment, then I would be a laughing stock amongst my colleagues. You no doubt, will take your leave and hop back on a train from whence you came. In other words: No.'

Mark stared in disbelief. Emma remained seated and stunned into silence again. Mark knew that she, like others on the ward, had guessed he was not taking his Haloperidol tablets. He had been credited for his skill in achieving this, because he had not been caught so far, and he always looked as if he had swallowed the damn things. The lack of side effects was the give away. Mark was well aware that Emma was on his side, but he wished Monica had been there.

Mark noticed by chance, Dr Siddiqui wearing a sad expression, and he wondered what on earth the doctor was thinking about. Was he feeling guilty regarding how Mark was being dealt with? He had signed the Section papers Mark assumed, and therefore had to take responsibility for his actions. It was of no help him sitting there looking sorrowful. Mark then noticed how Dr Siddiqui had the drug prescription chart in front of him, but that he hadn't written in it. Dr Sharman had handed it over with the clear expectation that Dr Siddiqui should complete his orders by writing out the prescription.

Dr Siddiqui closed the unaltered drug chart, and put it down on the pile with the others to go to the pharmacy. Dr Siddiqui caught Emma looking at him and he held her gaze long enough to identify that they were both in agreement and that nothing would be said. Mark caught this exchange, sighing internally with relief at the unexpected reprieve.

Dr Sharman then interrupted his thoughts by announcing sternly, 'Dr Siddiqui. You haven't completed that prescription. Pay attention, man! Just because lunch is late, there is no excuse for dozing. Give it here!'

Dr Sharman grabbed Mark's prescription chart and filled in the required areas for Droperidol liquid to be taken as he had instructed and he crossed out the previous prescription for Haloperidol. He launched the drug chart back in the general direction of the pile to go to the pharmacy, leaving Dr Siddiqui to pick it up from the floor and place it neatly on top of the other charts. A little power play for Dr Sharman's own amusement, Mark realised. Dr Siddiqui seemed as if he was about to cry.

*Short of a miracle, it looks as if I'm cornered*, concluded a shaking Mark as he was ushered out of the ward round. Taking the zombie liquid was inevitable. If he refused, then Mark knew he would undoubtedly be forced to have an injection. Anxiety was threatening to turn into panic.

*Christ. Not even Lewis can get me out in time to avoid this unscheduled part of the experiment.*

# Chapter 28

### Descent into Hell

Mark approached the hatch where Charlotte stood administering prescribed medication to each patient who required it, and she carefully explained to Mark exactly what his new medication was and the possible side effects. She emphasised how important it was to report any 'unexpected muscle stiffness or any unusual side effects.'

Mark looked straight into her with his blue eyes and wished she had the courage to pour the syrupy liquid down the sink, right in front of him.

'Any side effects, no matter how insignificant you think they might be, you let us know,' she said as she handed him the tiny plastic medicine pot. Mark hesitated for a moment or two and then, knowing that he had no choice, slugged it right back, but didn't swallow. He then took a beaker of water and pretended to wash it down as instructed, not actually sipping the water. He looked at Charlotte. She nodded vehemently, willing him on.

'Please, Mark. It's the safest option. Don't make him write you up for an injection. That takes forever to work its way out of your system.'

*God, I hadn't even thought of that. Shit, shit, fuck.*

Mark choked, and in doing so gulped the whole lot. He was trembling as he left the room.

Mark had one remaining intention. He made certain that he had his pad and pen at the ready to describe everything he was about to experience. He wanted to make this a special piece of personal journalism. What else could he do?

* * *

He felt fine for the first forty minutes or so, maybe a little anxious as would be expected. Insidiously over the next hour, a heavy slowness crept into his every muscle, and his mind became increasingly dulled.

At first, Mark tried to shake these feelings by having a strong coffee, followed by a second. He had to make do with putting three teaspoons of cheap tasteless coffee in a tall mug in an effort to gain any sort of stimulant effect. He now understood why he saw so many of his fellow patients with caffeine drinks or simply chain smoking. The need to maintain a degree of alertness drove this search for stimulants of any kind.

'Be Alert! Your Country Needs Lerts,' Mark said out loud as he stirred his coffee, recalling the words on his favourite t-shirt.

He wrote down, in fine detail, his feelings both physical and emotional, as they arose. As time went on, he was less able to find the vocabulary or formulate descriptions of these internal changes. It was as if he had a gargantuan sized ball of cotton wool being gradually crammed into his head, forcing his cognitive abilities to stagnate. Inexorably, he became incapable of creative thought or undertaking the task of committing descriptions to paper.

Mark realised that he was going to be in for a rough ride, but could not fight the tidal wave of fatigue, and an hour or so after he had swallowed his first ever dose of an antipsychotic medication, he gradually nodded off in a chair, not caring if he stayed awake.

* * *

Welsh Phil had been present in the dayroom when Mark had announced that he had just swallowed ten milligrams of Droperidol liquid. Phil watched as the effects caught hold of Mark.

As Mark slept Phil took the pad and pen from Mark's lap without him even stirring, but when Phil looked at the notepad, he couldn't read anything that Mark had written. To him, the shorthand looked like scrawl. 'Oh God, the meds have scrambled his brain!' Phil announced to his fellow patients. For this reason alone, he went to find one of the staff nurses to raise the alert.

He returned with Charlotte about ten minutes later, who gently roused Mark out of his drug-fuelled slumber.

As Mark came to, he appeared to have considerable trouble speaking, and his tongue had started to protrude out of his mouth as if he were rudely sticking it out in defiance.

The expression on Mark's face however, was not one of defiance but that of abject fear. He stood up out of the chair, leaning forward, trying to speak.

\* \* \*

Getting to the stage of panic breathing, he held his hands up to his throat. *Christ, what's happening? I can't breathe ... I can't talk.* Mark was freaking.

This made for an alarming sight.

Charlotte called urgently to Vance, the most composed, calm and collected of all the healthcare assistants on Pargiter Ward, who made his way into the dayroom. He talked Mark through the fear and anguish, giving him constant assurances that this would be dealt with in a matter of minutes. Mark was crying in fear of his life. His tongue had swollen to three times its normal size, his jaw had stiffened painfully, but with help from Vance, Mark realised that he could still breathe through his nose. He had to concentrate hard not to lose self-control. 'Breathe gentle and slow, man, like a Caribbean breeze ...'

Vance was a stockily built West Indian man with a voice like a warming hot chocolate drink on a cold winter's day, and it had magical qualities that you couldn't buy. He never panicked and he never broke into a sweat. Ever.

Charlotte meanwhile, had hightailed it to the office and bleeped the on-call psychiatrist urgently. She took instructions over the phone. This was a psychiatric emergency because Mark's airways were at risk of being compromised altogether. Charlotte shakily prepared an injection of Procyclidine ten milligrams, as instructed; to counteract the side effects that Mark was enduring. Mark didn't even wince when Charlotte administered the injection. His dread of needles had been trumped by the fear of death.

The on-call doctor ran straight to the ward to see Mark, who required another injection before the terrifying swelling and stiffness abated. As the effects of the first one wore off, the second one took twenty minutes to have any sort of lasting impact on his desperate situation. Without the remarkable soothing voice of Vance, Mark knew he would have been in all sorts of trouble. After what seemed an eternity, his tongue, jaw and throat torture subsided, but the damage was done. Mark had been psychologically shaken to the core by this experience.

So that Mark could have a side room, Vance organised a reshuffle of the men's dormitory, and sat with him throughout the night.

Surprisingly the Procyclidine injections had not only relaxed Mark's muscles, allowing his tongue to return to normal, but it had also made him much less sedated. It was a brief respite.

'Phil, I thought I was a goner ...' Mark mumbled.

'I thought you were too!'

Phil had been sitting outside Mark's side room door throughout the night, listening to Vance's calming words and to Mark's questions and gentle snoring. During this time he made notes in Mark's notepad. Mark managed to get some rest, but by the time the morning shift were arriving, he had begun to identify a new unfamiliar restlessness from within. He was uncertain as to whether it was a type of anxiety caused by the injection. Mark had then wondered if this unsettled feeling might simply be a response to the hours of tongue torture, but he recognised that he also felt tearful, physically weak and psychologically vulnerable.

Once Mark was up and about in the morning, in a drowsy state, Phil handed him back his writing pad and said honestly, 'I don't mind being your secretary a bit longer, if it helps.'

Mark gave him a weak smile, and thanked him for his concern and for 'being there.'

'Ah, that's no problem. It's a scary, lonely place. Mind you, Vance was amazing, wasn't he? Lovely man, heart of gold.'

# Chapter 29

## Watching

Emma and I emerged from the early morning handover meeting on Wednesday, and agreed that there should be a special request to review the plan to give Mark regular Droperidol. It was far too risky for him to have another dose. We both knew that young men were more prone to physically distressing side effects of antipsychotics, and that side effects were almost inevitable in patients where a mental illness was not at the heart of their problems. Mark fell into both of those categories.

I phoned immediately through to Lucy, Dr Sharman's secretary, to make an urgent request for our consultant to review Mark without delay. What that bastard had done was unforgivable. I was dreading having to speak to Charming in person, but that day I was determined not to be swayed or bullied.

Unexpectedly, it was Dr Siddiqui who returned my call later in the morning. Emma spoke to him, and he agreed to come to the ward immediately.

'Weird. He sounded truly concerned,' Emma said, 'which may have something to do with the news that Charming is away preparing for his "I'm an immensely important psychopharmacologist" conference on Friday, and he has given the Pargiter Ward deputising role to Dr Sticky. Did you know about that?'

'Don't be silly, they don't tell us mere mortals about such things, that would constitute good manners.'

Dr Sharman was in fact staying in a well-appointed hotel, being wined and dined at the expense of at least three pharmaceutical companies who were funding the National Psychopharmacology Conference. There were eminent professors and doctors who would be speaking to a room full of other academics and doctors for hours on end, congratulating themselves on their achievements.

I was immensely relieved to hear that Dr Sharman was away for the whole weekend. Dr Siddiqui, taking his new role seriously, met me in the goldfish bowl ward office, and we went through the events of the previous night as they had been recorded in Mark's patient notes. I thought that Dr Siddiqui was in an odd mood. Was that sadness? Guilt? I wasn't sure. We sat looking through the finer details of the impact of Droperidol on Mark, which included the fact that he had become dizzy and had fallen, banging his head against the arm of a chair in the dayroom. There were no indications that he had been knocked unconscious or sustained any injury, but it was not a good advert for patient safety.

Dr Siddiqui sighed loudly and turned to me speaking in earnest, and at length. I struggled with his accent at times, but his message was clear enough.

'Monica, I want to say that I have been thinking about what you did and what you said the other day, and you made me realise that I can't work here anymore.'

'Oh God, did I?' I asked, worried that whatever I had done had made this man so miserable that he was leaving. Had I turned into a bully?

'Yes. I have been belittled,' he went on, 'and I have had my confidence taken away by that man. So I am leaving. I will be gone in four weeks' time, and I wanted to thank you. You stand up for the patients and I am a coward. That man has a narcissistic personality, in my professional opinion, and he's dangerous, Monica. Be careful, or you could end up like me. But you are not me. I suspect that he has other plans for you, because you challenge him and he hates that.'

It was no surprise to me that Dr Sharman could have a personality disorder. What threw me was that another doctor had recognised it and viewed him as a bully.

'I don't know much about Narcissistic Personality Disorder,' I confessed, to which Dr Siddiqui instantly responded by fetching a book down from the shelf and handing it to me saying, 'Look it up. Know what you are dealing with. I think you will find it enlightening and of use to you all. I am sorry for being so weak. But now we shall see Mr El Amin and change his prescription. I will face the consequences on Monday.'

Dr Siddiqui did exactly that. He met with Mark in the side room, apologised, and reviewed how the poor exhausted man was feeling. He crossed out nearly all the medication on the drug chart. 'No more medication of any kind, other than the Procyclidine, is to be given to this man. Nothing, until such time as the side effects completely subside.'

Emma and I were even more delighted when we persuaded Dr Siddiqui to be braver and to allow Section 17 leave for Mark. Dr Siddiqui made it abundantly clear that this was 'solely for the purpose' of ensuring that Mark had his CT scan, which was arranged for Friday that week. Dr Siddiqui gave permission for two hours of escorted leave and asked me to ensure, without fail, that I was the escort. 'No one else,' he instructed.

I raised my eyebrows, smiled, and happily agreed. We had hoped to get more leave for Mark than that single two-hour window, even so Emma and I felt the stirrings of a rebellion and it excited us both.

* * *

Mark, on the other hand, was not feeling any excitement. He felt dreadful. It was as if an invisible hand had pulled the plug on his positive emotions, and left him at the "crest of a slump", if there was such a thing. The most miserable of thoughts invaded his every moment, and his previous negative life experiences were replayed in a gloomy monochrome, accompanied by the appalling feelings they invoked at the time. In addition, out came emotions of intense sadness and pain. These were the ones he usually kept safe in a psychological box at the back of his mind. They came darkly flooding back and he began to weep.

Mark was unable to assemble his thoughts in a useful order to write his feelings down, no matter how painful, and he had resigned himself to the fact that he was incapable of being any kind of journalist. He also decided that he was an unworthy soul, who would never find love.

Phil spent hours sitting with Mark, being comforting and gently positive. Emma put herself on watch, and carefully, from a distance, Mark knew she was observing for warning signs that could indicate if he was slipping into a dangerously low mood and headlong into suicide territory. He was.

By lunchtime on Wednesday, Mark's agitation was noticeable as it reared its ugly head. Mark began to pace. He paced up and down the green lino corridors for the rest of the day. He could not sit still even when Phil was reading to him from the newspaper or trying to engage Mark in completing a crossword that he was usually so good at solving. Mark was exhausted with the endless compulsion to move, and was talking to himself. 'This is hellish torture. Make it stop, someone.' The nursing staff had nothing to offer other than reassurance and Procyclidine.

It was a tense waiting game, which continued for a further two days, but by the Friday the worst of the effects were easing and Mark gradually poked his more positive self out from beneath a dreadful hangover feeling, sad emotions and negativity. This was much to the relief of patients and staff alike, including Dr Siddiqui who made sure he attended the ward everyday to see Mark and any other patients who needed their medication reviewing. Dr Siddiqui wore a smile as if he had at last gained a sense of pride in his work.

# Chapter 30

## The Right Thing is Wrong

'Listen up, everyone! We have two new arrivals who came in yesterday evening. One disturbed and disruptive young lady, determined to cut herself using any suitable item she can lay her hands on. She is Tania White. Some of you may remember her. We may have to organise additional staff for one-to-one specialing if she's true to previous form. So far we have not been directed to put her on close obs, but stand by.

'The other new guest, Wayne Parker, is an undernourished tracksuit-wearing and hostile gentleman, who is supposed to be voluntarily entering into an alcohol detox programme on the ward before he progresses to a highly sought after bed in a residential rehab unit in the depths of North Wales. Your guess is as good as mine as to whether he makes it that far.' Bob had a way of ensuring that we knew what to expect. His handovers were descriptive, but not necessarily subtle or polite.

I missed the rest of the information, as I was required to take a call from Richard Huntley. He apologised profusely for contacting me, but assured me that he had no other choice.

'Not a problem, Richard. How can I help?' I asked innocently assuming this was to do with a tribunal report or arrangements to access Mark's notes again.

'I'm sorry, I know that I asked you not to help me with Mark El Amin's case, but I'm at a real loss as to where else to go.' Richard went on to explain that he had searched through Mark's patient notes again, double checked the ward Section paper copies file, and even asked Harriet Morris in the Mental Health Act office for information, however, there was no sign of the original Section 3 recommendation made by Dr Giles Sharman, that he, Richard, knew existed because he had seen it. 'I saw it myself, with my own eyes,' he confirmed.

He had indeed seen it the previous Friday when he first met with Mark. I knew that, because it had been in the notes that I had provided for him, and in fact I had gone to a lot of trouble to ensure that the Section papers, copies of, were placed on the top of the patient notes. Richard had picked up rapidly that day that I had suspected a number of things were wrong with those Section papers.

'Yes, I remember it vividly,' he said. 'I even read it out to Mark at the time, to clear up the issue of whether he was already known to mental health services or not,' he recalled. 'And now I cannot find a single copy of that original Section paper.' Exasperation was getting to Richard. 'This is a cover up of astounding overconfidence,' he announced. 'That Section paper has been smoothly replaced by a Section 2 recommendation, as it should have appeared in the first place, and you have been blamed for misinforming the patient as to which Section he was under.' He then took a steady deep breath and asked, 'Monica, do you have any idea where I can find a copy of that original Section paper?'

'Yes I do, but I could be in the biggest possible trouble if anyone finds out where you got it from.' Still, in for a penny, I thought. I had already disclosed to Richard far more than would be acceptable from my employer's point of view.

'I took an additional copy at the time that I made the ward copies,' I told Richard frankly, 'and I put it in my pocket to read carefully later because what Harriet said at the time didn't make any sense.' I went on in an attempt to defend my actions. 'She said that the Section 3 paper which I had given to her, indicated that the patient, Mr Trainman, was known to Dr Sharman, which was not possible because we didn't even know his name then. I hadn't had time to read it before I took the paperwork to her office that day, so I took the copy out of curiosity … I say curiosity, but there was another reason. I don't know which word describes it, but Dr Sharman made my life hell that day and I wanted to find anything that might give me ammunition for revenge.' I was gabbling nervously. 'Oh God, that sounds so ridiculous now I've said it out loud … sorry Richard. In short, I still have that copy at home, in my flat. I can drop it in at your offices when I finish work if it helps.'

'I don't care why you have it, or how you got it, Monica, but you are a star, as far as I'm concerned. The ends will justify the means, so let's say no more about it. Put it in a plain envelope, address it "private and confidential" for my attention and write "by hand" in the left hand corner, then I will know it's from you. Monica, this information and your description of what happened in ward round on the day it was written, is enough to ensure that revenge will indeed be served up fairly soon. Please do not breathe a word to anyone. I have a couple more matters to put in place and hope my darling wife does not have the baby early.'

'Oh, Richard, I'm sorry. I forgot to ask when it's due!' I exclaimed, genuinely upset that I hadn't remembered the pending birth when we'd met again.

'Not for another week,' he replied 'but knowing my luck, junior will make an unscheduled appearance, just when I need him or her to arrive a little late if possible. Never mind, we will do what we need to, to get Mark released from his Section. It's illegal, or it was. I'm seeking expert advice from the Mental Health Commission regarding the legal points. Still, that's not your concern. You have done more than enough. Keep your head down and thanks again.'

\* \* \*

The Mental Health Act Commission contacted Richard Huntley later the same day and he was put in touch with an expert barrister by the name of Lewis James.

Richard didn't make the connection at first, until he actually spoke with Lewis on the phone and recognised the voice and accent of the man he knew as James Lewis. Lewis had to confess to the whole truth about his involvement with Mark 'El Amin' and about the research project.

Richard could not have been more delighted with this revelation. Justice, at last was going to be seen to be done, and by more than professionals and members of a tribunal. This was a national story in the making.

\* \* \*

Once I had finished speaking with Richard on the Wednesday morning, I phoned James Lewis, Mark's visitor and family lawyer. I hadn't spoken to him before, and I quite liked the sound of him. He was a bit of a character. He was one of those people who gave his surname first when he answered the phone. Or so I thought. 'Lewis James,' he said, when I rang the mobile number contained in the patient notes. I introduced myself as Mark's named nurse, which he appeared to find funny for some reason, and he made a flippant remark about the fact that in his view, 'everyone should have one of those.'

I carried on regardless, and informed him that Mark had experienced an unusual and significant reaction to the drugs he had been prescribed, and that although he was improving, Mark had asked that we let him know the situation. James Lewis, family friend and solicitor, seemed genuinely alarmed at this news.

'Bloody hell, when did this happen?'

I gave him the general gist of the events and he in turn apologised for not being able to attend the ward straight away. He said that he had a busy day scheduled and wouldn't be able to visit Mark until the next evening. I gave assurances to Mr Lewis that we were looking after Mark, and that I would let Mark know personally when he would be coming in to the ward to see him.

I wondered if Dr Sharman had picked up on the fact that James Lewis was a solicitor.

When I found Mark, he was in a sorry state, pacing endlessly up and down the corridor, agitated, with a look of emotional distress on his usually beautiful serene face. I walked with him for a while, and the longer I did so, the more enraged I became at what Dr Sharman had done to this man. It had been unnecessary to increase or change his medication.

'I can't face taking any more,' Mark said in a detached, but tearful way. 'I can't have any more of that stuff, Monica.'

'It's okay, Mark. Dr Siddiqui has crossed out that medication on your drugs chart, so you're not on anything now, nothing apart from Procyclidine if you need it. The effects will wear off soon, and then you'll be less restless. Try to keep talking to us, and distract yourself if you can. It will soon pass.'

'How soon? I can't do another ward round with that man, Monica. He'll be back on Monday and I'll be given a bloody injection, like every other poor sod he takes a dislike to. I can't do it. I can't. I have to get out of here.'

A charging Sicilian bull came at me, and I was given the telling off of the century in no uncertain terms by Gina the cleaner. She waved her mop at me viciously as she shouted and ranted with a furious look on her face.

She had been trying to clean the floor of the main corridor where Mark was creating endless footfall, almost to the point of wearing a trench into the pale green lino. Gina was seen earlier chatting away to him and trying in vain to persuade him to sit down for five minutes, so that she could complete this task. She was not a happy woman. She understood perfectly well that he was only pacing because of the medication and she gave me both barrels in Anglo-Sicilian swear words and gesticulations. She held me personally responsible.

I agreed with her. My heart was in pain and I could barely breathe. I looked again at Mark. The man was in despair at the threat of having to take more medication. He was right to fear the actions of Dr Sharman, come the following week. The doctor with a deficient conscience, the vindictive, heartless man who was supposed to help people get better, probably would order injections to be given to Mark. This would be done to reassert his power and undermine anything that Dr Siddiqui would have achieved over the weekend. It is the way of the professional bully.

'We'll think of something,' I offered lamely. I tried to reassure Mark, but I was rather distracted by endless intrusive thoughts that found their way into my head and which would not be denied attention. My mind was taking me to a place that I had never previously contemplated visiting. I went there nevertheless.

On Friday afternoon, I was to escort Mark for a CT scan, to the main hospital. I ran through, in my head, a variety of possibilities and the likely consequences to each of these options. They were plans in which I was to aid Mark to take his own discharge, to escape, to leave, to abscond.

It was illegal.

I had good justification for having these thoughts. In my view, if we didn't have a bully for a consultant, these ideas and plans wouldn't even have occurred to me. If we had senior managers who cared, then they wouldn't have employed a psycho as a consultant.

'How the hell would he like it?' I asked myself of The Charming One. 'He's never even tried Haloperidol or any of those medications he prescribes without consideration. Maybe he'll get his comeuppance when Richard gets the proof he needs, I thought.

Mark can't wait for next week. He has to get out of here on Friday. That's all there is to it. I had convinced myself of this even as I said the words in my head. I was in so much trouble anyway, or at least I would be, when I had delivered that copy of a Section paper that I had in my flat. In my flat! Shit and double shit! Confidential patient information was in my flat. What an idiot I'd been. That simple fact alone could result in my instant dismissal, even if I did not get caught for enabling a patient to abscond while under Section. Despite these sinking realisations, the most impressive conclusion that I reached was that rebellion felt so much better than conceding to the bully. Thus, in my eyes, it could easily be condoned.

I felt more in control having reasoned my way through that series of deep and meaningful concepts, and in the interests of maintaining my own sanity, I went back to the relative sanctuary of the ward office.

There, I had a good thumb through the diagnostic manual, within which Dr Siddiqui had suggested I would find information on narcissistic personality disorder.

What I discovered was painfully accurate. He had been right. The manual described Dr Giles Sharman perfectly.

It read: *'Narcissistic Personality Disorder; A long term pattern of abnormal behaviour, characterised by exaggerated feelings of self importance, an excessive need for admiration and a lack of understanding of others' feelings ... often take advantage of people around them ... disdain and lack of empathy for others ... arrogance ... a sense of superiority, power seeking behaviour ... expect to be treated as superiors ... inability to tolerate criticism ... belittling others ...'*

The manual then went on to state: *'These traits must differ from the cultural norms in order to qualify as symptoms.'*

This was him! Dr Giles Sharman.

Was it culturally normal for consultant psychiatrists to behave like this? I didn't think so. Dr B had not been cruel and callous, and certainly it wasn't acceptable for a professional with this sort of personality disorder to look after such vulnerable patients.

I thus made a promise to myself that if Richard Huntley had not taken action to ensure that Mark was removed from his Section by Friday lunchtime, then I would escort Mark for his scan, but not bring him back. If I was sacked or struck from the nursing register, it surely would be preferable to allowing any more targeted torture to happen.

Surprisingly, now that I had a plan, I felt lighter. I busied myself with the various tasks on the ward for the rest of the shift, and the whole place seemed to cheer up as a consequence of my positive attitude, and the fact Dr Sharman was not going to be around until the following week.

Emma and I had a brief chance for a catch up on our way home. She was undeniably worried about Mark's mental state, but both of us were optimistic that the effects of the Droperidol would naturally dissipate in the next couple of days.

Perhaps I should have done, but I gave not the slightest hint to her regarding my plans to help Mark to abscond. She was my good friend, and I did not want to put her in a compromising position. In all honesty, I didn't want to give her the opportunity to be rational and to talk me out of it, as she undoubtedly would have tried to do.

I popped home briefly to collect the precious copy of the missing Section 3 paper and delivered it, as Richard had instructed, to the offices of Huntley and Greaves, which were situated only a fifteen minutes walk from the hospital. I didn't even hesitate or give this a second thought. I even met Cheryl the efficient secretary for the first time, in person. We had spoken to each other over the phone for the last three years, and I had formed a picture of her in my imagination, but I had been wrong.

Her voice had made her sound thin and dark-haired to me. She was, in real life, almost the opposite. Cheryl had a smiling round face and a body to match. She wore standard office attire; a neat skirt to the knee with high-heeled court shoes and a smart blouse. We had a polite chat and I left feeling gratefully unburdened having deposited the evidence of my professional misconduct.

* * *

When I returned to my flat, having bought some essentials from the local shops on the way, I told Boris the cat about my plans and he seemed to approve, highly. I was certain that he would not even try to talk me out of my foolhardy intentions, and as usual he didn't let me down. Good old Boris was not the best at playing devil's advocate and he failed at debating important issues, such as how I was going to earn a living if I were caught colluding. Like every good cat, he was best at listening, purring, eating and then sleeping. It was more than likely that he would not have been able to deter me, even if he could speak.

I was about to settle down in front of the TV, when I noticed the answerphone machine flashing.

'Hello, Monica, it's Max Davis here. I've booked the tickets for The Bonus Bonas Band, just like I said I would, and to prove you wrong. Ring me please. How about a drink tomorrow? Emma says you're on an early shift.'

Suddenly I remembered the test that I had set when I'd had too much to drink at the rugby club. Max Davis was so full of himself that I had challenged him to get tickets for my favourite local band, in the hope that he would fail and never have reason to phone me. I didn't even give him my number. Emma must have done that. Sneaky cow.

I couldn't face dealing with his persistence that evening. He would have to wait. I had other things on my mind, which in themselves made watching the telly difficult. I couldn't concentrate.

Unusually, I was on the rota to cover the ward round on Monday, the thought of which made my heart sink into my slippers. If my plan was successful, then Mark would be officially absent without leave as from Friday afternoon. Dr Sharman, on the other hand, would be returning to the ward on Monday from his weekend of hobnobbing with the great and good of psychiatry at the national conference. I thus convinced myself that the conference was bound to be an overwhelming success, and that Dr Sharman would be glowing with pride and self-satisfaction to the degree that he wouldn't even notice or care that one of his patients had gone missing.

Mark's ward rounds had so far taken place on Tuesdays, and the next week that was to be my day off. So there was a slim chance that Dr Sharman wouldn't find out about Mark until then, which meant that I wasn't going to be there to witness the bomb of fury explode, if I was lucky.

Eventually, after much convoluted thinking, reality settled back in. 'No chance, you idiot.' I knew that was a stupid wishful thought. He would expect to be informed as soon as he returned to sit at his desk. Never mind. What could he do? We would have informed the police and reported Mark as a missing person by then anyway.

All Mark had to do was to avoid being caught for six months. After that, his Section would have lapsed and he would be a free man. I appreciated that this too seemed an impossible goal to achieve, unless Richard Huntley could pull a rabbit out of a hat and make the Section 3 disappear. Now, that would be magic.

# Chapter 31

### Time to Go

The next few days on Pargiter Ward, were reminiscent of the old times when Dr B was in charge. There was a lighter atmosphere altogether, and as Friday afternoon approached, no one seemed to notice that I had become nervous, fidgety, and that I was glancing at the clock far more than was necessary. There had been no news from Richard Huntley, and nothing from the offices downstairs, to inform us that Mark was no longer detained under the Mental Health Act. I therefore resolved to keep the promise I had made to myself.

When I found him at about a quarter to three on the Friday afternoon, Mark was grabbing a sweatshirt from his locker in the dormitory, to put on for our trip to the main hospital site. As it was raining, I sourced an old umbrella from lost property for us to shelter under on the way to the Medical Imaging Department. Mark's CT scan was booked for three pm. By good fortune, the timing of the appointment was perfect. I was due to finish my shift at three, so I could put on my raincoat, and take my handbag with me without raising suspicion. I was only expected to return Mark to the ward and sign him back in once he had finished at the general hospital, and then I could disappear home for a relaxing evening. Nothing would look out of the ordinary to the casual observer as we prepared to leave the ward.

I had suggested innocently to Mark that he should bring some money with him as 'we could stop at the WRVS shop in the hospital,' and he could treat himself to a newspaper.

'Don't forget that notepad and pen of yours,' I added 'and you can interview me while you're waiting for the scan. You and Phil seem to be enjoying this creative writing course. You've interviewed almost everyone on the ward … apart from me that is.' I signed us both out. We strolled sedately through the shabby ward entrance doors, and took the stairs to the main exit from the psychiatric block.

Mark was peering around intently, taking in his surroundings as if for the first time. He was still subdued in his mood, but he chatted pleasantly enough as we walked.

'I've no idea where I am.' He reminded me that he didn't have any recall of his admission other than a vague impression of fluorescent strip lighting on ceilings. There wasn't much of interest to see. 'Yeah, I don't exactly feel short changed' he conceded.

We didn't have far to go in the rain, which for Mark was a blessing as he was wearing his trusty sandals, as usual. As was always the way, we were kept waiting for the CT scan, and spent a good twenty minutes in the reception seating area. The conversation during my interview with Mark was non-specific at first, and Mark kept to safe subjects, asking me how long I had been a nurse for, and what my career plans were. He ventured into interesting territory when he talked about his admission to Pargiter Ward, and he thanked me for trying to help him. Despite his awful experiences with side effects and lack of sleep since his admission, he remained temptingly handsome. In that waiting room, he looked at me with those amazing blue eyes and wearing his gift of new aftershave from his friend Mr Lewis, Mark smelt delicious. I controlled my own impure unprofessional fantasies because there was work to be done, and in a radical departure from my moral code and fundamental life principles, I was about to knowingly break rules. I asked Mark to put the rest of the interview on hold, and to write down the vital information that I needed him to have.

He looked mystified at first when I handed him a business card for Huntley and Greaves. Folded up tightly with that card, I passed him a ten-pound note.

'Put that in your pocket,' I commanded firmly but quietly.

'Mark, I need you to listen and write this down so you don't forget. When we are finished here, we will stop at the WRVS shop, which is adjacent to the main hospital entrance. To get to the station from the WRVS shop exit, walk to the road and turn right. When you get to the big set of traffic lights, cross the road, turn right and then head left over a bridge. You will see pedestrian signs for the station. Got it? Good.

'Phone your friend, James Lewis, and also you should contact Richard Huntley. I think he's trying to get your Section revoked, but nothing has happened yet and unfortunately this may be your only opportunity to abscond. Please try not to get caught. Get as far away as you can, and dye your hair or something, so you look less like Jesus,' I added in desperation, knowing that the police would have to be stupid not to recognise Mark once they were given his description.

'I'll be distracted, looking at birthday cards for a while, so you can just leave. Here, take the brolly. Keep your face covered once you get outside in the rain. Good luck, and in the nicest possible way, I hope I never see you again.'

Mark had calmly jotted down the instructions and had nodded his understanding more than once. We both went mechanically through the motions of having the CT scan carried out, and once completed, we left the department, silently plodding through the hospital corridors. Walking into the WRVS shop, we took different directions, and in doing so Mark turned around briefly and simply mouthed the words, 'Thank you.'

I would like to think that I saw a tear or two, but that was nothing more than romantic invention on my part, and I headed, as promised, to the card section. I pulled out amusing birthday cards to peruse, but failed to read them properly. Instead, I watched surreptitiously as Mark bought a newspaper.

'Good thinking, Batman!' I said to myself as he then made his way to the main exit and into the rainy afternoon, putting the umbrella up as he did so.

'Goodbye, Jesus Trainman,' I whispered, feeling splendidly gratified despite the knots in my stomach.

I dragged time out by walking up and down various corridors, then back to the Medical Imaging Department pretending to search for my patient, who was long gone by then, and was hopefully getting on a train far, far, away.

Inevitably I had to gather my mental strength for the return to the ward. To put on a convincing act, I ran around the block several times getting wet and breathless before I entered the psychiatric unit, and pounded up the stairs to Pargiter Ward. I broke the news to my colleagues on the late shift that Mark had 'given me the slip.' I asked if he had perhaps returned to the ward under his own steam, which he hadn't, assuring my colleagues that I had already searched through the main hospital as far as I could. 'He just disappeared,' I said finally.

'You can't blame the man,' said Staff Nurse Bob. 'Not after what he has been through the last few days, poor sod. I'd run if I were in his sandals. Good luck to him. Monica, don't worry. Document what happened, and we'll report him as a missing person to the police, once we can get hold of them. It's a Friday and you know how busy they get, so it's likely he won't even get picked up this side of Christmas.'

I was visibly shaking due to the arrival of a whole butterfly house of fluttering nerves, and I remained on the ward long enough to write up the notes and have a hot cup of tea to settle my levels of tension. I was required to complete a risk incident form and let the on-call manager know that we had a missing Sectioned patient, but that was no great hardship. Bob eventually succeeded in getting through to Police Control, and gave them a description of Mark, which they did not seem to take seriously. They asked about risk to the public and whether the patient was a risk to himself. Overall they gave the impression that they were not pleased to have to go in search of a man resembling Jesus in Levi jeans, who sounded more sane and less risky than the ne'er-do-wells they usually had to deal with.

It was Bob's reasonable opinion that any risks Mark might have presented with, were lessened by the fact that he was no longer a patient on our ward. I had to agree with Bob; Mark was certainly less of a suicide risk away from the likes of Dr Sharman.

# Chapter 32

## Mark Goes to Ground for a While

Mark stepped out into the rain from the hospital's main exit and followed Monica's instructions, trudging through the damp and drizzle, huddled beneath the tatty umbrella until he arrived at the station. Once inside the building, he found a payphone.

Mark had seen Lewis James the previous evening, whose facial expression left Mark in no doubt as to his own welfare. 'You look like shit,' Lewis had said, as if he needed to add emphasis to Mark's dire situation. 'We should have you out in a couple of days. The legal side is not as straightforward as we had hoped, but nearly there.' Lewis again insisted that Mark find a way to escape. He had tried valiantly to persuade the ward staff to let Mark out with him for supper in town, but they were resolute, repeating endlessly that Mark had no agreed leave other than to be escorted for a scan by his named nurse the following day.

Lewis gave up trying to exert his legal authority, but then explored the possibility of using diversion tactics in order for Mark to 'slip past the guards.' Mark made him realise that the staff were skilled and good at their jobs, and opportunities for escape were few and far between. Mark reminded Lewis that he should have known better than to make such a suggestion. They had to settle for a takeaway pizza each, which Lewis arranged to be delivered to the unit. In a generous gesture, he ordered enough pizza to fill The Albert Hall, by way of a thank you to the staff, and to Mark's fellow patients for their excellent care and kindness.

When he phoned from Hollberry Station, Mark was sure that Lewis would be delighted to hear that he had managed to abscond with relative ease, and so soon. Lewis answered his mobile phone and did indeed sound thrilled to hear Mark's voice.

'Mark, we were just talking about you. How are you doing today?'

'We? Who's we?'

'I stayed over last night, at a cosy hotel. I'm with Richard Huntley at his office in town.'

'Are you? That's great. I'll meet you there. I'm out. Unofficially, you understand. I have the office address so I'll only be a short while. Wait for me?' Mark asked with a faint hint of anxiety, making his voice waver.

'Thank Christ for that. Of course I'll wait for you. See you when you get here.' Lewis beamed at Richard Huntley as he confirmed the latest news.

Mark, meanwhile, found a conveniently placed poster map of the town with a "you are here" marker on it. He needed to orientate himself and find out how to navigate to the offices of Huntley and Greaves. He took out from his pocket, the solicitors' business card given to him minutes earlier by Monica, praying that he did not have to walk back past the hospital. No. Good.

The offices were a short distance away, beyond the station, and when he arrived, Mark practically fell through the door to be greeted by Lewis and Richard personally who then ushered him into a warm dry office.

Within a short while, Cheryl, as efficient as ever, entered with the most heavenly cup of freshly ground coffee Mark had ever tasted. He sank into a comfortable office chair and let out a long sigh of relief. He hadn't realised how tense he had been since making good his escape, courtesy of the marvellous and brave Monica. He decided to keep her collusion a secret in order to protect her career. There was no point in the NHS losing an angel, so never once did he disclose this fact.

Lewis and Richard Huntley had been highly industrious over the course of that Friday, and they were about to go into glorious legal detail for Mark's benefit when Richard's personal mobile phone rang out loudly. When he answered it his face told the story.

'I'm on my way!' he said, bursting with excitement. As he ended the call he turned to Lewis and Mark to announce that he was dashing home to pick up his wife who had gone into labour with their first child. There was a mixture of panic, pride, and anticipation in his voice as he did so. His face beaming, he shouted to Cheryl to lock up at the end of the day, he was 'off to become a father.'

Mark, Lewis, and Cheryl shouted their good luck wishes to him as he careered out of the side door and into his car. Shouts also went up from behind various office doors at Huntley and Greaves as the news spread.

With that, Lewis and Mark decided to head in the direction of Mark's real parents' home by car. Mark made use of, and paid rent towards, a cottage annex at their house when he was back in the UK, which was an arrangement they all benefitted from. His parents had not been surprised when he disappeared to undertake another assignment within weeks of returning home in July. That had been the pattern of his life for years. He owned a flat in Oman where he used to make camp for the vast majority of the time between assignments, but once Penny had left him he lost interest, and had rented it out, becoming in effect an itinerant journalist. Any visit home to his parents was truly welcomed, especially by Mark's mother who loved to see her only son, of whom she was chest-achingly proud.

Lewis had his impractical but luxuriously comfortable V12 Daimler Double Six parked around the corner from Huntley and Greaves, and both men piled in rapidly, to avoid what they could of the rain. The downpour had increased both in quality and quantity.

'Don't look so worried,' Lewis said. 'The cops aren't out to get you, you know. They're far too busy with criminals. Besides which you're not Mark El Amin, and you do not live at number whatever it is do-dah street because it does not exist and neither do you. So relax, lets go to Suffolk.'

Mark had to explain to Lewis that he was a bit nervous but the anxiety was more agitation and restlessness, 'caused by the bloody medication.'

'I should have known. I wonder how much longer that will last, what do you think?' asked Lewis out of genuine concern.

'No idea. But it is a hell of a lot better now than it was, thank God. I thought I was done for.'

'Good job you got out when you did. How did you manage that, by the way? Pick a lock?'

Mark only gave Lewis a vague reply about an opportunity that had unexpectedly arisen which he took advantage of. Lewis didn't push for further details. Mark predicted that the subject would come up again, as he knew Lewis would not be satisfied with the deliberate attempt to side-step the question. *I'll have to come up with a solid story to keep him quiet*, Mark thought.

As they drove out of the town and headed east, Lewis suggested that Mark might like to read the information that had been gathered so far on the background of a certain Dr Giles Sharman. He directed Mark to a buff folder inside his briefcase. Contained within was a diagrammatical timeline and a career outline report. This indicated that Dr Sharman had become a consultant psychiatrist in his early forties.

His post at Farley Hill Hospital was recorded in brief, then according to the timeline, in 1987 a short gap appeared before he was employed as a research fellow at a renowned university in Northern Ireland, where he also apparently acquired a PhD in psychopharmacology.

'Nothing too unusual,' Mark noted.

Lewis agreed, and conceded that Giles Sharman had indeed earned a solid reputation in the world of psychiatric medicine by completing research studies published in professional journals with alarming regularity.

'The next report is more revealing,' Lewis hinted, thus inviting Mark to explore further, and Lewis allowed him ample time to read carefully through the pages contained in the rest of the folder.

Mark settled back into the Daimler's comfortable leather seats and as he scanned the details, he flipped back and forth between pages several times, occasionally letting out a whistle.

A while later, and without prior warning, Mark produced a string of expletives, and a look of abject disbelief crossed his face as he dropped the folder down on his lap. He looked across at Lewis, who was by then driving sedately along the A14 towards Ipswich at eighty miles an hour, despite the rain.

'You've got to be joking! He was struck off in 1987 for endangering the lives of patients during a drug trial and reinstated five years later! Is that legal?' Mark could barely get the words out he was so stunned at what he had read. 'I need to read this again. I must have missed something,' he said, scratching his head.

Lewis assured Mark that he had understood correctly the first time, and proceeded to enlighten him as to the true facts of Dr Giles Sharman's illustrious medical career. The information that Lewis was able to access from the records on the Medical Practitioners Tribunal in 1987 indicated that the General Medical Council was obliged to bring a case against Dr Giles Sharman as a direct consequence of two mental health patients being hospitalised with life-threatening side effects from drugs. They were part of a trial being overseen by Dr Sharman at Farley Hill Hospital.

Lewis tried to explain. 'The investigation revealed that Dr Sharman had taken the astounding decision to increase the dose of the trial drug in the case of these two, and other patients. Apparently, he believed their psychotic symptoms were subsiding, and had thus concluded that an increase in dose would be met by a corresponding increase in improvement. This was outside of his remit, unlicenced, and potentially dangerous or even fatal for the patients concerned, and he carried this out with impunity. He was only prevented from doing further harm when two patients developed severe cardiac problems and the consultant cardiologist raised the alarm. No one else reported him.'

Lewis had also uncovered that Giles Sharman had put forward a sound argument in his own defence at the Medical Practitioners Tribunal hearing. He had tried to implicate both the drugs company and the researchers who were leading the trial. As a result, holes were exposed which weakened the GMC's case against him. There was a lengthy debate as to whether the tribunal was to suspend his licence to practice medicine, but in the end they fully revoked it.

'I should bloody well hope so,' exclaimed Mark, who then wanted to understand how a professional, who had been struck off as a doctor, could still be registered and practicing seven years later.

'Most people wouldn't be aware, but a suspended doctor has a right to request reinstatement to the register after five years. They have to prove their fitness to practice and that they have kept clinically updated, which dear Giles did by virtue of his research fellowship, his PhD, and all that jazz. He was only offered that academic appointment because of the old school tie network. His great pal at medical school wangled the research post for him at the university.

'The scandal at Farley Hill was, it seems, inventively hushed up by the management, and Dr Giles Sharman was reborn five years later, although he waited for the most opportune moment before applying to his current post, where I believe they think the sun shines out of his nether regions,' Lewis asserted as he took a sweeping left turn. Lewis headed towards a service area, in need of refreshment and to alleviate the considerable pressure that had built up in his bladder, worsened by the relentless rain.

'Oh my God,' exclaimed Mark as a large penny dropped. 'So this is legal then. We can expose him and the scandal at Farley Hill but it is still all legal. The trial has in essence taken place, and he has already served his time … if you like.'

Once parked at the service station, both Lewis and Mark disappeared rapidly into the toilet facilities, and then met up in a brightly lit café area.

There they found a secluded table in the corner, away from prying ears. They looked suspiciously like a couple on a clandestine date, having an affair and huddling close together for the thrill of a snatched moment together. They realised that they had incendiary information in their hands but it took Lewis to put into context the most recent and illegal actions performed by Dr Giles Sharman as they related to Mark himself.

Mark slurped on a mug of strong coffee, as he was desperate to escape the remnants of the cotton wool effect in his brain. He had to be able to concentrate on the information that he needed to hear, understand, retain, and assimilate. Waiting for the caffeine to kick in, he took a few moments to phone his parents to forewarn them of his return home, and was relieved when his mother offered to provide a family dinner. One of enormous proportions, judging by the description of what she had in mind.

She often expressed her love through food, and liked nothing better than to entertain family and guests by force-feeding them with her delicious menus. Mark heard her joy over the phone, especially when she realised that he was bringing a guest for the night, and he smiled at the prospect of a bulging belly and indigestion. It would be bliss compared to hospital food. He promised to be home in the next hour or so.

Lewis called his tolerant wife to break the news that he was having yet another night away from home. She was well aware of the situation.

'Me again!' announced Lewis, when his wife answered.

'Hello, my lovely, did you get your man out?'

# Chapter 33

## A Man of the Utmost Importance

On the Friday that Mark had made good his escape from Pargiter Ward, Dr Giles Sharman was in his element, strutting around like a peacock at the National Psychopharmacology Conference being held at one of London's top hotel venues. The event was being covered by the national and international medical journals, and sponsored across the board by the big names in pharmaceuticals. They had an almighty vested interest in the marketing and selling of their products via the psychiatric profession worldwide.

Dr Giles Sharman had been invited to be one of the keynote speakers at the conference. In a huge twist of irony, he was due to be discussing the moral code for psychiatry in addressing the impacts of unwanted side effects in the long term use of antipsychotic medication for severe and enduring mental illness.

This was the hot topic of the year, and was certain to gain him respect and admiration from his peers. It was also a guaranteed way of attracting worthwhile gifts from the large pharmaceutical companies, several of whom had been known to sponsor conferences in the Caribbean or other exotic corners of the world. After all, Dr Sharman was to recommend use of the newest antipsychotic drugs in his speech the next day. He would therefore deserve special attention from the pharmaceutical industry's marketing managers. Giles Sharman revelled in this belief. His main aim however, was to eventually secure himself a position in the higher echelons of the NHS itself, perhaps as a Mental

Health Tsar, through which he could gain ultimate international recognition. His chest puffed out at the exciting thought.

A lot of mingling and social networking happened at such conferences, during which endless self-congratulation and cronyism took place amongst the top psychiatrists. On this occasion, interest was coming from across the world.

Dr Sharman was delighted to be introduced to a reporter from the Daily Albion newspaper, a diminutive Scottish chap with a rather strong accent, by the name of Jock Mackenzie. Jock said he was 'thrilled to meet such an influential psychiatrist,' and requested time to interview Giles Sharman, who without hesitation snapped up the chance of more notoriety and fame.

Lewis James and John Starkey had swiftly brought Jock into service as soon as they were informed, by Mark, of the scandal surrounding this particular consultant psychiatrist. It was like a gift from the gods when they were alerted to the fact that he was to speak at the weekend conference. They realised that if they could secure a press pass, they could meet the man himself, interview him if they were lucky, and have a few words with his psychiatry colleagues. There would be the ideal opportunity to take some excellent photographs into the bargain, and all in the name of sound journalism.

During the interview with Jock, Giles Sharman barely noticed that the focus was not only on the contents of the speech he was to give the next day, but that Jock steered the conversation towards the psychiatrist's past career and achievements to-date. Jock neatly pried into Dr Sharman's private life where, despite his efforts, the barriers remained firmly in place, with only vague generalisations forthcoming. The doctor, it appeared, had no wife, no children, and was wary about discussing relationships other than professional friendships.

Without too much effort, Jock managed to secure the relevant details that would support the background research being carried out by Prof Hugo's team. He wasn't particularly seeking out salacious gossip, so he left questions about Dr Sharman's private life alone for the time being.

Later in the day at the bar, it was easy for him to extract snippets of information from Dr Sharman's inebriated peers that would eventually lead to Jock delving deeper into a seedy world increasingly inhabited by Giles Sharman. For now, this was information that he did not desperately require.

Jock was excelling at ingratiating himself with Dr Giles Sharman, rapidly catching on to how the man lapped up praise and adulation by the boatload. Giles Sharman was on boastful form. Jock took full advantage, and pushed his luck by requesting permission to take additional photo shots at the hospital and of one of the wards at Hollberry Hospital Psychiatric Unit.

The timing of this request was immaculate, and Giles Sharman was gushing with self-importance as he immediately reached inside his briefcase for his mobile phone. With an audience to hand, he contacted Gordon Bygraves, instructing him to make welcoming arrangements for a photographer from the Daily Albion to visit Pargiter Ward on Sunday. Thus he ensured that the pictures would be available for the newspaper to go to print on the Monday, when the weekly health section appeared.

Over the phone to Gordon Bygraves, he went to loud and detailed lengths to describe the news that he, Dr Giles Sharman, was to be a central feature in the Monday edition of the Daily Albion. Jock had hooked him with assurances that he would be ideal for their series on "Medical Trail Blazers" and that he had been sent especially to meet with Dr Sharman at the conference to ensure that as much accurate and interesting fact as possible found its way into the feature article.

* * *

At the other end of the phone, Gordon Bygraves' face fell and he sat forward in his chair in an attempt to contain his anxiety. He had been backed into a corner and not given any leeway to negotiate the management of this intrusion. Added to this was his sure and certain knowledge that the whole building looked tired and unloved. Nothing short of a miracle was required if the place were to be acceptable enough to appear in the national press. Despite these reasons for declining the demand from Dr Sharman, he could do nothing other than to give his weak approval. 'Yes, that should be fine, we'll expect a photographer on Sunday then.'

As soon as he ended the call from Dr Giles Sharman, Gordon picked up the phone again and rang as many of the hospital board members that he could find on a Friday, those who weren't playing golf or on a long weekend. The ones he did manage to speak to, seemed unconcerned and mostly flattered by the attention that the hospital was about to receive. Gordon was given the green light to spend money on superficial cosmetics to smarten the place up. His first response was to call Harriet Morris from the Mental Health Act department into his office and he asked her to bring a few of the medical secretaries with her. Between them they rapidly pulled ideas together. This was done far too swiftly, even for a most basic plan for upgrading and improving the overall ambience and the outside initial impression of the unit building.

Not until the end of the day did it occur to Gordon Bygraves that he would need to inform the staff and patients of Pargiter Ward, and the other wards and departments contained within the unit, that they were to expect a visit from the press.

He only thought to do that, because he had been informed that Mark El Amin, their mystery man who looked like Jesus, had gone AWOL. He hoped the police would have returned him before Sunday, and that the coppers did not appear on the doorstep with a man in handcuffs when photographs were being taken by the press, that would not be the sort of publicity he was anticipating.

Thankfully he had a positive response from the occupational therapy department, whose staff offered to come in on their days off, the next day, to create one or two large posters and to put artwork on the walls. They had a number of designs in mind that Gordon was certain would be useful, and he gratefully accepted their offers of help.

The Pargiter Ward staff nurse in charge, Bob, was not so enthusiastic and he raised a stream of queries about how the press visit was to be managed in terms of safety, confidentiality, dignity, and timing of the usual ward routines. He also wiped the floor with Gordon's plan to paint the corridors and ward doors before Sunday.

'That's not even remotely possible. Painting has to be carried out with estates staff doing the work in stages, and the paint will not be dry on the ward doors in time for Sunday as you are about two weeks' short for the requisitions to be put in place.'

Gordon Bygraves felt embarrassed because he had not even thought through the vast majority of these issues, and had less than two days to ensure that he had a well-designed plan for each contingency. Gordon bluffed his way through Bob's queries by outlining that in the morning, on Saturday, a team of staff and helpers would be arriving with the intention of making the place look 'a little more welcoming' and he updated Bob with the offer from the occupational therapy department which seemed to be well received.

'Yep, big old posters, that should hide a multitude of sins.' Bob was, in reality, rolling his eyes and shaking his head in despair at the other end of the phone line.

It was suggested by Bob, to Gordon Bygraves that the most obvious first step would be to alert the staff members who were to be on duty on Saturday and on Sunday, including the night staff.

'Of course,' replied Gordon, writing down each of the valuable points that Bob was coming up with, while simultaneously acknowledging that the staff nurse seemed to have a lot of common sense. Gordon himself was sadly lacking this characteristic. He had no idea how he had ended up as unit manager, and neither had any of the nursing staff. They assumed he was one of those sideways promotions that happened in the NHS because senior management didn't know what else to do with him. Most of the nurses on the unit thought he was a nice enough chap, who used to be an average nurse, but was simply not very good as a manager.

* * *

'I tell you what, I'll ring the ward staff to warn them. You concentrate on organising tomorrow's redecoration efforts,' said Bob. Undertaking the whole task was more than Gordon was capable of on his own.

Bob had a habit of singing tunes relating to whatever had been said in a conversation, or which related to certain people. In this case, he left the office to tell the staff the news and could be heard singing an old track, by Jilted John, which contained the immortal line 'Gordon is a moron ...'

* * *

On Saturday morning, hours after the routine handover meeting, pandemonium struck Pargiter Ward. It came in the shape of Gordon Bygraves, Harriet Morris, and one or two unfamiliar faces, who arrived carrying armfuls of new bed spreads, scatter cushions, plastic flowers, vases, and framed pictures. Gordon announced that there was a box van full of other items yet to be transferred up to the ward.

Emma had been due on the late shift, but when Bob had spoken to her at home, she had volunteered to start much earlier in anticipation of extra help being required. It was more than helpful. She and one of the more-experienced healthcare assistants found themselves policing the plans that had been made to dress-up the ward.

The office staff and the management team had, in their infinite wisdom, failed to ask for input from the staff on the ward, and thus had singularly failed to take into account the issue of risk when it came to items considered safe enough to have on an acute psychiatric ward.

The occupational therapy staff were pressganged into helping, not only in the creation of posters, but in redesigning items, particularly the paintings and pictures that had been purchased that day and brought on to the ward. These were immediately diverted back downstairs to the OT art rooms to have the glass removed. The pictures could not be hung using wire and picture hooks, and had to have mirror hangers screwed on to them for safe and secure attachment to the walls of the corridors.

* * *

'Which bright spark decided that buying a mini pool table was a good idea to have in the large dayroom?' Emma shouted above the mayhem that was taking place in the main reception area downstairs. She had taken on the role of head controller in deciding the safety of each item being unloaded from the van.

* * *

There was no help offered from the security guard who sat at the reception desk by the entrance to the unit.

That was pretty much all he did.

He sat.

He would rise from his seat to ensure that the main unit doors were locked at nine pm, when his replacement took over until the Sunday morning. Then he came back and sat for another twelve hours doing nothing. He said hello to everyone who entered, asked them to sign in and sign out, and that was his contribution to security. If the alarms sounded he did not react, as he was not permitted to leave his desk other than to go to the toilet.

On that Saturday he sat and watched the proceedings with fascination.

'Don't you worry, Rocky, you just sit there and watch us do the hard work!' shouted Emma. She received a big grin, a nod and no comprehension of her sarcasm.

Emma diverted several items to OT staff for modification, and others she returned immediately to the van.

The mini pool table was one of the items returned.

Gordon Bygraves challenged Emma's decision making, until she asked him if he had ever experienced being on the receiving end of a sock full of snooker balls. 'Effing idiot,' she muttered as he walked off in embarrassment at his own stupidity.

She then sent back, using a few ripe phrases to emphasise how astounded she was, the box of glass vases. 'Anyone for wrist slashing? Glass available here, free of charge! But try not to make a bloody mess on the effing carpet because the effing press might notice!'

It was indeed fortunate that, as usual, the vast majority of the patients were on day or weekend leave because the chaos of the to-ing and fro-ing made management of ward safety troublesome for the staff. Emma, having taken overall control of proceedings, had ensured that the ward revamp took place in sensible stages to offset the increase in disruption.

They had to wait for a man from the estates department to arrive with his special secure toolbox and a drill, before the pictures could be hung on the walls. Meanwhile, the focus was on new bedspreads, new chairs, scatter cushions, and putting plants around in giant planters. The planters had to be filled with additional weight to make them too heavy for an angry person to launch. Gordon was therefore dispatched to the local builder's merchants for heavy ballast. The plants were only plastic so this was not difficult to achieve.

New soft furnishings in the shape of chairs for visitors and patients replaced the ancient vinyl ones in the dayrooms. It had not occurred to Gordon Bygraves that the reason the vinyl chairs were so old, was because they had withstood the tests of time and damage, and were specifically designed for use in hospital dayrooms. Cheap furniture was not going to survive much beyond six months, if that.

Emma instructed that the old vinyl chairs be stored in one of the unused rooms in the basement, knowing that they would have to be returned to their rightful places on the ward in the not too distant future. She had more sense than the whole makeover team put together. She also knew that the scatter cushions would be gone as soon as the photographer had finished his assignment on the ward. They were too tempting as a hiding place for contraband, for self-harming tools, or drug paraphernalia.

There were new board games, packs of cards, second-hand books, and magazines being unloaded. Once scrutinised by Emma, these were taken to the ward, to the delight of the patients who were stuck there for the weekend. They were given the special task of trying out these items, and did not hesitate in giving their valued opinion. There was an overwhelmingly positive response.

Once the OT staff had completed the required modifications to the items sent to them, they turned their attention to creating their artwork and made posters from pieces of creative writing that the patients had produced over the previous few months. The vast majority of patients took their artwork home when they were discharged from hospital, but others left their creative efforts to decorate the OT department walls and provide inspiration for others.

By the time the end of Saturday arrived, the place was feeling more homely, depending of course on what sort of home you came from. It wasn't luxurious but the unit was definitely not so dreary or soulless as it had been previously.

The final instruction from Gordon had been to create a ward supplies shop where patients could purchase toiletries and washing powder, and borrow second-hand clothing. This had been magically provided through use of a storeroom full of broken furniture which had been forgotten about and left undealt with. This was mainly because the requisition form, for removal of these items, had been swallowed up in the chasm of endless processes required to get any simple practical task achieved in the inefficient leviathan of the NHS.

Emma could not get the old and dusty contents of that room into the back of the hired van speedily enough. She instructed the husband of one of the secretaries, who had been bribed to drive the hire van, that he was to take these items to the tip. The other items were for return to whichever shop they had come from, and the glass vases needed 'replacing by plastic ones please.'

Gina the cleaner was like a terrier down a rat hole. Straight into the storeroom, she had it scrubbed and sparkling in no time. It was lined with shelves and would be immensely useful in future. The OT staff made a lovely sign for the door: *Ward Shop and Clothing Store*. They then made a neat square blackboard to go below the sign, to indicate the opening times, once it had been decided what they were to be.

The store was stocked with toothpaste, soap, toothbrushes, ladies sanitary items, tissues, shampoo, and the like. This only served as a reminder of the lack of basic patient provision to-date. The staff team on the ward was delighted with the result, but painfully aware that the task of managing the shop had yet to be thought through.

* * *

When the mayhem settled down and the mess tidied up, Emma found time to phone me at home to give me an update on what to expect when I arrived for the Sunday early shift. Emma was proud of herself for leading on the formidable undertaking on Pargiter Ward that day, and she let me know what a trial it had been to ensure dangerous items were not 'dumped on an acute psychiatric ward by people who should know better.'

I had been in a hell of a stew all day long. I had tried to keep myself busy at home, catching up with mundane household chores and shopping, mainly to keep my mind from dwelling on the distinct possibility that I could get the sack any day. I demanded to know from Emma if the police had returned Mark El Amin to the ward yet.

'No. We haven't heard a peep. I think they may have more important things to do. Besides which everyone here has other things on their minds. I think he's been forgotten about. He's probably miles away if he has any sense. Anyway, Mon, he's better off out of here. It was chaos earlier.'

\* \* \*

'Now then, tomorrow …' Emma prompted. 'The photographer man is coming late morning and has been told he can only stay for one hour. He's not allowed to take proper photos of the patients or staff, so he's going to take shots from behind and out of focus in an arty-farty way. I think Gordon Bygraves is in charge of escorting him around, so there should be no specific impact on our staff. What a bloody fuss for a few photos.'

\* \* \*

I agreed, a right bloody fuss. I chatted with Emma about what she feared Dr Sharman's reaction would be, when he found out that Mark had gone AWOL.

'I shouldn't think he will be bothered one way or the other. He'll be far too busy revelling in the press attention. The article is supposed to be in Monday's paper, so we may not even see him in ward round,' suggested Emma after time to reflect.

'Oh. I never even considered that possibility, Em. What a relief that would be. If he does turn up he'll be unbearable, insufferable, and other adjectives that I can't think of, but they probably end in …able.'

\* \* \*

We were both of the opinion that Dr Sharman's horse was getting higher and it would take something spectacular to knock him off it. We even made suggestions to each other, and amused ourselves for many minutes inventing a new game called 'knock the git from his high horse'.

# Chapter 34

## Photographic Evidence

Sunday morning arrived, and the newly purchased plastic plants, plastic vases containing plastic flowers, posters and pictures remained as they had been strategically placed the day before. I was in charge of the morning shift, and there were more than one or two issues to contend with.

The new admission, the young lady by the name of Tania, had managed to get hold of a craft knife left unattended by one of the helpers during the ward tart-up. During the night, Tania had done a fine job of carving up her left arm and had been taken over to A&E by the night staff to be stitched back together. I had to review the situation, and assess the level of risk that Tania was presenting with, in order to update the on-call doctor.

The decision had been made the night before to place Tania under close observations, but this, I knew, could be detrimental, as it often resulted in lots of positive attention being given in response to an unhelpful self-harming strategy. A bit like rewarding bad behaviour. It was a difficult decision because not enough attention in reaction to self-harming, could every so often result in the person upping the ante. Result? More blood.

There were probably long and complicated psychological theories to describe that particular set of dilemmas and behaviour, but I tended to be more practical in my analysis. To me, Tania was a person who didn't understand or recognise her own emotional responses and who could therefore not talk about them. She acted out her feelings by demonstrating hurt or anger, offending others and by injuring herself. Simple.

I decided that it would be wise to be cautious, rather than have a dramatic blood bath for a press photographer to take sneaky snaps of. Tania would be kept out of the way in a side room with the brilliant Margaret for company. There were lots of new books to be read that day and Margaret was keen to share out loud the gift of a good story.

All was calm when Gordon Bygraves entered the ward accompanied by a middle-aged man in a crumpled suit carrying an expensive-looking camera. He was introduced to me as, 'John Starkey from the Daily Albion newspaper, who has come to take photos to support the article about Dr Sharman. It's due to be published in Monday's edition of the paper.' I tried to look impressed as I double-checked with both men that they knew they 'should not enter the female dormitory area', and that no photos of patients or staff were permitted; although out of focus, or shots from behind, would be acceptable. 'These requirements must be explained to any of the patients who try to get into a shot, or who happen to appear in front of the lens. That is vital,' I asserted.

Gordon Bygraves, once more out of his depth, asked me if I would kindly escort Mr Starkey around the ward, and ensure that the agreed parameters were kept to, regarding confidentiality and privacy.

'Right, well, if I'm doing that, then you will have to stay in the office and cover the phone. Just take a message and I'll deal with it later,' I advised, reminding him to ensure that he kept an eye on the ward exit doors, and to make sure that no one left without him checking whether they had permission to do so.

'I'll give you a top tip,' I whispered. 'Don't let anyone leave …'

* * *

John Starkey had not, for many years, been a reporter in the field, and he was relishing every moment. Gordon Bygraves had been under the false impression that he was a photographer, and had therefore fallen for the simplest of approaches. Gordon had found himself explaining lots of things to a person that he assumed didn't understand, not knowing that the man in front of him was a reporter, or in this case the editor of a national newspaper. All John Starkey had to do was pretend he was a bit dim.

\* \* \*

The photographer asked lots of questions about the unit including, 'How many patients are there here usually?' And when Gordon replied, he said, 'Oh really? And where are all the patients today, Mr Bygraves, it seems a bit quiet?' and, 'what about the doctors where are they?'

Gordon didn't hesitate to give the answers, and more besides, but John had no such luck with me. I'm too smart for that old trick.

'Do you know Dr Sharman well?' he asked me directly as we turned the corner into the main corridor.

'I don't think anyone does,' came my short reply. I then manoeuvred him in the direction of the dayrooms, the new ward shop, and a lovely a view of the corridor with the artwork on display.

It was then that I spied a short poem in the corner of the creative writing poster.

*There was a consultant called Sharman*
*Whose actions were somewhat alarmin'*
*He gave lots of pills*
*To those with no ills*
*And that's why they nicknamed him Charmin'*
It was signed *Mr Trainman*.

I couldn't help gasping, alerting John Starkey who, in an instant, was taking the shot before I could stop him.

He made light of it. 'Great. Funny … The whole poster is inspiring. I'll get one or two close ups, and a couple of long shots down the corridor.'

I caught him as he managed to sneak a picture of the male dormitory, chancing that it was in focus. He unsuccessfully tried to reassure me that this was not the case, and that the most important photographs would be of the outside of the building, and the plaque on Dr Sharman's office door.

I was certain about that. The plaque showed streams of letters after Dr Sharman's name, adding to his legendary gravitas, and reputation as the man of utmost importance to the hospital.

As we made our way back towards the ward office, Gordon popped his head out to inform me that the security guard on reception downstairs had taken delivery of two boxes of chocolates for the staff and patients on Pargiter Ward, and could I please collect them. I persuaded Gordon to stay on the ward while I did so, and I escorted John Starkey to the main unit exit, ensuring he did not linger anywhere he was not supposed to. I had the distinct feeling that he had another agenda, and not one as simple as taking publicity shots for a newspaper article. I was not prepared to be implicated in whatever that might be. I was in quite enough trouble as it was.

Making a show of it, I waved goodbye to John Starkey who seemed resigned to the fact that his tour of the premises was over, and he fired off a couple more camera shots of the main entrance as he departed.

Doing as I was asked, I went to reception to collect a large tin of Quality Street chocolates with a label stuck to it indicating it was for consumption by the ward staff and patients. The second smaller box was wrapped in paper with an envelope addressed to *Welsh Phil, Pargiter Ward.*

Intrigued, I returned to the ward, and once I had relieved Gordon of his duties in the ward office, I delivered the smaller box to Phil, who was at the time getting ready to go out for lunch with friends and family.

'Birthday, is it?' I asked.

It wasn't Phil's birthday but he was thrilled to receive a present, whoever it was from. As I left, he opened the envelope to find out. Phil read it out loud for me to hear.

*'Phil, Thank you once again for your kindness and help. I am safe and well. Please look out for next Saturday's copy of the Daily Albion. You will like it immensely. In the meantime please enjoy the chocolates. M.R.'*

'M.R. ?' queried Phil. He knew it was from Mark, but why M.R.?

Phil and I ruminated over this riddle for some time. How could Mark know what was going to appear in a newspaper a week into the future? Unable to answer these questions, Phil resolved to ensure that he got hold of a copy of the Daily Albion first thing the next Saturday morning.

I survived the Sunday early shift with no major calamities despite the fact that I was suffering from the negative impact of sleepless nights. I was living with the nail-biting consequences of my breach of confidentiality, which carried with it the likelihood of immediate suspension and probable dismissal. On top of that, I had colluded in an absconding. No, I had facilitated a Section patient's absconding. That was worse. I anticipated that I would soon be exposed as being unfit to practice, of professional misconduct, and breaking the law. Still, where was the proof?

Once I had finished for the day, I was left dealing not only with the anxiety of managing the pending ward round, but also attention from the press, both due to occur on the very next day. I barely slept a wink on Sunday night.

# Chapter 35

## More Coffee, Nurse!

I was trembling with adrenalin overload as I walked onto the ward on that fateful Monday morning. I had convinced myself that it would be my last day as a registered nurse, and although I was fearful of the consequences of my actions over the previous week or so, I lay the blame firmly at the feet of Dr Giles Sharman. The thought of seeing him that morning filled me with a bitter hatred of which I had not previously been so painfully aware.

Charlotte was the other staff nurse on duty with me for the early shift, and she emerged from the locker room looking nervous. 'You alright, Charlotte? You look worse than I feel.' On enquiry, it became apparent that she had assumed that she was to be in charge of running the ward round that Monday morning, and I gladly let her continue to believe this. What a reprieve!

I felt a pang of guilt, which lasted for less than a second.

'Don't worry, Charlotte, I'll help you as much as I can.'

Which I did, in all fairness. Between us, we prepared the notes, the drug charts, and I lay the coffee and tea trays that day. The selection of biscuits was of a particularly high standard, as one of the secretaries had donated a selection box at the weekend, to help the workers through the task of upgrading the décor in the ward on Saturday. It seemed that two or three helpers had the same idea, and as a result the ward was awash with biscuits and chocolate. What unhealthy fare for a hospital ward.

Dr Sharman and his entourage of trainees, followed at a distance by Dr Siddiqui, entered the ward at full volume.

All anyone could hear was 'guffaw guffaw, phwa phwa phwa … and they all loved it of course …'

There was The Charming One at the head of the procession, expounding his own magnificence, carrying a pile of newspapers. He took these with him through to the large meeting room where the ward round was due to be held, and handed them to Charlotte, with instructions to distribute them to the relatives of the patients who were to be attending the ward round that day.

'What about the patients?' she asked innocently.

'If you must,' came the reply.

As Charlotte brought the newspapers out of the meeting room, I entered with the first tray of refreshments, and I depressed the plunger in the cafetière, shakily pouring Dr Sharman one of his many cups of coffee that morning. He didn't even acknowledge my existence, which was fortunate for him, because I might have been tempted to fast-track my imminent dismissal, by giving him the benefit of my sleep deprived foul temper that morning.

He was busy soaking up admiration from his fawning juniors, as he read out pertinent paragraphs from the article that had appeared, as expected, in the Daily Albion.

When I walked back into the ward office, I had a brief look through the article with the accompanying photographs. The photos were underwhelming in their simplicity, and only four appeared with the article. A splendid tableau of Dr Giles Sharman giving his speech to the delegates gathered at the national conference, a decent photo of the outside of the unit, where the plastic plants in plastic planters looked strangely realistic, and there was also a simple shot of the main ward corridor with a couple of out of focus patients at the end, colourful artwork on the walls. Finally there was the shot of the plaque on Dr Giles Sharman's office door, with the attendant string of letters after his name.

The article outlined the contents of his keynote speech at the National Psychopharmacology Conference. Nothing out of the ordinary, but enough exaggerated accolades to make Dr Sharman's head so big he might have struggled to keep it upright without a neck brace.

I then read the article in more detail, and nearly reached for the phone there and then. If only I had known who to complain to, or which law had been broken, I would have done. The article outlined that *'Dr Giles Sharman advocates the use of more modern and less harmful antipsychotics in the management of severe mental illness, such as for schizophrenia.'*

This was a work of fiction!

Dr Sharman had been reported as saying that his clinical practice *'was an example for all,'* and that he was *'mindful every day of the impact treatment decisions had on individuals and families.'* The end of the article insinuated that because of his outstanding reputation, the Hollberry Psychiatric Unit was to become a Centre of Excellence for Psychiatry.

Utter twaddle! Bollocks. What dreadful lies! How could he get away with saying these things, and yet doing the opposite?

I was stabbing the desk with my biro. As I was enjoying doing so, the ward doors swung wildly open when Sue the CPN, preceded by an irate-looking woman, marched onto the ward and headed smartly towards the ward office. Sue managed to speak first. She apologised for the direct approach, and introduced the lady with her as 'Rodney Wells' sister.' Rodney's sister then launched her attack.

'My brother is in A&E, and I want to see that man. Now! I know he's here, and I demand an explanation for the lies he told to the newspapers.' She had a copy of the Daily Albion in her hand, rolled up, and being used as a tool of intimidation as she waved it in my face. I needed time to absorb the information being fired at me, so I answered softly, keeping a cool head.

'Sorry, I didn't catch your name. I'm Monica, one of the staff nurses, and I think you said that Rodney is in A&E.'

'Nicola. I'm Nicola,' she replied sitting down in the chair I had offered her. I shut the office door in order that we would not be disturbed, while Sue helped to fill in the missing pieces of the puzzle for me. Rodney had taken an overdose and been found by his sister first thing that morning. He had left a suicide note, which not only implicated, but also named Dr Sharman in Rodney's decision to take his own life. It was Nicola's view that Rodney had become hopeless, despairing that his life could ever improve. In short, she believed that the effects of the injection that he had been forced to take in order to secure his discharge the previous week, had contributed to his suicide attempt. He was now in intensive care.

I asked Nicola and Sue to wait in the area outside the kitchen, where there were a couple of new chairs strategically placed. I made an urgent call to the unit manager.

\* \* \*

After minutes of heated negotiation, I persuaded Gordon Bygraves to see Nicola in his downstairs office and to take her through the formal complaint procedures. Sue accompanied Rodney's sister, taking a letter she had written in response to Dr Sharman's 'unprofessional behaviour' the previous week, when he unceremoniously sent her out of the ward round. She was still fuming about that.

I interrupted the ward round, between patients, to confidently inform Dr Sharman that Rodney Wells was in intensive care, and I gave him fair warning that Rodney's irate sister was in the unit making a formal complaint. I relished this opportunity to take a shot at Charming.

His response was curt. 'Thank you. Duly noted, Nurse Morris. Now could I have a fresh pot of coffee, and take my cup and wash it as well.'

What an arrogant unfeeling bastard. 'Please?' I reminded him, without thinking. He glared at me as I left the room. As sorely tempted as I was to smash his cup and sodding saucer against the nearest wall: I didn't.

A few moments after I had retreated from the meeting room, there were raised voices. Firstly the new patient, Wayne, who had been admitted for alcohol detox, came stomping out, announcing that he was leaving us.

'Yeah well, fuck you too, you dick!' He slammed the door before racing away to collect his personal belongings. Then quite unexpectedly Dr Siddiqui came storming out. I had never seen him storm before, and was reasonably astounded at the sight. I checked with Charlotte, who appeared in the doorway of the large meeting room, that our newest arrival was permitted to leave earlier than planned. She nodded vehemently, and confirmed that he could leave unhindered by a discharge care plan or by any medication. She then sighed and returned to the court of Dr Sharman.

Dr Siddiqui marched towards me obviously in a furious mood, and he was a most peculiar colour. He had found me in the kitchen, swilling coffee grounds from the cafetière, and I offered him a glass of cold water, which I then fetched in a plastic cup, from the corridor water dispenser. As I did so, I said a cheery goodbye to our detox man who passed me by, leaving the ward without further ado.

Once he had regained his composure in the confines of the ward kitchen, Dr Siddiqui thanked me for the water, and confessed that he had finally snapped in the face of, 'endless hypocrisy and insult.' He was still shaking with rage, which made two of us.

It was Dr Siddiqui who then updated me with the events that had led to a double storm-out from ward round. Dr Sharman had taken one look at the notes for Wayne Parker, who was now marching out of the ward doors with his worldly possessions in a carrier bag, and discharged him. He had informed the gentleman that if he wanted to stop drinking then he should 'get on with it', and not take up valuable bed space in hospital.

Job done.

Neither concern about alcohol withdrawal symptoms, nor appreciation for the efforts to secure funding for a placement in North Wales, nothing. Dr Siddiqui had snapped, raged and departed from the ward round in the same manner as the man before him had done.

'I couldn't listen to any more. He makes me feel sick.'

Thanking him for his honesty, I took advantage of Dr Siddiqui's appearance, to access sedation for Tania, the young lady who had self-harmed on Saturday night. She was incredibly agitated that morning, having struggled with the indignity of being watched as she went to the toilet, washed, and dressed. It has to be said, she was also difficult to negotiate with. Being a ward round day, we were so short staffed that the path of least resistance lay with Lorazepam or Diazepam.

Dr Siddiqui gladly joined me at the drugs trolley in the medication room to prescribe and dispense a tablet for Tania. As I was taking this to her, Dr Siddiqui announced that he had left his posh Parker pen in the clinic room, so I handed over the keys for him to retrieve this, while I continued on my way to find Tania. She didn't protest at the offer of the sedative, making me cross that I had caved in so easily to this course of action, which was usually a last resort. Somewhat mean-spiritedly, I assumed that this had been her aim in the first place. Wonderful stuff, Lorazepam.

I shook myself out of this distraction, as I suddenly realised that I had not yet returned to the ward round with the fresh coffee and his lordship's clean cup and saucer. I raced back to the kitchen where I found Dr Siddiqui sipping his water, and he handed me back the hefty bunch of ward keys. The nurses in charge of the ward usually wore a hole in their pockets from carrying the large selection of keys around on each shift. We rarely let them out of our sight unless to another nurse.

'I hope you locked up properly.'

'I think I did.'

'Are you sure, absolutely sure?'

I shouldn't have doubted Dr Siddiqui. Of course he was capable of locking the door behind him, but it was certainty I needed to have in my mind, and for this reason, I dashed back to check. Vance, our magical mellow healthcare assistant confirmed this for me. He was ever watchful, and had seen all the clinic room movements from his vantage point.

'No worries, Monica. The man locked up again.'

\* \* \*

I felt foolish when I returned to the kitchen. 'Sorry, I didn't mean to doubt you. Force of habit.'

I gave the coffee a brief swirl, pushed the plunger half an inch, and then took the pot, cup, and saucer in to Dr Sharman. I didn't hang around this time. I poured a cup of coffee for The Charming One, and left without even looking at Charlotte to see how she was holding up in the face of the day's adversities.

Dr Siddiqui had left the ward when I came out. He was nowhere to be seen. I wondered briefly whether he had gone to pack his bags, pre-empting the need for any more shouting.

There had been no eruption so far to the news of Mark El Amin's disappearance, although I had been on tenterhooks for the whole morning. Lulled into a false sense of security, I thought that the day's dramas had finished, but as the clock indicated that lunchtime would soon require organising, there were more shouts from the large meeting room, and Charlotte burst through the door.

Here it comes, I thought, bracing myself for the slow walk to face the inquisition.

'Call an ambulance! Dr Sharman is having a fit.'

As the words were coming out of Charlotte's mouth, I headed into the meeting room to be greeted by the unexpected sight of three junior doctors looking at each other, then at Dr Sharman who was slumped in his chair with his head tilted to one side, muttering that he was having a stroke.

It was farcical. We had to call an ambulance even though A&E was within walking distance. None of the doctors wanted to take responsibility for transferring Dr Sharman in a wheelchair and phoning A&E to advise them of the situation, so Charlotte phoned for an ambulance.

I took Dr Sharman's pulse, and spoke reassuringly to him, for want of an activity that looked as if I was concerned for the man's welfare, as a proper nurse would do, and because none of the doctors made any effort to examine the stricken consultant in front of them.

Feelings of sympathy were absent. I merely went through the pretence of nursing actions. I remember distinctly trying not to smile when a hilarious cartoon popped into my mind. In my marvellous imagination, I saw that Dr Sharman's head had become too big, and was so heavy that his neck had collapsed under the strain. The humongous head had wobbled from the vertical, and eventually come to rest on his left shoulder.

Ward round was abandoned.

Despite the turmoil, Charlotte and I maintained the integrity of the ward safety and its functions, by carrying on as if nothing had happened, and once Dr Sharman was wheeled to A&E by a couple of bemused paramedics, we ensured that the lunch service went as planned.

The post-lunch medication administration was next on the list of tasks, which I undertook out of concern for Charlotte. She appeared to be exhibiting signs of nervous exhaustion.

I also phoned Gordon Bygraves to tell him of the events, and in doing so caused him to crumble under the weight of the responsibility I had given him. He would take steps to contact family members, he assured me. Did Dr Sharman have any family? I wondered.

Charlotte and I made valiant efforts to sustain harmonious order on the ward as well as our own dignity. We made it through to the usual shift handover meeting before we had time for a proper debrief about the events of the morning. It was incongruous to see, but both of us were smiling as we sat down to break the news to the ward team.

Emma arrived bright and fresh and ready for the late shift, but once she had absorbed the details of the morning's dramas, she was unsurprisingly unsympathetic. Although she verged on the inappropriate at times, I was past caring what she said.

'It couldn't have happened to a nicer bastard.'

The response from the whole nursing team at that meeting was irreverent, in true mental health nurse style and tradition.

'You have to be careful what you wish for … and I don't think that was the kind of stroke he dreams about.'

'Fat-headed man anyway.'

'Pride comes before a stroke.'

'It's what happens when you tell lies to newspapers …'

Sadly and predictably, there was not a lot of concern shown by the good people of Pargiter Ward that day. There was instead, a collective sigh of relief that Dr Giles Sharman, bully and tyrant, had left the building.

# Chapter 36

## Who Did What?

I was reliably informed, by my friend and colleague, Sharon, staff nurse in A&E, that Dr Sharman had become the centre of a small controversy on his arrival within the general hospital building. There had been a difference of opinion amongst the A&E medical team as to what he was presenting with. One Smart Alec accused him of taking his own medication.

'It looks remarkably like a dystonic reaction to me,' he had said, apparently.

Sharon's colleagues could only agree that it was 'a dystonia of some sort,' but as they were debating the likelihood of whether it was a stroke, and deciding that it was not; Dr Sharman had a heart attack. He ended up in intensive care in the bed adjacent to Rodney Wells.

\* \* \*

Rodney died that night.

\* \* \*

Days went by without interesting news filtering through to the ward about Dr Sharman's condition. However, by the end of the week, a solemn Gordon Bygraves furnished us with an update. He announced that while Dr Sharman had responded well to treatment, his full recovery was by no means certain, and there was to be an investigation by the police into a number of matters. Gordon took a deep breath as he asked the staff to keep this information confidential.

'Evidence has come to light that Dr Sharman may have been poisoned.'

Leading up to Gordon's statement, my heart had been in my mouth. I had assumed that the announcement was going to be about Rodney Wells, who we knew had died, but most of the staff team were unaware of his sister's accusations aimed at Dr Sharman. The speed at which inside information is shared in a hospital is usually supersonic, so I then panicked that the truth about Mark El Amin's escape had come to light. But no, it was about the man that we despised. The news was good.

'How do we know he was poisoned?' Bob asked, ever the sensible one.

'A person or persons unknown sent him a note to inform him,' Gordon replied before he rapidly put his hand in the air as if directing traffic, and asked for no more questions. He had remembered, a little late in proceedings, that the police had asked him to avoid giving details to anyone who might potentially be implicated. As usual, Gordon had not thought through the consequences of his actions. Idiot. Every member of staff and every patient past and present would be a suspect. There had not been so much excitement since we accidentally admitted a member of her Majesty's Secret Intelligence Services, at least that is what he told us.

Everyone had a theory or named a prime suspect in the poisoning of Dr Giles Sharman, and the excitement was unbearable as we waited for more news. We put in special requests to colleagues in the general hospital to gather information for us about police activity, and there was plenty to report. Our sources reliably informed us that police had visited the cardiology department several times in the last day or so.

Dr Sharman had produced the note declaring that he had been poisoned with Droperidol. Droperidol had been identified as the possible cause of the cardiac arrest, as well as the other collapse and muscle spasms. However there was no conclusive evidence of Droperidol being found in his blood when they tested for it, several days after his admission. Most interestingly, according to reports, the police had been seen talking to Dr Sharman at his bedside to inform him that he was being charged with something ... but none of the general hospital nursing spies knew what he had been charged with. None of us on Pargiter Ward could imagine what that would be either.

The police came to the hospital on the Friday, and they spoke to those of us who were present on the Monday when Dr Sharman was taken ill. We were called in to work, if not already on duty, and I was timetabled to speak to police at four o'clock, giving me a whole day's worth of worry.

I was shaking in my sensible shoes, waiting to be called in to help with enquiries. Directed to wait outside a consultation room on the ground floor, I sat alone on one of a long line of chairs, gently sweating. Why were hospitals always so hot and stuffy? I could hear the police talking from beyond a closed door in front of me. Now and again, I heard Bob's voice as he answered questions. The police couldn't possibly have realised that the door was paper-thin, which meant that I was party to confidential discussions.

'With respect, nobody actually liked the man. He was a bully,' I heard Bob say.

'Your colleague, Monica Morris, how would you describe her?' a female voice asked.

'Monica? She's solid. By the book. If I was admitted, I'd want her as my named nurse.'

Despite my nerves, I was chuffed to bits to hear Bob say that about me. It gave me much needed confidence.

Finally he emerged unflustered, producing a comforting wink at me as he closed the door behind him. Dependable Bob had a Teflon coating. Nothing seemed to penetrate his calm and tough exterior.

While I awaited my inevitable call to enter, I could still hear the discussions from within. It seemed that the police had concluded that 'any evidence which could prove a poisoning with prescribed drugs, is probably long gone,' and they wondered 'was the note a weird hoax by a deranged patient?' They debated the possibilities for a while and mumbled on about motives, means, and methods. 'Possibly. If there actually was a poisoning, the prime suspect is Dr Siddiqui, although let's see how Nurse Morris shapes up.'

It was my turn. After gentle opening queries, the more probing questions came my way.

'Were you the only nurse to hold the keys to the drug trolley that day?' I was asked.

The detectives sat opposite me. There was one fragrant female who should have been on the perfume counter at Debenhams, accompanied by her grey middle-aged male partner who was destined to burst out of his shabby suit, imminently. I was unsettled by how disinterested they both seemed.

'I doubt it. We quite often need to pass the keys to each other during a shift, and that day I gave them briefly to Dr Siddiqui, as well as to Charlotte Quinn.'

'Ah yes. They've both confirmed that with us,' said the Debenhams Detective. Her partner asked about the drugs trolley security and then predictably asked if anyone that I knew of would want to harm Dr Sharman.

'Oh dear ... erm, I can think of quite a few people who dislike the man intensely. I'm not sure anyone would go so far as to poison him though.' Neither detective seemed to have picked up on my trembling hands and quavering voice. I couldn't help it. I was so nervous.

'Dr Sharman, what was he like to work with? A fair-minded sort of chap, would you say?'

I struggled to answer and barely managed an intelligible reply.

'Let's put that another way; have you ever had cause to disagree with Dr Sharman recently perhaps?'

I couldn't lie. 'Yes. I had a difficult time accepting his clinical decisions sometimes.'

'Where would you usually document these objections? In the patient notes?'

Oh God, where was this going?

'Yes.'

In front of them I spied copies of nursing notes, off-duty records, pharmacy orders, letters, and photographs of the ward. These were laid out plain for me to see, shuffled and referred to. I couldn't miss them.

'You were having a difficult time leading up to Dr Sharman's collapse.' A statement. Not a question.

'Was I? I don't think so ...'

'We have a letter here indicating that you had inadvertently misinformed a patient about what Section they were on. Were you reprimanded for this?'

'Yes, but it was not my error. Dr Sharman had ... confused me.'

'Bad week for you, wasn't it? Didn't you lose a patient in your charge a matter of days after that? The same patient in fact.' Debenhams Detective leant forward over the desk.

Oh shit! Here we go. 'Oh yes. I was escorting him for a scan.'

'Are you in the habit of mislaying your patients?' With a hint of the offensive, Debenhams woman caught me with a sneaky jab at my reputation.

'No. I've never had anyone abscond on my watch, until then.' I wanted her to know that a lack of make up was no indication of poor professional standards.

'So, what was it this time that allowed such an unusual lapse? I only ask because, by all accounts, your colleagues see you as dependable and thorough. Not someone who would be prone to inattention shall we say?' She was incisive in her approach and hurtful. I had been wrong. She was over-qualified for Debenhams. Her make up masked her intelligence.

'I feel ashamed to say that I slipped up. Birthday cards in the WRVS shop distracted me. I let the patient buy a newspaper. He hadn't been out of the ward doors for over a week, so I felt sorry for him.'

What a ridiculously banal excuse, which made me represent myself as a thoughtless imbecile! Idiot Monica.

'Whose birthday was it?'

'What? Oh, I can't remember exactly.' She had me. I looked and sounded guilty. I assumed that the truth had been revealed. I was going to be charged with abetting a Sectioned patient to abscond. I became cold and clammy with fear, but the two detectives only nodded and changed the subject. Having revealed me as a liar, they moved smartly back to the day of Dr Sharman's collapse.

'And you prepared the teas and coffees that day?' they probed.

'Yes.'

'Who would usually have access to the pots of tea and coffee?'

'They're kept in a locked cupboard and only the staff have access.' Is that what they meant?

'And who are the drinks served to?'

'All the doctors usually, the staff nurse in the ward round and community staff sometimes. Anyone who's there I suppose, apart from patients and relatives.'

'Right, so anyone can access the contents of these coffee and teapots? Is that the usual case?'

'Yes.'

The two detectives leafed through more papers before scribbling down a word or two on a pad. Ending the interview, they thanked me for my valuable contribution to their enquiries, and I slid mercifully from my chair. Enough sweat had pooled in the small of my back to make an embarrassing squelch as I did so.

* * *

I returned to the ward none the wiser, predicting that there would be a memorable Colombo moment when the guilty person was revealed, but it never happened.

Welsh Phil was watching these various occurrences with a great deal of interest. He had hypothesised that Mark El Amin must be the prime suspect, because Saturday was the next day, and the poisoning was bound to be the story that Phil was supposed to read in the Saturday edition of the Daily Albion. Phil knew his theory had a number of gaping holes in it. Mark had left on the Friday before the poisoning, and although he would have had a fine motive for poisoning a consultant psychiatrist, he did not have the means.

\* \* \*

Vance had decided that it was Dr Siddiqui who was the poisoner. He had motive and means, and had accessed the drugs trolley on that day. Vance kept quiet to the police about his suspicions, so did Welsh Phil.

\* \* \*

The possibilities were endless, and not taken at all seriously amongst the staff in the hospital who had a book running, taking bets on 'whodunit'.

As no one was ever charged or even identified, the proceeds went to Children in Need.

# Chapter 37

## What the Papers Said

On Saturday morning, I was on the early shift. I stopped at the newsagents as usual to collect newspapers and magazines for the ward. The newsagent was bursting to talk to me.

'Strike a light! I always wondered what went on behind those doors,' he announced. 'They'll be closing you down after this little lot.'

He realised by my blank expression that I was clueless as to what he was referring to, so he flashed me the headline in the Saturday Albion.

*'Is he Insane? Psychiatrist Charged with Fraud and Manslaughter had False Qualifications.'*

Alongside this were columns and columns of writing, with subheadings and quotes, and a picture of Dr Giles Sharman, grinning charmingly at the camera. I was so shocked that I scooped up the pile of papers only saying a mumbled 'thanks' as I left, and headed across to the hospital.

It was only six-thirty am when I rushed up to the ward, where Welsh Phil greeted me. I had promised faithfully to get him his own copy of the Saturday Albion, and he had given me the money up front.

I handed it over, with trepidation. Predictably, Phil let out a stream of swear words, which sounded fabulously musical in a Welsh accent. We both sat together over a cup of tea, and trawled through every column and every sentence. The larger article was to be found in the centre of the paper, and even before reading the content, we gave each other a sequence of stunned looks.

The articles had been written by a man called Mark Randall.

'Bloody hell Phil, Mark is a journalist.' All at once I was overwhelmed by the implications of this astounding fact.

\* \* \*

*Our undercover reporter was asked to form part of a national research experiment. What he found within the grey imposing walls of Hollberry Hospital Psychiatric Unit is so shocking that The Albion Newspaper Group is calling for a public enquiry.*

'Christ,' Phil said, immediately apologising for blaspheming.

\* \* \*

*Our reporter managed to gain admission as a patient under the name of Mark El Amin.* Phil and I knew the details of Mark El Amin's admission experiences at first hand.

The way Mark had written about them in the article for the paper was honest and frank, and there could be no accusations of poetic licence or exaggeration, yet it made difficult reading. He had been complimentary about the nursing staff, and most admirably he had been incredibly thoughtful about his reporting when it came to describing other patients. Welsh Phil became slightly tearful and reached for my hand as we continued to read together.

Down the corridor, Margaret was reading the article out loud to everyone who gathered around her in the large dayroom. It was an electrifying atmosphere that morning.

One revelation described in the article was that Dr Sharman had been charged with forgery regarding the Section papers, which related to Mark's detention under The Mental Health Act. There were not too many details on this matter, possibly to avoid compromising an investigation by police, I assumed. Underneath that section there appeared a photo of the plaque on Dr Sharman's office door, and a paragraph explaining that the letters after his name were not necessarily factually accurate, neither were one or two of his qualifications. Most shamefully and '*In a shock exposé!*' it was reported that Dr Giles Sharman had previously been struck off as a doctor.

'How the hell is that possible?' I asked aloud.

Welsh Phil couldn't answer that question, but he was delighted to read that the scandal at Farley Hill Hospital had been an outrageous cover-up of patient harm, and abuse. 'I knew I was on to something. I'm not as mad as they think I am!' he said with an emotion-laden laugh. We both sat, with our chins almost touching the table, reading the newspaper. It was hard to comprehend how a doctor without the qualifications he purported to have acquired, and who had already been struck off, could be working in our unit, and on our ward.

'You had your doubts about his credentials, didn't you, Monica?'

'Was it that obvious?'

'No, not really. I read your lips through the glass.' Phil pointed in the general direction of the goldfish bowl of an office. 'I'm sure you were doubting whether he was a qualified doctor … or was I wrong?'

'Guilty your honour … but keep that to yourself.' Good grief. I hadn't thought about that. Lip reading. Phil wasn't even deaf.

The article in the Saturday Albion detailed why it was that Rodney Wells' sister had accused Dr Sharman of medical negligence and the manslaughter of her brother. Police were reportedly following up with a full investigation at the Coroner's request. That was a depressing added bonus.

I eventually left Phil with other patients, sharing his own theories about the downfall of Dr Sharman, as I was keen to read my own copy of the Saturday Albion extremely thoroughly. I checked and double-checked, but there was no mention of my role in Mark's escape. There was also no reference to my guilt in supplying a copy of confidential Section paperwork to Mark's solicitor Richard Huntley. According to the newspaper, Richard had reported Dr Sharman to the police for fraud under the Mental Health Act, on behalf of his client. The expression 'irrefutable evidence' was used.

The article did emphasise and enlighten me as to how much trouble I was in.

I was painfully aware that what I had carried out would be considered to be a case of gross misconduct, and instant dismissal would undoubtedly ensue if anyone ever found out that I had enabled Mark to abscond while on a Section; but I didn't know that it had a Section number of its own. Section 128 according to the newspaper was *the offence of assisting someone under the Mental Health Act 1983 to go AWOL.*' Mark had carefully woven the facts into his article, without any specific member of staff being referred to in relation to his escape. In fact he appeared to have fabricated that part of his story, matching my fictional version of events at the time.

*' I made a dramatic bid for freedom whilst my escort's back was turned. It was my only chance to escape from the hospital and into the freedom of the driving rain outside...'* Good grief, surely someone would ask questions about who the escort was and why they had been so negligent. Pressure was building up inside me, threatening to turn into a screaming eruption of biblical proportions.

Then, gathering myself, I read in depth the detail of Dr Sharman's formal charges of forgery, and I finally grasped the seriousness of what else I had done.

*'Under Section 126 of the Mental Health Act 1983 is the Offence of Forgery. This applies to forgery of documents used in the administration of the Act, such as, forgery of signatures on Section papers, but also applies when false information is knowingly written on the papers with the deliberate intention of deceiving others. It is an offence to knowingly possess them as well as to forge them.'*

Oh my God! I had committed another crime. I'd had a copy of an illegal Section paper in my possession, and I knew the information had been a lie. Heartsinkingly, I therefore concluded that I was guilty of fraud, or was it forgery? Or was it possession of forged documents under the Mental Health Act?

I read on in a state of despair for my career as a nurse. My only consolation was, that if it could be proved that Mark had been illegally detained, then he would not be considered to have been under a Section. If that were the case, then I perhaps could avoid the issue of enabling a patient to abscond. Wishful thinking on my part, I was sure, but it helped to quell the unholy scream, which still threatened to explode.

* * *

Days and weeks went by, as the newspaper disclosed more sordid details about Dr Sharman's past, and eventually produced the scandalous results of the national research project *'into the integrity and robustness of the psychiatric profession.'*

The results were damning, and with them came a salvo of rebuttals: *'Research method was biased and morally questionable'* said psychiatry.

*'Psychiatry is based on sound clinical evidence,'* came the strong message from the Royal College.

Conversely the papers announced that the *'Psychiatric Abuse Research Experiment reveals Psychiatric Services to be Fundamentally Flawed.'*

However hard they tried to defend themselves, or refute the findings, the damage was done to the reputation of the psychiatric profession and to public confidence. Not one of the pretend patients participating in the experiment was exposed as an imposter. None of them were even accused of malingering. Each one attracted a diagnostic label and were expected to engage in treatment with medication. On a cheerful note, three experimenters were offered psychological therapy for management of voice hearing, despite not having any hallucinatory voices to contend with.

It was a repeat performance of the Rosenhan Experiment twenty years previously.

*'Psychiatry is still in the dark ages,'* concluded Mark Randall in one of his final pieces for the Daily Albion.

The exposure of coercion and abuse of consultant powers galvanised a clamour of debate in the press, which called for a radical overhaul of the Mental Health Act. While the debate raged, at Hollberry Hospital not one person was arrested or charged with poisoning. It felt as if nobody cared enough to ask about that particular incident after a while, even though it could have killed Dr Sharman.

\* \* \*

Not one detail about my role in supplying confidential information as evidence appeared in the press. Richard Huntley never mentioned it.

Dr Siddiqui passed his exams, and became a considerate consultant psychiatrist.

Gordon Bygraves and Harriet Morris, no relation, were dismissed.

Welsh Phil went home, as did every other patient. No one stays on a psychiatric ward forever. Not even the nurses.

Dr Sharman recovered from his heart attack, and was formally arrested on his discharge from hospital. His court hearings and trials were reported in the national press, and he drew enough attention and notoriety, to fulfil the needs of his narcissistic personality disorder even though he was never seen working in psychiatry again. He was the only doctor in this country to have been removed from the GMC register twice, and to be found guilty of forgery under the Mental Health Act requiring him to briefly serve time at her Majesty's pleasure, most of it suspended.

A few people were of the opinion that he was not punished enough.

# Chapter 38

### Phil Lynott, Che Guevara, and Jesus Go to a Bar

Twenty years or so later, I found myself in a cosy pub with my husband Max and our good friends Dave and Carol Williams. I had also arranged to meet an old acquaintance, but he and his wife had not yet arrived. They had tracked me down through the power of the Internet, and by good fortune lived a short taxi ride away.

We had barely arrived in our favourite watering hole, when I noticed, sitting at the corner table, by the fireplace, a group of bright chatty young people in their late twenties or thereabouts. My grandmother was right, the older I become, the more difficult it is to identify the age of those younger than myself. One of the group struck me as having a disconcerting likeness to a young Phil Lynott, the long-since-dead lead singer of the band Thin Lizzy. I mentioned this to Dave, who, as an easily excitable person, burst into his own rendition of "The boys are back in town" which he thought was comical.

Dave is funny. He's a salt of the earth Essex man, with a ripe and fruity sense of humour and a generosity of spirit that is often hard to find in others. He's taller than Max, and walks with an untrendy walking stick as a result of a motorbike accident years ago.

After a short interlude, during which Dave exhausted his repertoire of Thin Lizzy songs, badly sung with a lot of la-la-la-ing at forgotten lyrics, we noticed another famous lookalike.

'Bugger me,' Dave said to Max, pointing rudely in the direction of a man at the other end of the bar. 'It's Che Guevara! Look. He's got the beret and a beard. He's got the combat trousers. He's even got one of those tea towel scarf things round his neck!'

'And would you believe it,' added Max, caught up in Dave's childlike joyfulness, 'El Che's wearing a T-shirt with his own picture on it!'

The whole scene caused a lot of amusement, to the extent that Carol and I joined in with the witty banter as we tried to make a joke from 'Che Guevara and Phil Lynott walk into a bar ...' but nothing even remotely funny fitted with the opening line. All four of us sidetracked ourselves into a series of "man walks into a bar" jokes, for a while, until Max, slurping at his beer announced that 'Jesus's dad has just walked in.'

Dave was thrilled, and looked round immediately. 'It is Jesus! Hasn't he got old? He's a bit grey and look he's married! He's coming over. Carol ...'

Dave has a habit of thinking things out loud. He speaks in a booming voice, and behaves as if he's watching television, rather than part of the scene that he's commentating on. At times, he inadvertently causes offence, but mostly he's hilariously entertaining. It was his usual ploy, if he had overstepped the mark, to alert Carol that she might have to stand by to diffuse the situation. He may put on a tough act, but he's a real softie underneath it all, and hates confrontation. He was at his most mischievous because Max was about. They egged each other on something terrible.

Carol, is a woman with endless patience, and like her husband, she has a heart of solid gold. Being the type of person who is interested in what other people have to say, she includes everyone in conversations, and has a warmth and friendliness that makes it a privilege to be counted as one of her true friends. She also has a special gift: an ability to extract information, to negotiate a deal, and to haggle a discount like no other woman I have ever met. She does this with an innocent air that wrong-foots the opponent. When she has completed the transaction, whether it be compensation for a complaint, or to agree a price on a new handbag, the defeated party is more often than not seen scratching their heads and trying to determine how she deprived them of the upper hand.

Carol prepared herself to humorously fend off the approaching stranger who resembled what Jesus might have looked like if he had lived into his half century.

The man walked towards us, and I recognised him immediately. He was staring directly at me as he reached for his wallet. Every man reaches for their wallet as they get to the bar in a pub, which is normal, but on this occasion this particular man took out a ten-pound note and offered it to me. A huge smile lit up my face. 'Mark! I'd forgotten that you owe me a tenner! That's brilliant!' and then I laughed as I took the money.

Just for a moment, Max was confused until he realised that Jesus was the journalist I had been expecting. I made introductions all round, and tried hurriedly and sensibly, to explain to Carol and Dave why Jesus had walked into a bar with a ten-pound note to give to me. I had told them all, including Max, that I had arranged to meet up with a journalist – which was true – also that the journalist and his wife wanted to do a documentary based on a true story about medical malpractice and they needed to interview me. We had planned to meet so that the details could be explained to me before the filming took place. I wanted Carol to be there because she was not afraid to ask questions that I wouldn't even have thought of. Max hadn't been listening when I tried to explain it to him. He couldn't understand why I wanted to discuss this in a pub.

'Why do you need to discuss it at all? Do the documentary and be on the telly. Anyway, what if these people are boring? They'll mess up the whole evening.'

Max soon forgot about his objections. The evening passed in a blur of beer, wine, cider, and stories of such detail and entertainment value that the time seemed to whiz by. Mark and I informed the rest of the group, that we had not seen each other for about twenty years. Not since the day I gave Mark ten pounds and allowed him to abscond from my care and from Hollberry Hospital.

Although I had never spoken to anyone about the events of that September twenty years previously, for an unfathomable reason I felt able to confess my sins in a welcoming pub in deepest darkest Essex by the sea.

Mark took up parts of the story telling, to fill in the details that I had not known about until I read them in the Daily and Saturday Albion newspapers. Max, Dave, and Carol didn't even seem to remember the case of the scandalous Dr Giles Sharman. Then, as we recounted the unsavoury details, vague memories of the story in the press came back to Carol, and she probed in more depth. She loved a bit of intrigue. She asked how the idea for the research project had come about, and how Mark and the team had managed to get away without having to give an NHS patient number.

'Our administrative system was rubbish, that's why,' I recollected. 'We had an old computer system, but not a national database or anything of real practical use. We were lucky if we had an address and telephone number accurately recorded.'

Once he had regaled us with his own naked exploits at Hollberry Station, Mark told us about the other journalists, the research team, and how they had fared during their time in hospitals across the country. We cried with laughter to hear about how Linda had caused a traffic jam dressed as a queen, but even more so when he told us about Jock's Monty Python attempt. Then Mark disclosed that it was Jock who had interviewed Dr Sharman at the National Conference, as a complete set-up.

He also revealed that Jock kept the man in his sights for a lot longer than the assignment had required, and had uncovered more than he had bargained for when it came to revealing Dr Giles Sharman's sexual depravity. It had only required a bribe to a couple of well-paid prostitutes to reveal the unwholesome truth. 'Jock became obsessed with dishing as much dirt as possible when it came to Dr Giles Sharman,' Mark said. 'Meeting the man in person unnerved him so much that exposing him became a life's work for our Jock.'

Carol pushed for more information. 'When you say sexual depravity, what sort of thing do you mean?'

Mark would only offer one example: Dr Giles Sharman had regularly paid a suspender-clad woman to throw cream cakes at his genitals, while he was naked, and he paid extra for every direct hit.

Dave and Max were beside themselves with this salacious titbit. They begged for more, but were declined. They threatened to trawl the Internet to find the rest of the twisted sexual antics that would surely be found in glorious Technicolor.

'That's all you're getting. The rest is unspeakable and not for discussion in a pub.' We were left hanging.

In contrast to the howls of laughter, the mood between us became quietly reflective. When Mark described how it had actually felt when he took the liquid antipsychotic medication, his description brought a tear to my eye, which Carol did not fail to notice. In order to regain composure, I excused myself and went to the ladies toilet, and I caught her understanding expression when I returned. I smiled weakly in response. Emotional memories seemed harder to contain after a cider or two.

The second brief, but sombre mood, came when we talked about how Rodney Wells had killed himself. Carol was again asking questions about how consultants were allowed to get away with that level of abuse, especially as nowadays there would be an expectation that other staff would blow the whistle. She then realised that she had answered her own queries.

'Oh, I see. The research project brought to everyone's attention that there was bullying and abuse going on, because it was brushed under the carpet. The bullying was covered up. Monica, I can't imagine you ever being bullied.'

Mark answered for me. 'She wasn't. She was the only one who stood up to Dr Sharman. That's why we want her for this documentary. It will be twenty years since the research project, and we want to do a comparison between then and now. Monica took real risks to protect her patients and we can't do the documentary without her.'

Mark asked my permission to discuss the finer points of his escape from hospital, and I had no reason to be concerned that this disclosure in The Queen's Head, amongst friends, would cause me a significant problem. Mark's perspective was fascinating to hear. He had been stunned at what I'd had planned for him in order for him to abscond from the hospital, and shocked that I had given him money, an umbrella, and a means to contact for help.

'I'm not sure how you're going to take this.' Mark said to me directly. 'But I had planned to run anyway. I was caught like a rat in a trap and desperate to escape, whatever the cost.'

My face must have been a picture.

'But I couldn't do it,' Mark revealed.

'Why not?' Carol queried, before I could ask the same.

'Oh, I wanted to, in my head, but that hideous medication sucks the life out of you. I couldn't get myself together enough to plan my escape. I could barely imagine giving Monica the slip. I had no energy and no motivation.'

'Now you tell me!' I pretended to find this fact funny.

* * *

Max, Dave, Carol, and Mark's wife Julia listened politely, and gave supportive nods and comments until I revealed that what I had done on that day in 1994 was illegal.

'In truth I shouldn't still be a nurse. In fact I should have been charged, and sacked from my job and removed from the nursing register.'

There were a variety of facial expressions around the table, not least from my husband who, it seemed, was not impressed.

'You've kept that a secret for over twenty years?' he exclaimed, eyes wide, eyebrows raised.

'Yes.'

'Unbelievable. I thought I knew everything about you.'

'Maybe you don't …'

Max laughed. I had completely misunderstood him.

'I never knew you could keep a secret!'

Carol was astounded that I had carried out such a risky strategy, even if it was to help a patient. She had always seen me as a rule keeper, not a rule breaker.

'I had to. Mark could have ended up dead, and the senior managers weren't listening to us, so I was left with my conscience to deal with, and I've never regretted it.'

'And I have never forgotten what you did. Even though I wasn't a real patient,' Mark added, lightening the mood once again by ordering another round of drinks.

'That's two Hop Heads, one Betty Stogs, a pint of Weston's Family Reserve, a large Pinot Grigio and a glass of water for Carol please.'

# Chapter 39

## Pub Battleships

There we were in the Queen's Head, Burnham on Crouch, relative strangers recounting from two different perspectives, the same outrageous and almost unbelievable story, that we had been a part of.

Dave and Max continued to behave like naughty schoolboys throughout the evening, asking endlessly for more details of Dr Sharman's smutty sexual exploits. They were given short shrift, mostly from me. 'It wasn't a Carry On film, you nellies!'

I had given them a game to play, a mistake on my part.

'Oh, Carry on Bonkers … Carry On Nut Crackers … Carry On Basket Case,' they offered, 'and my personal favourite, Carry on Round the Bend,' added Dave.

'No, that's rubbish, it sounds as if it's about plumbers.'

'Oh yeah …'

'Shut up the pair of you!' Carol took charge of the playground as usual, and then turned to Julia to help quench her thirst for more information.

'Now, Julia, tell me how you met Mark. Did you know him when he was locked up in the mental hospital, or did you meet later?'

Julia generously filled in a few years' worth of information for Carol and me. Mark had decided to continue his interest in the mental health injustices that had been exposed by the research project, and he had also recognised his personal requirement to take a break from war zones. He moved back to the UK, and in that time encountered Julia who happened to be a researcher for the BBC. They had met, by happy accident, through an assignment.

Our reunion was not serendipity; Mark had managed to find me and had emailed asking me to consider participating in the documentary Julia was making. I had read his articles in the papers over the years and seen him on the news a couple of times. I wasn't too keen on the idea of a documentary appearance, but how could I resist seeing Mark again in person?

Being wary of what I was letting myself in for, I agreed to consider his proposal, only if he met with Carol, Max, and me. As much as I loved Dave, he wasn't much use in this situation. If you needed a survey of your sewers doing, he was your man.

Mark's wife, Julia, was lovely, and she was enthralled at the tales we told. She had never heard the specifics of my involvement in helping her husband to escape from hospital. Taking their cue, Mark and Julia outlined what they had in mind as my contribution to the documentary. I expressed my reservations, requiring all Julia's powers of persuasion to convince me that I would not be committing career suicide. After several minutes of debate and uncertainty I eventually acquiesced.

'Good,' Max said, giving my shoulders a squeeze. 'Now can we get on and enjoy the rest of the evening?'

\* \* \*

At about eight pm, we ordered snacks in a sensible effort to soak up some of the alcohol. While we nibbled, we talked.

Mark wanted to know what had happened to Welsh Phil, which lifted the mood again, because we had to tell the tale of the Chocolate Wars bringing those times flooding back to both of us. Dave and Max decided that chocolate sounded good, and they purchased four walnut whips. Then, after a huddled discussion, they rapidly returned to the bar to buy a selection of alcoholic drinks.

With permission from Diane the tolerant landlady, they commandeered a decent-sized scrubbed top table. Taking a couple of large bar menus, they created a barrier across the middle of the table. Diane allowed them use of her dartboard chalk with which to draw out a grid either side of the central menu barrier, and they labelled each axis with letters and numbers. In doing so they invented their own version of "Pub Battleships".

This was highly entertaining, and a small crowd gathered behind each player. When a successful hit was achieved, the winner ate the chocolate or drank the drink contained in that square of the board. By the time Max succeeded in sinking Dave's last Walnut Whip they were both slurring their words.

I didn't have any update on Welsh Phil to give to Mark, other than to say how thrilled he had been when he'd received the box of expensive chocolates that Mark had sent as a thank you. Phil was never admitted again to Pargiter Ward, as far as I was aware, and I had to assume that he had moved out of the area, as I never came across him again.

I was able to assure Mark that I was still in touch with Emma after all these years, despite our career paths veering in different directions. Mark was pleased to hear that she had been a bridesmaid at our wedding, when Max and I married years earlier, and that she had made it her business to outdo the best man by performing her own unforgettable speech; as only Emma could. After all it was her fault that Max and I met, and his fault for pestering me to the point of submission. Even though he behaved like an overgrown child, I couldn't imagine life without him.

Once Pub Battleships had finished, we returned to the subject of Dr Sharman's comeuppance.

I skirted neatly around my involvement in supplying confidential Section papers, as I didn't have to confess my offence in that regard: the secret had remained firmly with Richard Huntley.

Carol asked a string of questions about Section papers and types of Section, fascinated by the whole legal tangle. Mark and I had to confess that we were still not experts in mental health law, so Mark suggested that if she wanted to know more, then his great pal Lewis James was still alive and kicking. Mark was certain that he would like nothing better than to join us for a drink one evening.

He then glanced approvingly across at Max and Dave who were suffering from a fit of the giggles. They had been unable to resist checking Max's smartphone for the Giles Sharman kinky sex story.

'Carol, have we got a whip at home anywhere, or a ping pong bat?'

Carol shook her head, and sighed.

Mark and I eventually reached the end of our story, as far as I could remember it. At least I had thought so, but rather surprisingly, Mark had more up-to-date information about Dr Sharman. Of course he had been found guilty of the fraud, but not of the manslaughter charge, that sadly did not stick. But Giles Sharman was found grossly negligent, and the NHS had to pay a vast sum of money to Rodney Wells' family.

The six of us, including Jesus, sitting drinking in a pub with Che Guevara and Phil Lynott in the same room, explored the biggest mystery:

The poisoning of Dr Sharman.

Mark had not been privy to the events of the ward round when Dr Sharman had been taken ill, and had missed the on-the-spot drama at the time. He was hoping for new information to present as part of the documentary.

I had managed to piece together important chronological detail from Charlotte, who had been in the large meeting room for the duration that day. I had only seen the aftermath.

According to her, Dr Sharman had gradually become more lethargic throughout the morning of that fateful ward round, which is why he had consumed the greater part of a pot of coffee and was demanding a second.

He had apparently commented that he was exhausted by the weekend's events at the National Psychopharmacology

Conference, and was regretting the fact that he had not taken an extra day or two to recuperate. He was seen shaking his head, and then stretching his neck from left to right before eventually it became obvious that something was wrong, and he shouted that he was having a stroke.

Subsequently, Dr Sharman's secretary, Lucy, had told me that it was she who had first opened the note from the culprit, announcing the poisoning of Dr Sharman. This had been in a plain envelope with a simple typed instruction: *For the Attention of Dr Giles Sharman*. She had not even read it properly before adding the letter to a pile of post that she then delivered by hand to the main hospital, where Dr Sharman was recovering from his heart attack. He had demanded to see his correspondence that day, as he was expecting to receive a special invitation to appear at a week-long conference in the Costa Brava, Spain: all expenses paid.

'She threw the envelope away, so there were no fingerprints for the police to find.'

'Were there any fingerprints on the letter itself?' Carol asked.

Then everyone joined in. Apart from Carol, we were all a little inebriated.

'How was the poison given to him without him noticing?'

'It has got to have been in his coffee, for sure.'

'Too obvious, and why didn't anyone else get sick?'

'Who were the main suspects?'

'Was it Dr Siddiqui?'

'Was it Rodney whatsit's sister?'

'Was it you?' Max joked, looking at me.

\* \* \*

If Dr Giles Sharman had died when he had that heart attack, the police would have explored, in more depth, the events leading up to his collapse. They would have undertaken a full murder enquiry. Instead, they had as good as ignored the poisoning.

If they had examined the evidence in detail, then I would have been the prime suspect.

I had a motive, I had the means, and I gave Dr Giles Sharman a double dose of his own favourite medicine, Droperidol, in his coffee to make certain that he suffered. This was not difficult. I had drawn up a syringe-full of Droperidol liquid and put each dose in the bottom of his cup. Twice. The liquid was in the cup before I even entered the ward round, so no one ever saw me. Dozens of eyes watched me pour out the drinks. Those witnesses were adamant I could not have possibly poisoned Dr Sharman. The gutter press stuck with the story that he had pretended to be poisoned in an attempt to avoid arrest and gain sympathy. Rubbish. It was only a matter of luck that he didn't die. Who knew he had a heart condition? I'm not a doctor.

His comeuppance, courtesy of the press, was as big a surprise to me as it was to anyone. But I had meant to poison him, and I had meant for him to know he had been poisoned.

My secret could never be revealed. I could so easily have unintentionally killed him.

* * *

'Monica, you should write a book. This is a fascinating whodunit!' Carol said. She was right.

'Yes, but Jesus, tell me, what happened to Dr Sharman in the end, do you know?' Dave asked, staring intently and drunkenly at Mark.

Mark did know. He had saved the best for last. Apparently the fact that he was not allowed to practice, as a medical doctor, did not stop Dr Giles Sharman from being called a doctor. Mark's information, via Jock, was that Giles Sharman had moved to Australia and worked for a small manufacturer of health products, which although harmless, were not the panacea for all ills that he professed them to be via numerous television adverts as 'clinical expert' Dr Sharman.

'He spent years deceiving innocent people, by selling them drugs they did not need. There's a theme here you'll notice. He still basked in notoriety, which once again fed his narcissistic soul. He retired and lived alone until his death.'

'Yes. But how did he die?' begged Dave, who was perched so precariously on a bar stool that he was in danger of falling.

\* \* \*

'Well ... it's not pleasant. Jock Mackenzie sent me the gory photos, although needless to say, I haven't brought them with me. We're saving those for the documentary. To cut a disgusting story short, no one had complained about a nasty smell, but Dr Sharman was found, by Australian police, in a decomposed state. He'd been at home for about 6 weeks after his death with a large dildo wedged in his rectum, a plastic bag over his head, and a bottle of amyl nitrate close by. No one, it seemed, could bear to live with him, and he had resorted to playing dangerous sex games all alone.'

For a man who had loved himself so intensely, this was poetic justice.

## THE END

# Acknowledgements

This book was inspired by true events.

The Rosenhan Experiment took place in the 1970s in the US, and only partial details of that research are outlined in this story.

Lightning Source UK Ltd.
Milton Keynes UK
UKOW04f2227130917
309144UK00001B/144/P